Twisted Fate
#5, Rhyn Eternal Series

Lizzy Ford

Cover design by Eden Crane Design
www.EdenCraneDesign.com

Twisted Fate copyright © 2015 by Lizzy Ford
www.LizzyFord.com

All rights reserved.

No part of this book may be reproduced in any form or by any electronic or mechanical means including information storage and retrieval systems, without permission in writing from the author. The only exception is by a reviewer, who may quote short excerpts in a review.

This is a work of fiction. Names, characters, places and incidents either are products of the author's imagination or are used fictitiously. Any resemblance to actual events or locales or persons, living or dead, is entirely coincidental.

Published by Kettlecorn Press
ISBN-13: 978-1-62378-229-0

DEDICATION

For my husband, Matt, who keeps me from floating away into my imagination

CHAPTER ONE

Stephanie finished unloading the back of the SUV with a grunt. They were late, and the festival's private security had refused to let them drive to the stall where her roommate was exhibiting.

"Last one!" she called and straightened. Already her lower back was stiff from the combination of a long drive down the coast and lifting boxes of handmade journals.

Her friend, Olivia, waved her hand out the window of the car and drove away from the sawhorses dividing the festival from the parking area.

Stephanie arched back – and ran into someone. "Oh, sorry," she murmured and turned.

"I'm cheating on my wife with the babysitter," the man said and continued walking. His dog shied away from her, staring at her over its shoulder until they were swallowed by the crowd.

She rolled her eyes. Dogs hated her and people … well, they went weird around her. They'd always just told her things. She'd never understood the dynamics of her life except that she had a strange effect on everyone she met. Tall, trim and dark haired with eyes that appeared teal or aqua, depending on what she wore, she didn't draw crowds like her blond-haired sister or looks of appreciation and envy like her fashionably perfect mother. She was, as far as she could tell, normal.

Maybe that's why they tell me strange things. I look harmless. Boring, she thought, gaze lingering in the direction the handsome man and his dog had gone.

"Next time we'll bring a dolly," Olivia, said, joining her. She bent to lift two boxes and began walking through the crowd.

Stephanie followed her lead, and they quickly found the small booth reserved for them. Olivia sprang into action the moment the boxes were down, and Stephanie stepped out of her way.

"You need help?" she asked, already knowing the answer.

"Nope!" Olivia's possessiveness and OCD meant Stephanie was there mainly for companionship and lifting purposes. "You want to get us some water?"

Stephanie left the booth and began wandering through the festival towards the small section of food vendors. The book festival featured an eclectic mix of small, local presses with niche publications and larger, polished displays by major publishing houses. Libraries, used books shops, rare book displays, and tables filled with artwork lined the street. Authors' booths ran along the backside of the main strip, near the food vendors.

The festival was already crowded, and guitar music spilled out of the open doors of a studio. The seaside town of Carmel was a mix of wealth and art, ocean and towering trees, hills and beaches. She found herself liking the place she'd never visited before.

She barely registered the people who bumped her as she walked the packed streets. At least, not until someone smacked straight into her and knocked her onto her behind.

She landed hard enough for her teeth to slam together. "Hey," she grumbled, looking up.

The woman was staring down at her, as startled as she was. "I am so sorry!" she exclaimed. "I hope you don't notice I'm missing a hand."

"What?" Stephanie asked.

"I said, I'm sorry about running into you." The blonde offered her hand.

Stephanie accepted it and let the tall woman pull her up. The beautiful blonde with striking green eyes was toned, willowy and perfect in every way. She was also missing a hand. Stephanie did her best not to look.

"Are you okay?" the blonde asked.

"Yeah. Happens a lot," Stephanie replied.

"Does it?"

"Yeah. No problem."

"We can't let him find you."

Stephanie met her gaze. "Come again?"

"Sorry again." The blonde smiled. "Nice bumping into you. Have a nice day."

Stephanie watched her maneuver through the crowd, perplexed by the interaction. She dusted off her backside and thighs. The growl of a dog drew her focus from the strange woman, and she instinctively moved away from the sound. She didn't bother looking at the animal. It only seemed to antagonize those that went so far as to growl or snap at her instead of avoiding her.

She loved the idea of dogs and cats as companions but had never been able to get one, because they all hated her.

With a shake of her head, she continued towards the food vendors. Her gaze skimmed over the exhibits and rested on one of them. A psychic had a table displaying books she wrote about the mind, future and universe. Stephanie stepped out of the throng of people passing down the street to the table.

She picked up a business card.

"That's not for you." The woman seated behind the table snatched it back, brushing Stephanie's hand. "If he finds me, he'll take my daughter away."

"Um, okay. I'm sorry." Stephanie stared at her. *Today is weirder than usual.* Maybe the upper class, enlightened hippies of Carmel were more in tune to whatever *vibes* she gave off. Or maybe, she hadn't been out in too long and forgot how people seemed to like to trust her with personal details that made her uncomfortable.

"Keep walking," the psychic said.

"Actually, I need one of these for my friend," Stephanie replied and picked up another card. "She likes this kind of stuff."

"You will take nothing of mine with you." The psychic snatched the card once again.

"Look, just a word of advice, but you can't come to a festival and refuse to hand out your cards! I mean how can you possibly sell anything with a business model like that?" Stephanie retorted. "I'm taking a damn card, and I'm giving it to my friend." This time, she swiped the card and started away before the crazy psychic could take it back.

"If you hex me, I will find you!" cried the psychic.

What is it with this place? Stephanie made her way to the food vendors to buy a couple bottles of water and started back towards the booth where Olivia was waiting.

"Excuse me," said a male voice behind her. "You dropped this."

She turned, patting down her pockets as she did so.

The tall man behind her had chiseled, Asian features, turquoise eyes and an expression that appeared serious to the point of grim. He held out a wadded up dollar that could've been hers or not.

"I don't think I did," she replied.

"No, you did."

"Fine. Keep it."

"I can't."

"Because …"

His eyes slid to the side and he shifted feet. "I just can't. Take it back."

"I'm never coming back to this place," Stephanie muttered and grabbed the dollar from him. As she did so, he gripped her wrist with his other hand and tapped the meat of her palm with a tiny needle. "What the hell?" She yanked away.

"Please don't be her," he said.

Don't be who? She almost asked.

He handed her the money once more. "Here's your dollar."

She shook her stinging hand and shifted away. "Keep it." She watched him slide away into the crowd and turned in the direction of Olivia's booth, determined to drop off the water and report the psycho who just drew her blood.

Olivia's booth was hopping, and Stephanie soon forgot the weird interactions with strangers to help her friend sell journals. The mad rush lasted until the four boxes of journals were gone. Stephanie sat down several hours later to relax while Olivia hurried to the car to retrieve another box.

Her gaze fell to the pinprick on her palm, and she sighed. She was used to people acting weird around her but no one before today had drawn her blood. Was her own uniqueness amplified in a place that prided itself on being eclectic?

"What's wrong?" Olivia asked cheerfully as she plopped another large box on the table.

"Nothing. This place is so you." Stephanie pulled the psychic's card from her pocket. "This lady is super crazy. You might like her."

Olivia took it with a good-natured smile. Everything about her was the opposite of Stephanie. She was bright, happy and loved by everyone she met. "I'm surprised you haven't asked to sit in the car yet," Olivia admitted. "You're too goth for this place."

Stephanie glanced down at her dark clothing. "Not goth. I just don't believe in the same stuff you do."

"Someone needs to meditate."

"I do like meditating," Stephanie admitted. "It helps me relax. But I don't see the things you tell me I should in my head."

"It takes time and imagination, one of which you have plenty of and the other none!"

Stephanie smiled. "You got all the creativity." In truth, she often envied Olivia's carefree attitude towards life and her ability to design and mold journal cover designs out of thin air. She lifted one of the treasures and ran her fingers over a pattern made from no less than ten different kinds of material. "How do you make these?" she asked a little enviously. "I have no creativity, no imagination whatsoever."

"It's my thing," Olivia said with a shrug and sat down beside her to watch the crowd. "Your thing is …" She cleared her throat. "Well, you're special."

Stephanie laughed.

"And not in a bad way!" Olivia retorted. "You're definitely a lot more uptight than I am and too analytical about everything. You have no aura but you're a good person. From what I read, you're an anomaly. I'm just learning to be more psychic. I can't figure you out but I've made you my mission to help."

"Gee, thanks," Stephanie said. "I'm your charity case."

"You know that's not true. My live-in experiment maybe."

Stephanie smiled once more, hurt even her new roommate thought she was weird. She'd moved out of her mother's apartment in the hope of being like every other college student.

"Maybe you should talk to this lady." Olivia motioned to the business card.

"No, thanks," Stephanie replied, not wanting another confrontation with the crazy psychic lady. "I know I'm different. I want to be creative like you but …" She shrugged. "Maybe my talent is to make everyone around me look good. I'm surrounded by such gifted people. You, my sister, my mom, even my dad, wherever he is.

He was the lead neurologist in the world before he disappeared two months after knocking up my mom."

"No," Olivia objected. "I think you're working off some sort of karmic debt from another life. It's why you have all these issues." She waved a hand at Stephanie's non-existent aura.

"I don't believe in past lives," she reminded her. "I believe in what I can see, hear, and touch. None of this aura business. I'm more like my dad than my mom and sister: total left brain with a knack for physical stuff instead of art. I'm a normal, boring person who graduates with a Masters in engineering next year, whose name no one ever remembers, who dogs can't stand, and who gets yelled at by psychics at book festivals."

"Oh. You had another incident?" Olivia frowned. "Are you keeping a log like I told you to? I wanted to take your issues to my reiki teacher."

"It's constant. I can't track all of it," Stephanie said. "Anyway, moving on to a happy topic, you sold, like, fifty journals so far!"

Olivia's face lit up. She began describing ideas for future projects. Stephanie half listened, disappointed to have had her day ruined by the local crazies. This was supposed to be a mini-vacation, and she was already looking forward to going home to the apartment she shared with Olivia and hiding away once more.

CHAPTER TWO

FATE KNELT BESIDE THE HOMELESS MAN WHO REEKED OF BODY FLUIDS and alcohol. The passed out human's features were obscured by an unkempt beard and dirt, and his home consisted of a soggy box recently collapsed under the spring rains.

"You have a point zero, zero four per cent chance of making your life better before Death comes for you," Fate said to the unconscious man. "I wish you luck."

"My brother, the optimist," said the woman with curly red hair and bright eyes behind him.

"On the contrary, I wish him a speedy death," Fate said and rose. He tended to focus on the chains of events that interested him the most rather than the likeliest. "There are days when I wonder if tolerating so much free will is a disservice rather than the alleged respect for their decisions our father claimed we must honor."

"You killed Father. I assumed you knew he was full of shit."

"And there are moments when I'm reminded the fate of humanity is better left in their hands than ours," he said pointedly. "Deities are generally assholes but at times, they have a point."

Karma rolled her eyes. "Which was why you locked me up for a millennium. To teach me a lesson."

"True," he said with a quick smile. "You failed to learn the other lesson I took away from Father. Timing is everything. You can't just balance whomever you want at a whim. You have to choose the right time to interfere in the life of a human, Immortal or deity."

"Or, I can do whatever the fuck I want," she replied and looped her arm through his. "What does timing matter when everyone has something coming to them?"

Fate chuckled, always amused by his reckless sister. "You want another thousand years in a tiny cell in the Underworld?"

She made a face at him.

They left the alley and joined the crowd in the streets, which had been closed off for a street festival. The scent of the ocean was in the air and its blue waves peeking through trees at the bottom of the town built on a hill. The pricey boutiques lining the main street of wealthy Carmel, California, had thrown open their doors to welcome the visitors.

The moment they joined the throng of humanity, Fate absently began calculating the destinies of everyone around him. It wasn't a conscious doing, and he rarely paid the business of his mind much heed, unless there was something truly interesting about someone he ran across.

Which was rare anymore. The seventh oldest deity in existence, he'd generally grown bored with his job and safeguarding the fate of the entirety of humanity. Humans did what they wanted – and he had long since stopped caring.

Only two chains of events were capable of arresting his attention for long. Whenever he thought of the first, his focus went to Karma, and he became concerned about his inability to shift her Future.

The Immortal society had been dangling over the edge of a pit filled with demons for too long. He'd seen the tiny thread holding them in place snap, and the demons begin to rampage as they had many, many ages before. Neither his manipulations nor his brilliance had corrected the destiny the Immortals were barreling towards. There was always a way to change the Future, but sacrificing his sister to do it – the only solution he'd seen thus far – was out of the question. He had to keep looking, keep tweaking. The Future was a combination of many variables. He just had to pluck the right thread and alter the chain of events.

The second chain of events seemed both inevitable and indecipherable. Some part of it was obscured from his Sight, and he'd already done all he knew to do in order to prevent it from occurring. Vexing, this Future was impossible, at least for now, leaving him free to help his sister before it was too late.

"Ohhhh!" Beautiful, lethal Karma came to life beside him the moment the energy of humanity reached her. Her eyes and hair began to shift colors, depending upon how well balanced the people nearest her were. The darker their past deeds, the darker her hair and eyes.

"Watch yourself, sister," he warned her, holding back a laugh as the people nearest them stopped to look twice at her rainbow hair. "Your true colors are showing."

It took her some effort to rein in her almost rabid urge to balance anyone who crossed her path. Her eyes glowed with predatory curiosity, but she managed to quell the physical changes caused by her inherent power. Her self-control had come a long way in the year since she'd managed to escape the Underworld. She no longer shorted out in public.

"She loves this soooo much," she growled in a voice barely human.

"Don't start with that Gollum shit," he chided. "Be civilized. Or pretend to be anyway."

Since seeing the *Lord of the Rings* movies, she'd gotten worse about talking in the third person. Now when she did her best Gollum impression, she scared people off.

Not that he left much of a better impression. Those nearest him, either sensing his energy or simply noticing he was very different, tended to move away quickly. Just over six feet tall, lean with light brown hair and eyes that turned from white to black to every hue in between, Fate was by no means fully ordinary in appearance. He wore dark sunglasses when he visited the human world, though it was next to impossible for him to pass as a human, which he often found disappointing.

He didn't consider himself the predator other deities often did. He usually had no intention of interfering with – or ending – anyone's life, and he wasn't trying to lure humans or Immortals into Hell or mess with them in any way. If anything, he was a good guy, an aloof ally to everyone around him, willing to help along someone's Future for the right price.

"What is it you wanted to show me?" he asked. "This isn't my normal scene."

"Not *civilized* enough?" Karma asked mockingly.

"It's boring," he replied with a charming smile. "I can do uncivilized if it's interesting."

"Still not peeking into your own future," she asked.

He shrugged. "More of the same. I stopped looking a while ago. My life is more boring than that of any of these humans. Besides, if something interesting happens, I want to be surprised." And … he'd taken care of the only surprise in his own path that could derail the life he preferred to live.

"Then I guess you'll see, won't you?" she said with a mischievous twinkle in her gaze.

The world held little capable of surprising him or ensnaring his attention for long. He privately doubted anything in the mortal world his too easily amused sister wanted to show him was going to be remotely worth his time. He went along with her, though, because he had nothing better to do. The normal tug of war between Immortals and demons was unusually calm. Even the deals made among deities failed to impress him, and he'd spent a few weeks in the jungles of South America doing manual labor alongside an undiscovered, primitive civilization that still viewed him as a god.

Unable to alter the chains of events he needed to, he'd resigned himself to waiting for the right opportunity. At least the trip to a festival was enough to keep him occupied for half a day.

The constant calculations of the destinies of those around him streamed through his thoughts like background music.

Ten percent chance of tripping over the speed bump.

Eighty three percent chance of bumping into the man she'll marry.

Fifty two percent chance of being hit by a car before the end of the day.

Fate purposely nudged the man about to trip out of the way of the speed bump and stopped fast enough to ensure the woman behind him was certain to smack into her future husband.

The last calculation made him pause, and he turned his focus to the person who had triggered it. The married mother of two was standing in front of a booth texting. Fate considered her for a moment, accessing the chain of events of her destiny to see what happened later to give her such a high percentage of dying. He then approached and smacked into her.

Her phone clattered to the ground. Pretending to be off balance, he crushed the screen with his heel and then stepped back. "My goodness!" he exclaimed, feigning surprise. "I'm so sorry!" He bent to retrieve the phone and verify it was indeed inoperable.

"Oh, damn," the woman replied, frowning. She accepted it back.

Zero percent chance of being hit by a car before the end of the day.

"Here. Let me reimburse you," Fate said and handed her a few hundred dollar bills.

She started to protest.

"No, take it," he said.

Charmed by his smile, she didn't object again, and he moved on.

"And you lecture me about interfering," Karma said, joining him several steps later.

"I'm done playing for today," he said with a shrug. "Beside, she's got two kids. Might as well save someone some grief."

"And if you knew she beat one of them and was scheduled to be balanced today?"

"You'll get her eventually." He glanced at her. "We aren't competing, Karma."

"Whatever."

Fate dwelled for a split second on the new information before dismissing it. His job was the Future; Karma's was balance. They could be at odds, if they chose to be. But as siblings, their tiffs tended to last many years without leaving scars between the two of them. They always ended up together again. The bond of family was thicker than that of their inherited duties.

He trailed her, looking for something interesting among the booths and exhibits while Karma made a beeline through the crowd to somewhere specific.

Ninety nine percent ...

Three percent ...

Seventy nine percent ...

The numbers continued to float through his mind. He saw Karma had stopped several booths ahead and continued at the leisurely pace towards her.

Eighty three percent ...

Point zero four percent ...

Silence.

Twenty percent ...

He stopped, jarred by the interruption in the flow of numbers.

Fate searched the crowd for the anomaly. Karma was retreating towards him, a puzzled expression on her face. He stepped back.

Eighty three percent ...

Point zero four percent ...

Silence.

Twenty percent ...

Following the odd break in predictions, he drew near a booth with several customers in front of it. He plucked the threads of each person's destiny and dismissed them just as fast. He hit the brick wall of someone whose destiny he couldn't see, who had no thread to pull, no chain of events and no calculations whatsoever.

The attractive young woman was seated at the booth behind a stack of colorful journals. Her large eyes were bright blue-green, her silky hair blue-black, her high cheekbones and jawline refined and her smooth skin the color of dark honey. Hers was an understated, simple beauty grounded in the symmetry of her features and striking eyes. He'd had his pick of women across the millennia – and decided quickly her looks ranked towards the top of those he'd known. He hadn't felt the spark of instant attraction in a very long time.

Karma joined him, and together they stared long enough for the two women at the booth to exchange a look with one another.

"Can we help you?" asked the woman with no future, standing.

"What is it, precious?" Karma hissed.

Teal eyes slid to his sister and back to him. "Journals, Gollum," she responded, unfazed by Karma's oddness. She picked up two and handed one to each of them.

Fate took it without bothering to look at it. His fingers grazed the stranger's as he did, and a flutter of warm electricity shot through him. He gazed down at her, trying to place the sensation and what it meant about the woman before him.

She froze, as if feeling it as well.

"Hello, gorgeous," he murmured with a half smile.

The woman flushed red deep beneath her dark complexion. But she didn't look away, didn't move, as if trapped in the same strange spell he was.

"These are so wonderful!" Karma's near squeal jarred him out of the trance. She ran her hands over the textured cover with interest before lifting her eyes to the pretty stranger. "But what are you?"

For once, Fate was happy for Karma's uncivilized candidness. Never in all his time had he ever run into someone who had no future – yet still lived. He'd been looking for something to intrigue him and found it where he didn't expect to.

As if realizing she was staring at him, the pretty woman cleared her throat and released the journal. The warm current stopped when they no longer touched.

"Another one," she said and rolled her eyes at her friend. "All yours." She turned her back to them and moved to the back of the booth, crossing her arms unhappily.

"You'll have to forgive my sister," Fate said with a smile. "She's different." He pretended to look over the journal, more interested in the brooding woman dressed in black. "This isn't really to my taste." He set the journal down. "I tend to like something a little more … polished. Leather usually. Do you have anything like that?"

"No." The face of the auburn-hair woman before him turned pink. "These are made from ecologically sustainable materials and vegan friendly."

"I'm definitely not vegan," he said.

"Then maybe you're at the wrong booth," the woman in the back snapped at him. Her eyes were fiery, her jaw clenched. She left the shadows for the table.

"I'm certain they're fine journals," he said.

"My brother doesn't like handmade stuff," Karma explained. "He's too civilized."

"Civilized or arrogant?" challenged the woman with no future.

"You don't normally stop by someone's table to insult what they're displaying. Olivia spent at least ten hours on each one of these."

Realizing his mistake, Fate offered an absent smile. "I didn't realize they were handmade. The quality is exceptional, just not what I prefer."

"It's cool, Stephanie," said Olivia with a smile. "Like you said. This place is full of strange people."

"I think I said assholes," Stephanie muttered under her breath.

"Assholes?" Fate raised an eyebrow. "A rather harsh judgment for a potential customer, isn't it?"

"I don't think we want the money of someone who can't appreciate something uncivilized," Stephanie responded.

Olivia laughed nervously. "I'm sorry. Steph is having a rough day."

"My fault," Fate replied. "Your friend is right. I've managed to offend the creator of these beautiful journals, and I apologize."

Olivia grinned.

Normally adept at handling people and situations, Fate was finding himself unable to figure out what to say to improve the current situation. By peeking into someone's future, he was usually able to discern enough about them to know how to talk to them. But this Stephanie was an enigma. He wasn't even able to tell if she were a true human, Immortal, or demon.

They gazed at one another, he curious and she angry he'd insulted her friend.

"I love them!" Karma exclaimed, oblivious to the tense, silent exchange, and picked up another. "I want four, one for each day of the week. Is that okay?" She peered up at him. "Brother?"

"Of course," he replied, realizing all of them were staring at him while he gazed at Stephanie.

"How about seven?" Stephanie asked his sister. "That's almost two week's worth."

"Even better!" Karma agreed.

He watched Stephanie deftly handle Karma's odd requests for colors and textures without so much as a blink. The woman with no future helped his sister sort through the journals and choose those she was buying.

It was rare when he met someone who could tolerate Karma's absurdities let alone politely respond to her. Fate found himself impressed. The protective brother in him appreciated someone else making the effort to help Karma feel like she wasn't the outlier she was.

And … there was something about Stephanie that left him unwilling to look away. She held some sort of magic, whatever she was.

At a loss of what to say to someone who clearly didn't know she was different, Fate checked the prices on the sign and paid Olivia, who seemed far less likely to throw his money back at him than Stephanie.

"Are you from around here?" he asked.

"We're from up the coast. Newport, Oregon," Olivia answered.

"Ah. Known for the lighthouse, correct?" He smiled, and Olivia's angst from earlier melted away in response.

"Exactly!" she replied. "No one knows about Newport."

"I've traveled extensively the past few years. What part of Newport?"

Olivia opened her mouth to respond when Stephanie nudged her. "He told you your journals suck. Are you really going to tell him where we live?" she demanded.

His charisma wasn't working on Stephanie at all. This wasn't normal, either. "You're right," Fate said smoothly, unfazed. "I've been incredibly rude. Can I make it up to both of you? Buy you a drink? Coffee?"

Stephanie's anger softened visibly. She glanced at Olivia, who seemed to be waiting for her to decide.

"Um, it's okay," Stephanie said. "I was rude, too. Let's just call it even."

"It would be my pleasure to have a drink with you."

She cleared her throat uncomfortably under his steady look and ducked her head. Opening her mouth for what he suspected was going to be a rejection, she had no chance to speak before Olivia piped up.

"Yes," she said. "We'd love to. We're staying in town at a bed and breakfast." She scribbled down the name on her business card and handed it to him. "You can drop by at seven. There's a bar next door."

Fate accepted the note with a smile. "Thanks."

Karma scooped up her new treasures with a grin, and the two of them left the booth.

"Good thinking," she said when they were out of earshot. "I was wondering how we'd get a chance to talk to the strange one."

"Were you able to read her?" he asked.

"No. Completely nothing."

"Same."

"What is she?" Karma gazed up at him curiously.

"I have no idea."

"She's a mystery!"

He chuckled. "Yeah. She is."

"We likeses mysteries," she said in her creepy voice. "Do you think she's a zombie?"

"I hadn't considered a zombie," he replied with a grin. "It'd be an awesome discovery."

"Yeah." Karma was already distracted by something else. She shoved the journals into his arms. "Hold these. I'm gonna go fuck with a psychic."

Fate accepted them and watched her approach another booth. He kept his distance, letting her have her fun while he was preoccupied with Stephanie. Nothing he'd experienced in his extensive lifetime explained someone who couldn't be read by Fate or Karma, the two deities capable of reading any living being in existence, from human to deity to demon. No, it didn't seem possible someone like Stephanie existed.

A familiar face drew his attention from his thoughts, and he followed the dark-haired man's progress through the crowd with interest.

"Karma, I'll be back," he called to his sister. He didn't wait for her response but shifted the journals and trailed the Ancient Immortal he'd never bothered meeting. Immortals in general didn't rank a visit from Fate, even though he dutifully tracked the Ancients who sat on the ruling Council That Was Seven. Responsible for managing the Immortal society and combating the Dark One's attempt to dominate humanity, the Council ranked high enough in importance for Fate to keep tabs on its members from time to time.

Their activities here in Carmel wouldn't have interested him in the slightest, if he didn't think it too convenient to find an Ancient within a hundred meters of a certain woman with no future.

Fate didn't believe in coincidences.

The Ancient entered a dark bar and sat at the counter next to a leggy blonde missing one hand. Fate took a seat several stools down and placed the journals on the stool next to him.

Kiki. The Ancient was one of seven illegitimate sons of Wynn, the oldest Immortal in existence, a creature even Fate was wary of crossing. Anyone sitting on two breaches between the mortal world and Hell – and unstable enough to open them in the name of self-preservation – was treated with caution even by deities.

The Ancient Wynn fathered seven sons, three of which were dead and one that was currently exiled. From what Fate knew of their dealings, Kiki was one of three remaining sons currently in favor by the new head of the Council.

The Immortals spoke too quietly for him to make out their words. He watched the two and pulled their threads from the webbing of destiny to check the choices they were about to make.

Eighty nine percent chance Kiki won't reveal their discovery to his father.

Fourteen percent chance Ileana takes their discovery to the Sanctuary.

What, or who, was important enough to hide from Wynn? Or to be taken to the Sanctuary, one of four neutral zones in the world where fighting and the presence of any creature with power were forbidden?

The two got up soon after and left. Fate remained, dwelling on the day that had turned more interesting than he expected. None of whatever was happening was his business. But he was curious. Karma was right; as different as their temperaments were, they both loved mysteries and surprises, and neither of them paid any attention to boundaries.

He sensed his sister enter and waited for her. She plopped down at the bar.

"So you brought me here to show me what?" he asked. "The woman we found?"

Karma shook her head. "I brought you here because I thought you'd like this place."

"It's nice," he said. "Not the first time I visited, either. It's a good choice."

She was gazing at him closely. "You approve?"

"Sure. Great day trip."

"What if it's longer than a day? Would you still like it?"

"I rarely like being anywhere long."

"But there's a mystery here. You could solve it."

"Could." He studied her. "Is this your way of saying you want us to stay here for a while?"

"Sorta."

"Hmm." Karma often did things he didn't understand, which he assumed was because she was reintegrating to the world after a thousand year stint in prison. The modern world was filled with delight and discoveries for her. That she wanted to stay longer than usual didn't surprise him, but her thoughtful expression did. "This means a lot to you?"

"I have to tell you something," she said. "I don't want you to be mad again like you were a thousand years ago."

"I promise not to get mad again so soon," he replied, amused. "What's wrong?"

"So I was thinking about what I do and why I do it," she began. "The noblest thing I can do for someone is to balance them, to give them a chance to start over. I help people. I have a very important job."

"You do," he agreed.

"I know I'm not the best at it yet. I know I disappoint you sometimes and our father wouldn't approve of how or when I balance people."

"You don't disappoint me, Karma," he replied. "You have more to learn about who you are and your duties. You also have an eternity to figure it out."

She was studying him again, unusually pensive.

"What's bothering you?" he prodded. "You want to spend some time among humans?"

"Well, first, I want you to know there's no hard feelings about you putting me in prison. What you did was help balance me."

"Exactly. I'm glad you see it my way." Not everyone would come to the same conclusion after being sentenced to prison for a millennium.

"I do. You're always right. Second." She hesitated then took his hands in hers. Her eyes were growing dark once more, her hair as well. She was starting to short out, probably from all the exposure to the humans needing balancing around her. "You're my brother. I do this because I want to help you the way you did me."

Until that moment, he hadn't bothered to guess where she was headed with the trip, odd questions or thoughtfulness. He hadn't bothered today to put the immense effort required into reading the destiny of a fellow deity. He'd checked her destiny yesterday, concerned about her involvement with the Immortals.

Yesterday, his sister had no intention of doing what she was doing right now. Fate pulled his hands from her grip, about to lecture her once more about timing, when a flash of cool energy zipped through him.

The calculations in his mind stopped so suddenly, he was temporarily distracted by the abrupt quiet where he'd never known silence before.

Her hair was returning to normal, though her eyes glowed unnaturally.

"Karma, what did you do?" he asked cautiously.

"You need to be balanced, brother."

His heartbeat accelerated. He tried to access his powers and found them gone. Not blocked, not hard to reach – gone.

"You have forgotten what it means to be you," she said almost gently. "I love you. I'm going to help you remember."

"Karma, this is not funny."

"No, but it's necessary." She stood and stacked the journals. "You're human, brother. Well, human-ish," she corrected herself. "You're deity born, turned temporary human. Whatever that makes you. Anyway, your destiny is yours again."

Her words sank into him slowly. "I don't understand. My reward for a lifetime of safeguarding humanity is *this*? To become one of them?"

She nodded.

"This is punishment. You're saying I was so off balance I deserved to be a human?" he asked, rare astonishment creeping into his voice.

"It's not punishment. It's balancing," she corrected him. "I was gentler than I could have been. I may not have timing, but I have compassion, which you've clearly lost since I went to prison."

He blinked, not expecting the rebuke from his younger, wild sister.

"Don't worry. Your power and status can be returned," she added.

"When?"

"When you earn them back." She shrugged. "So it depends on you."

"What does that even mean?"

"It means, when you're balanced, you'll be you again." With a cheerful smile, she started away, carting off her journals.

Unable to swallow the idea he was truly *human,* Fate trailed her. "How do I earn my power back?"

"I dunno. Try being a good human," she suggested. "Oh, and I reserved you a room at that bed and breakfast where the girls are staying. There's three hundred dollars in cash on the nightstand in your room. That'll last you ... how long? Ten years?"

"Not even close."

"Hopefully it doesn't take that long," she said. "I have faith in you, brother. You won't be stuck here for a thousand years like I was. You're stronger than me."

Coldness sank into his belly. Fate stood frozen, unable to digest what just happened. Karma stepped outside, and he forced himself to follow, not about to be abandoned in the mortal realm by his madwoman of a sister.

Stepping outside, he shielded his eyes against the sun and looked around.

Just like that, Karma was gone.

Shit. He waited for her to return, to tell him it was one of her pranks. When she didn't, he started to feel ill.

People passed him on their path into the bar, and he held his breath, hoping to hear their fates calculated in his head as usual.

Nothing. It was quiet.

And he was completely alone. Powerless. Exiled to the human world by none other than his sister. His thoughts went to his history of dealings with Immortals, humans and deities alike, and he glanced at the sky.

"I think I'll be here for quite some time," he murmured to himself. He had forgotten more misdeeds than he could remember.

At least he was comfortable in the mortal realm. What disturbed him: not knowing how quickly those he'd pissed off over the years would find out what Karma did.

This will be the ultimate adventure.

CHAPTER THREE

"You're not ready!" Olivia exclaimed later that evening.

"I'm not going," Stephanie replied. Sprawled on her belly across her bed, she was busy texting pictures of the leftover journal stock to her sister, who was one of Olivia's biggest fans.

"He was totally into you, not me."

"A sign he's an even bigger asshole than he acted."

"But he's hot. Like, really hot."

Stephanie's fingers paused as an image of the charismatic yet rude man from earlier flashed through her thoughts. Tall, athletic, handsome and charming, the asshole was sexy with golden skin, wide shoulders and a smile that probably knocked normal girls off their feet straight into his bed. He'd been wearing sunglasses, but she could imagine his eyes – whatever color they were – had to be as flawless as the rest of him. She'd felt the intensity of his look, and the memory made butterflies flutter in her stomach. It was a rare day when she considered wanting something to do with a guy. She noticed a lot of guys, but they never, ever noticed her.

"He's not my type," she said.

"So, what?" Olivia countered. "Don't read into this or overanalyze it. You're not marrying him. We're just having a drink."

Stephanie twisted to see her. Olivia was wearing a bright yellow dress and had taken the time to put on her makeup tonight. Naturally gorgeous, her eyes were as large as a doll's and her plump lips wine colored.

"Why do you even want to go?" Stephanie asked. "He was a total jerk to you."

"He apologized."

"So that makes it okay?"

"No, Steph!" Olivia sat down on her bed with an exasperated sigh. "I just want to have a little fun, and I'm not going to hold grudges against a complete stranger. If some guy wants to buy us a drink, why not just go and have fun then come back here. We don't ever have to see him again."

Olivia made sense. Stephanie knew when she was being unreasonably stubborn, but something about the guy made her uncomfortable. Maybe it was how he looked at her, through her. She'd spent her whole life begrudging the human race for overlooking her but if this was what it felt like to be noticed by someone else, she began to think she was better off being ignored.

"I'm allergic to fun," she said and shifted back to her belly.

"You're impossible!" Olivia rose. "I will drag you out of that shell one day and force feed you fun if it kills me."

"You've been saying that since I moved in a month ago."

"I got you to go on a road trip, didn't I?"

Stephanie rolled her eyes. "You can have fun for both of us," she replied. "People really freak me out telling me their weird secrets. I'm so awkward anyway."

"You're intense. There's a difference."

"Okay."

Olivia laughed. "All right. I'll be back by nine."

Steph nodded. She waited until she heard the door close before sitting up. A small part of her wanted to go with Olivia, to sit with the pretentious man and let him charm her, just to experience what it was like to be the center of attention to someone as devastatingly handsome as he was. She'd know it wasn't real, that someone like him wouldn't ever truly care about someone like her, but it would be nice to let herself believe she might one day meet someone who would treat her like she was the *good* kind of special for once.

Could she really tolerate being around someone so fake, though, even for a couple of hours?

A flicker of envy went through her when she considered how often her sister and Olivia went out on dates. She hated being different but feared taking a chance at changing her life. What did that make her?

Fighting with herself, she nonetheless stood and went to the dresser she was sharing with Olivia. She didn't have party clothes or sundresses. The best she had was the gray skirt made of soft t-shirt material she wore on laundry days and weekend mornings to run errands. Was it dark enough in the bar for people not to notice it wasn't exactly a formal skirt?

She sighed, torn between wearing it or jeans. The mid-summer humidity and heat was worse here than in northern Oregon, so she went with the skirt and a simple, dark t-shirt. Not entirely satisfied with how she looked, Stephanie slid her feet into sandals and pulled her hair into a ponytail before leaving the room. It was a quarter past seven. With any luck, the stranger was running late, and she wouldn't have to stand awkwardly in the bar looking for her party.

She checked the lobby first to make sure Olivia hadn't been stood up by the handsome stranger. She didn't see her friend and left the bed and breakfast for the cozily lit street outside.

The night was warm and air heavy. Fog hung low over the town, blocking the sky and creating fuzzy halos around street lamps. It smelled of flowers, and several people were out walking on the sidewalks past closed boutiques and open restaurants and bars.

Beautiful and tranquil, the tiny town was as charming during the night as it was during the day.

Except for the surplus of weirdos. Stephanie shook her head ruefully and started next door to the small English pub nestled between the bed and breakfast and an art gallery. She passed the middle of the alleyway between buildings. The sounds of a scuffle pulled her attention from her phone, and she paused.

Four men surrounded a fifth. Three of the five were fighting. One spoke in a language she didn't recognize.

Her heart took off. "Hey!" she called. "Hey!"

They ignored her.

She pulled out her phone. "I'm calling the police!" she shouted at the top of her lungs and waved the cell.

One glanced her way, but it was the sixth figure lifting itself off the ground that made her breath catch.

"Olivia," she whispered.

Her roommate was dazed and wobbling, her sunny dress torn. She began staggering down the alley, in the opposite direction of Stephanie.

The four attackers stood between Stephanie and her roommate. She debated what to do for a split second before sprinting away. Stephanie slammed the door to the bed and breakfast's lobby open then tore through the downstairs area, through the dining room closed for the evening and to the entrance onto the patio leading to the quaint courtyard. She hurried through the courtyard and to the back fence entrance the registration clerk told them stayed open until ten every night.

Stephanie raced out the gate to the alley to the left and hesitated once more at the mouth of the alley. Olivia had stopped walking and sagged against the wall of one building. She'd made it about five meters from the men who were beating the crap out of the fifth.

Without giving herself too long to think about it, Stephanie ran to Olivia's side.

"Olivia!" she hissed. "Can you walk?" She wrapped an arm around her friend as she spoke.

Olivia lifted her head, eyes glassy. She wasn't bleeding that Stephanie could see, though one hand was pressed to her forehead.

"Y…yeah," she murmured.

"Come on." Stephanie cast a quick glance at the men nearby and half dragged, half walked her friend the first few steps.

Olivia caught her balance and began to move.

Before they'd gotten far, however, someone ahead of them spoke.

"What's this? Dinner escaping?"

Stephanie's gaze flew up. If she hadn't known better, she'd have sworn the man had fangs. Before she could get a better look at him, he had shoved her back and grabbed Olivia. She hit the ground, one hand splashing into a puddle. She wiped away droplets of water from her face and scrambled up, facing the exit and Olivia once more.

She stood, too shocked to register what she was seeing.

The man *did* have fangs. Not only that, but he sank them into Olivia's neck while Stephanie watched and began to drink her blood.

"Run!" someone shouted from behind her.

She looked over her shoulder and saw the striking stranger from earlier. He'd managed to take out two of his attackers. The other two were on their feet, and they had fangs, too. But his eyes … they were out of a dream or movie. Glowing, filled with color yet colorless, the hue was like the iridescent reflection of light off the surface of a polished pearl, indescribably beautiful – and creepy as hell.

What the fuck? If not for the stinging of her wrist from the fall, she'd think this was a nightmare.

Olivia's faint cry of pain snapped Stephanie back into the moment. She balled up her fists the way her kickboxing sister had taught her and strode up to the man who had Olivia. Without stopping to aim, she punched him in the side of the head hard enough to knock him away from Olivia's neck then smashed a roundhouse kick high into the back of his neck.

He slammed into the wall, releasing Olivia, who dropped to the ground hard.

Eyes on the man struggling to recover, Stephanie knelt beside her. "Come, on, Olivia! We gotta go! Now!" she urged and tugged at her friend's arm.

Blood spurted out of Olivia's neck. In the few short moments since he'd bitten her, half of the material covering her torso was soaked with red, and blood pooled around her head and neck.

Stephanie rolled her friend onto her back and gasped.

Olivia's eyes were open and blank.

"Olivia! We have to go!" she said, shaking her.

The man who attacked Olivia snatched her arm and hauled her up. Stephanie punched him hard and drove her knee into his crotch. He doubled over, and she yanked loose, dropping beside Olivia one more.

"Come on, Olivia," she said and numbly shook her friend again.

She heard the sound of struggle behind her and hunched, waiting for the crazy man with fangs to grab her once more. He didn't, and seconds later, he dropped unconscious beside her. She jerked away and shook her friend again.

"Where'd you learn to fight?" the handsome stranger who visited their booth asked as he dropped to one knee beside her.

"My sister." She tried to lift Olivia. "Come on, Olivia!"

"We gotta go, gorgeous."

"Not without Olivia."

"There are a dozen demons waiting to eat us."

She stared at him, uncertain which stunned her more, his claim or … "What's wrong with your eyes?" she whispered. They were rapidly changing hues beneath the iridescent shimmer, mesmerizing and too surreal for any of this to be real.

"I can explain," he said with a smile laced with some of his earlier charm. He touched her arm. "But not here." For a moment, it was just the two of them – and a strange, warm electricity feeding from him into her. It was as intense as his gaze, exhilarating, compelling with a strange edge of familiarity, as if they'd always known one another, or were meant to meet.

"Oliv-" she started to object.

"- is dead," he said gently. "We will be, too, if they have anything to do with it." He pointed down the alley, where several more men waited. Streetlight glinted off their fangs. "Trust me. We need to go." He held out his hand.

She blinked the spell away and shook her head. "Olivia's not ..." She stopped. Tears blurred her eyes as she peered down at her friend's lifeless body.

"I can't leave you here." He took her arm and stood, pulling her up with him.

The strange current of warmth emitted by the stranger soothed her. Stephanie didn't resist. At a loss as to what to do, she let him guide her out of the alley, away from danger. She gazed at Olivia's still body until the stranger pulled her around a corner.

"We need to hurry," he said with quiet urgency.

She reigned in what she could of her horror and concentrated on escaping the freak show behind them. He held her hand, and together, they ran through the streets of Carmel, down the hill towards the ocean. At one point, she heard someone shouting as the men gave chase. The stranger ran faster and turned a corner, and the sounds of pursuit were soon lost.

They ran until they reached the beach then ducked behind a lifeguard post. Panting and trembling, Stephanie bent over, gasping in air.

"I have ... I have to call ... police," she managed and reached for her pocket.

"No." The man gripped her wrist, renewing the current of warmth between them.

She straightened, once more weirded out by his eyes but not wanting to break the strange bond of his touch. She stared up at him, overly aware of his nearness in a way she'd never noticed anyone else's before. He smelled of sandalwood and brown sugar, and the sense of familiarity was somehow stronger. But she'd never met this man. She'd remember if she had.

"Police can't fight demons," he added with a tight smile.

"You keep saying that word," she said.

"Demons?"

She nodded.

"It's hard to explain," he said.

She waited.

The enigmatic man gazed down at her, breathing heavily yet nowhere near as freaked out as she was starting to feel. He seemed as lost to the moment as she was.

"This is weird, isn't it?" he asked finally.

"Yeah."

"Are you hurt?" He tipped her chin up to peer at her neck, as if he, too, had seen one of the fanged men bite Olivia's neck.

Stephanie didn't answer. The logical side of her mind was working on rationalizing away the unusual display in the alley, which was hard when confronted with the colorful eyes of the man standing close enough for her to smell his faint musk. He was warm, his athletic frame a buffer against the cool ocean breeze. She had the sudden urge to be closer, to trace her fingertips along his chiseled jaw and across his full lips.

What the hell is wrong with me? My friend just died! Baffled, she pulled away from him and stepped back.

"You're handling this well," he said. "That's good. We might be partnered up for the time being."

Partnered up. As if they were working on a science project after school and not running from men with fangs.

Stephanie couldn't muster a response. She watched him move a meter away before seating himself on the sand and drawing up a bloodied calf for inspection.

"Would you believe this is the first time in several dozen ages I've been nicked like this?" he asked, amusement and irritation in his tone. "The last time I was in a physical altercation, I was wrestling my sister into a cell in the Underworld. That was before your time. Waaaay before your time."

I'm losing it. Nothing was making sense. Not the men from the alley, not Olivia's lifeless body, not the enticing man chatting calmly about nonsense. How was this real?

Stephanie looked around for something to defend herself with. Since coming to Carmel, she'd been accosted by insanity.

"I have to ask you a few questions you're going to find odd," he said, oblivious to her internal struggle.

"Odd?" she echoed. "You're talking about demons and you think anything about me is odd?"

"I hear a note of hysteria. Perhaps the questions can wait."

"Ya think?" Stephanie retorted. "Is this … is this a prank? Is my roomie really lying in a puddle of her own blood or is this … a joke?" She choked on the words, eyes hot with tears. She swiped them away only for more to form and soon found herself near-choking as she tried to keep her head long enough to figure out what the fuck was going on.

"I'm afraid it's real." His voice was closer. The stranger with the amazing eyes had drawn nearer.

"W… *what* is real?" she stammered.

"This may not be the right time."

"I need to know!" She glared at him through her tears. "I need to know if Olivia is … is really …" She swallowed the sob that wanted to escape, struggling to understand anything she'd seen tonight, including why one look from this man could make her forget watching her roommate die.

"I have a soft spot for humans in pain." He lifted her chin once more and offered a small smile. His warm palms rested on her cheeks, and he gently wiped the tears from her face with his thumb. "But don't tell anyone, okay?"

He'd been smiling, joking or entertained since their first meeting. She sensed an edge this time, something darker, buried beneath the faint smile and the natural charisma trying to usurp her anger and fear. She'd noticed it earlier, too, how he'd blatantly insulted Olivia then had her best friend eating out of his hand. She fought the strange charisma that made her want to sigh and trust whatever came out of his mouth next.

The stranger's touch calmed her, though, and her fascination with his color changing eyes prevented her from sinking into her emotions. They stood in quiet long enough for her to grow uncomfortable with the tension stretched between them.

"Your friend is dead," he said softly. "You made the mistake of helping me, which means you're on the demons' radar as well."

Her brow furrowed at his mention of demons.

"Are you up for an explanation?" he asked. The dark edge sank beneath his surface once more, replaced by amusement. "I've got all the time in the world to wait. I'm working off a debt to Karma. Might be stuck here for a while."

His words nudged her from her spell, and Stephanie shifted back, leaving his warmth. "This … no," she said finally. "I'm done." Turning, she started up the beach towards the road once more. "I'm going to my room and calling the police."

"Steph, there's no going back."

"Whatever this is, I can't handle it!"

"Look, I don't exactly know what to do next either," he said, trailing her. "But I know facing demons, when I've got no power and you're … well, a human, the bottom of the food chain –"

"What the hell are you even talking about? What powers? Food chain?" she demanded, whirling. "Do you hear the level of crazy you're at?"

He smiled, unruffled by her once more, as he had been earlier in the day when she called him an asshole. It was blunt, even by her standards, but his calmness managed to deflate the intensity behind her emotions. Like Olivia, he was non-confrontational, and his calm took the edge off her anger.

"I agree. It's madness," he admitted. "But it's real, if you'd give me a chance to talk to you."

She hesitated.

"I have a unique gift to see the Future," he claimed.

"You and every other psychic Olivia's dragged me to."

"Clearly a human can't see the Future. But I can."

She folded her arms across her chest. "Then what's going to happen next?"

"That's the problem. I seem to have temporarily lost my power."

What the hell am I prolonging this? Because he's the sexiest man I've ever met? Stephanie spun. "It doesn't take a psychic to know I'm leaving your ass right here and going back to the hotel! You're going back to the psych ward you escaped from."

"Hear me out." He circled her and held out his hands, not touching her but blocking her path. "You're wondering why you've had more wackos in your life today than usual. You've run into more than me today, haven't you?"

She eyed him.

"A blonde missing a hand maybe and an Asian gentleman with blue eyes?"

"How do you know that?" she asked. "Were you following me?"

"They're different, like me. They're in town, the demons are in town, I'm in town. It's not a coincidence you're here, too, a woman with no aura, with no destiny or karmic load. I'm different, but so are you. Your friend knew it."

She listened, unable to shake the deep resonance left in the wake of his explanation.

"Olivia was a good person. Death is a gentleman. He'll take good care of her," he added.

The horror of seeing her friend killed replayed in her head. Sorrow replaced her anger. She'd never felt so much like exploding or losing control or flinging her arms around a sensual stranger.

"There's a diner nearby. We can get pie and talk," he offered.

"I don't want pie," she whispered. "I want Olivia back."

"The demons are going to be waiting for you if you go back," he warned her once more. "You saw what they did to her. They'll do the same to you. My ability to protect you through conventional means is currently challenged. I'd rather sit with you and discuss this than risk your life confronting demons." He backed away as he spoke, in the direction opposite that of the bed and breakfast. "Either way, it's your choice. Fate is in your hands."

He turned and began walking away. His madness held her ensnared. Had she ever spoken with half his confidence about anything in life let alone *demons*?

Stephanie stared after him, unable to wrap her head around anything that had happened or the man with the intriguing eyes. She wanted to block the existence of men with fangs from her memories but whenever the image of Olivia dying crossed her thoughts, she saw one of them again. Her gaze went to the hill, at the top of which ran the street leading to the bed and breakfast, and then to the athletic man with a natural spring in his step striding confidently down the street.

Her adrenaline was wearing off, leaving her shaking from the ocean chill and shock. She'd dropped her phone along the run from the alley; if nothing else, the diner would have one she could borrow to call the police. Whatever was going on, there had to be a logical explanation, one that didn't involve demons or her best friend dying. Maybe if she pushed, he'd break down and tell her the truth.

With reservations that shook her to the core, she forced her body to move finally and followed the mysterious man with the otherworldly eyes.

Instead of going into the diner at the end of the street, the stranger stopped and leaned against the railing overlooking the ocean.

She drew as near as she dared, all of two meters away, hugging herself.

"Where do you want me to start?" he asked, his low, soft voice soothing her jumping nerves.

She dwelt on the deceptively easy question for a moment. "Who are you?"

"I think we should start somewhere simpler," he replied.

"What's simpler than a name?"

"We'll get to it." He flashed her a smile. "The two people you met today, they're Immortals. There are four main divisions of living beings that cross through the mortal realm: humans, Immortals, demons, and deities. At first glance, it's difficult to tell everyone apart. Demons are the easiest to spot. They're usually trying to make a meal out of you. The ruling race of Immortals are dead ringers for humans, except they tend to live thousands of years, if not forever. They coexist among humans in a subculture of their own. The other races of Immortals generally choose to remain hidden."

Stephanie listened, too stunned by his claims to leave.

"So, basically, you had two Immortals and a handful of demons in town. It's not infrequent, but I happen to know you being here isn't a coincidence, either. Whatever you are, you're unlike any creature I've met in any realm," he added. "Every living being has a destiny. You don't. I'm curious. What other sort of side effects have you experienced from being unusual?"

"A man with chameleon eyes is asking me what it's like to be weird?" she murmured and shook her head.

"Humor me." A smile tugged up the corner of his lips and sparkled in his eyes.

"Well." She cleared her throat. Whether it was his charisma or the fact someone might actually have an explanation for her uniqueness, she found herself answering. "Animals hate me. People trust me with their secrets or overlook me completely. Like I can be walking down the street and someone will stare straight at me and still run into me. Psychics are afraid of me." She shrugged. "Olivia always said I was really different but she couldn't figure out why."

He listened intently.

"That asshole drew my blood today," she said and glanced down at her palm at the memory. "Then you and your sister showed up and life went downhill from there."

"Interesting," he said. "I've never heard of any of this. My sister asked if you were a zombie. A life with no future?" He was pensive. "I've never heard of zombies being real but it wouldn't surprise me to see a new addition to the types of creatures in existence."

"When you say shit like that, you really freak me out." She was gripping the handrail of the boardwalk tightly enough for one knuckle to pop.

"My apologies." His focus was elsewhere. His gaze sharpened, and his relaxed stance shifted. He moved closer to her, tense where he'd been at ease, the dark edge back and his intent gaze on something beside the diner. "You'll adjust."

"What's wrong?" She held her breath, alarmed at the subtle change in him. "Adjust to what?"

"He means, we really don't have any other choice but to tell you everything you shouldn't know."

She spun at the male voice. The Asian man with teal eyes – who had taken her blood earlier – and his blonde partner stood beside the diner. Stephanie backpedaled, her back meeting the railing. The enigmatic man shifted with deceptive casualness between her and the newcomers. He steadied her with a light touch, and another trickle of warm energy fluttered through her.

Why did she feel safe around someone who babbled about demons and immortals like they were real?

"Your intentions?" His tone was friendly yet cautious.

"To take her home," the blonde woman replied. "Where she belongs."

"She's one of you."

"Yes."

"Who the fuck are you?" the man asked with a frown.

The stranger turned to gaze down at her. "Stephanie, meet Kiki and Ileana," he said. "They'll protect you."

She moved away from his touch, overly conscious of the warmth in her cheeks. Did he notice the spark at all when their skin met?

"Immortals," Stephanie said before she could stop herself. She studied the two people. How was she almost believing the outrageous story about them being immortal? They looked every bit as normal as she did.

They, however, were staring with varying levels of unease at the man she was with.

"Seriously. Who the fuck are you?" Ileana asked again, addressing the stranger.

"That's a story for another time," he replied smoothly. He turned Stephanie to face him. "Rest assured I'll make certain your friend is taken care of in the most respectful way possible. You'll be safer with these two than anyone else."

"I'm not going with them," Stephanie said. "I'm not going with

39

any of you."

"I'm afraid you have to," Kiki replied to her before shifting his focus back to the stranger. "But seriously, why are you involved?"

How were they more interested in the stranger than her? The only person not surprised by anything happening was the stranger who refused to give his name. The two parties exchanged looks over her head, one amused and the other wary.

"Is anyone going to tell me what's going on?" she asked.

"Sorry." Ileana offered a smile. "What's going on is you have a meeting to attend."

"Meeting?"

"With your father." Kiki spoke the words reluctantly.

"Ah, and there's the reason everyone is in town," the stranger said with satisfaction. "It's an honor, Stephanie. Our paths aren't likely to cross again, though. But I wish you well and much luck with that lot."

She found herself starting to wish him farewell before it clicked what Kiki had said.

"My *father*?" she echoed. "The man who left my mom when she was two months pregnant and never sent child support or called in twenty one years?"

The two exchanged a look.

"Trust me. You're better off for not having him in your life before now," the stranger spoke first. "But my good deed is done. I'm off to find some balance. Take care, gorgeous." He started away with a wink.

She watched him go before turning to the remaining two strangers. "You're seriously taking me to my father?"

"Did he tell you who he was?" Kiki's focus was once more on the man walking down the street.

"What? No. Why?"

"He's a deity," Ileana said with a shake of her head. "You can't trust those bastards. They're shady and shifty and more interested in personal achievement than anything else."

"Deity. Like a god?" Stephanie echoed. "He's a *god*?"

"Open a portal. We lost the element of surprise," Kiki said to his partner, the reserved note in his voice once more.

Ileana nodded and moved away, into the shadows of the restaurant.

"There's no good way to say this," Kiki said, facing Stephanie. "Welcome to the family. I'm sorry you're involved and even sorrier we found you. Just know you're not the only one our father is tormenting."

"Um, thanks." Stephanie peered more closely up at him. The trim man seemed too serious to smile. His eyes were similar in color to hers but otherwise, she saw no resemblance. "You and I are ... what?"

"Brother-sister. Half brother, half sister," he replied. "None of us share the same mother."

"How many of us are there?"

"There were seven boys and you. Three are dead, one exiled, one in training to become a death dealer and one ..." He drifted off. "Basically, I'm the only one living at home right now."

The insanity was falling harder upon her, but she somehow managed to block it from reaching her emotions and instead, found herself numbed and attentive, especially after the mention of the father she'd tried to find three times since she turned eighteen.

"You're doing good." He patted her shoulder awkwardly and then moved away. "It's time to go."

She watched him join his partner in the shadows of the restaurant on the side opposite the parking lot. They just stood there. Morbid curiosity got the best of her, and she ventured closer, waiting in borderline hysteria to see if they had a spaceship or something.

What she saw was worse. A hole in the world yawned open. On the other side weren't the hedges lining the boardwalk, but a cavern with glowing, yellow doors.

Ileana stepped through first, while Kiki stood aside, waiting for Stephanie.

Maybe I died in the alley. She inched closer, unable to comprehend how there was a hole in the world.

"It's the place-between-places," Kiki explained. "You can go anywhere from inside."

"That makes no sense."

"You get used to it. Better than driving or flying somewhere." He motioned her inside.

Ileana had already crossed the cavern, headed towards one of the glowing doors.

Her nerves were near the breaking point, but she was also acutely aware of something else, an instinct deep inside her stirring with increasing insistence the longer the night progressed.

She wasn't surprised by the mode of travel the purported Immortals had or even that Immortals existed. If anything, the news seemed supported by a newfound feeling that this was the way things were supposed to be, after a lifetime of not fitting in anywhere.

She stepped into the cavern. It was cool, and a mist coated the ground. It didn't feel like leaving the beach.

"That answers that question," Ileana called from the portal she stood in front of.

"Normal humans can't go through here without dying," Kiki explained. "But we already knew you'd be fine."

Stephanie stopped in place, a chill working down her spine. He walked past her, at ease telling her she could've died. Stephanie turned around to run back to the beach only to find the portal behind them had closed.

"Come on," Ileana said.

When she turned, the woman was disappearing through the portal. Uncertain where else to go, Stephanie followed them.

And emerged somewhere where it was daylight, next to a window overlooking a wide expanse of green forest. It was cooler here. The stone hall was flanked on one side by massive windows and the other by tall, wooden doors, currently closed. She seemed to be in a castle, if she had to guess.

"Where are we?" she asked.

"French Alps," Ileana said. "Home."

"Seriously?" Stephanie raised her eyebrows.

Neither of them appeared pleased to be there. They began walking down the hallway, and she trailed.

"Whatever happens, don't piss him off," Kiki whispered over his shoulder.

"Our father?"

He nodded.

Was her lifelong curiosity about her father about to be over?

Dread sank into her stomach. What was going on? How was any of this real? What about her suitcase in Carmel? Olivia's body? With some dismay, she realized she didn't even know Olivia's middle name or birthday. They'd been roommates but not really friends yet. As she progressed through a castle in the Alps mere minutes after being in California, Stephanie wasn't certain which was stronger, her guilt or the sense of familiarity that was growing stronger. She knew this world or at least, felt like she did.

CHAPTER FOUR

As promised, Fate returned to the scene of Olivia's death. The dead-dead demons were gone, taken away by their brethren, though they'd left the human where she fell. He assumed part of his Karma-balancing was to do as many good deeds as he could, and keeping his promise to the pretty woman with bright eyes was part of it. He hadn't really wanted to turn her over to the Immortals before satisfying his curiosity about what she was, but there'd been little choice. If demons were in town, she was safer with the Immortals.

If she were truly the daughter of Wynn, he didn't want to be further involved anyway. The dangerous leader of the Immortals was not what Fate needed at the moment, not when he'd played a hand in having Wynn killed the first time around and was vulnerable to anyone seeking revenge. His mind went to the chain of events he'd been puzzling over how to alter for years. The run-in with Wynn's daughter held double meaning. It was a warning, a reminder he hadn't yet corrected the path the single-minded Wynn was on.

Fate doubted the soul collectors would be long in coming, but he decided to call the man in charge, hoping it would add a few Karma points to his debt.

Gabriel. He spoke the word in his mind and waited, curious to see if Death himself could hear him since he was now human-ish. A light breeze touched him, and seconds later, the towering, muscular figure of Death appeared.

"She's already on the list," he said brusquely and checked the list of souls his death dealers were obligated to collect this night. Only he could see the names scrawling across his arm.

"I told someone I'd make sure this one was taken care of," Fate answered and stepped aside for Gabriel to collect the soul.

The large man with dark hair and eyes knelt. "Demons?" he asked, looking over the woman's throat wounds.

"Unfortunately."

"It's been quiet for a while. Haven't seen many demon incursions."

"Darkyn used up a great deal of power to cause that second breach in the mortal world before we went gallivanting to the Underworld," Fate said, referring to the last adventure he'd gone on with Death.

"I wonder if this means he's starting to recover."

"It's possible. Something's going on." Fate replied. "You missed a party today. Demons, Immortals, an Ancient … everyone was in town, including me and Karma."

Gabriel muttered something about Karma being crazy, which Fate chose to ignore. Even the foreboding figure of Death knew to be wary of Karma, for no one – even a deity – was immune from balancing.

Green mist formed around Olivia's body and coiled around Gabriel's hand as he coaxed the human's soul free. He glanced up at Fate as he worked and then back, tilting his head.

"Long story," Fate said before he could ask.

The soul coalesced and solidified, turning from fog into a flawless emerald dwarfed by Gabriel's large hand. He rose and eyed Fate. Fate didn't have to have his powers to know Gabriel was debating whether he should ask.

"What's wrong with you?" Death asked finally. "You aren't reading as a deity."

"Because I'm temporarily not one," Fate replied.

A glimmer of amusement, if not satisfaction, crossed Gabriel's gaze. "Now I do want to know."

Their relationship was better than Fate's dealings with most, partially because Gabriel had been a little more than a year, nowhere near long enough for Fate to have fucked him over in the course of his normal political maneuverings. If anything, Gabriel was an ally.

"My sister balanced me," Fate admitted.

Gabriel laughed loudly.

"I seem to be stuck here. It's a good place to be. Tons of interesting events today."

Death flashed a rare grin and tucked the soul into his pocket.

"Pie?" Fate asked. "I know a good diner."

As a deity, he ate rarely, if at all. Food was an indulgence. But since being human for almost half a day, he found himself craving human food, and his stomach felt empty.

"Why not." Gabriel started walking down the alley. "I gotta hear this story."

They left Olivia's body for the police to discover. Fate was more interested in saving her soul from the demons, who were known to steal them before Gabriel could take them someplace safe for eternity in his Underworld.

Returning to the diner at the bottom of the hill, Fate wasn't surprised to find Death a good companion. The only deity since the time-before-time to start out as a human, Gabriel's compassion had both alienated some Immortals and deities and attracted others. Fate found him a curiosity, hence his interest in him initially when Gabriel was abruptly appointed as Death by the outgoing goddess who then became his mate.

They sat in a booth in the corner and ordered.

"Karma may not be the bitch I thought she was," Gabriel said. Too genuine to gloat, he did smile. "How's life as a human?"

"Different," Fate replied. "Not entirely too bad, though I noticed your kind doesn't heal quickly." He lifted his bruised hand. He'd cut his knuckles punching a demon. The bleeding had slowed to a trickle.

"There's something humans do called a pressure dressing," Gabriel said. He took Fate's hand and wrapped a napkin around it. "Put pressure on it and hold it above the level of your heart to stop the bleeding."

Fate listened.

"You might need to learn a few more first aid tips," Gabriel advised. "I think I'm the only deity or Immortal in existence that likes you."

"Ah, but you do like me," Fate said with a wink.

"You can't riddle or maneuver your way out of this one."

Fate said nothing, beginning to suspect the same.

"What happens to the future if you're not you?" Gabriel asked. "How does the mates-blood-fate laws from the time-before-time play into there being no Fate?"

Fate dwelt on the response for a moment. Immortals liked to make up rules and had a Code with several hundred thousand different laws governing their kind and their interactions with other beings.

But deities were bound by only three bonds, known as the original laws, that survived from the time-before-time: mates, blood, fate. The sacred three bonds were generally open to interpretation as to what they actually meant. The only catch: all three had to exist. Without his power, a leg of the sacred trinity was missing.

"The three original bonds are necessary to hold the universe and all its laws together. I imagine life goes on. At least, for a period of time," he replied. "I imagine there's a possibility of cataclysmic failure of the universe if I don't work off my karmic debt fast enough."

Gabriel stared at him. "Are you serious?"

"Very. Every living being on the planet has a bond to Fate. How can they exist, if I don't?" Fate mused.

Gabriel sat back, too stoic to show the alarm Fate knew he felt.

"Whenever a deity is prevented from his duty, the world pays," Fate said. "You learned this first hand when you became Death and got locked out of your underworld."

"You mean, when you locked me out," Gabriel corrected him. "It was a fucking daily nightmare. And yes, I know now you were right to do it. You helped guide me in the right direction so I didn't destroy the universe. Can anyone help you that way?"

"Not to my knowledge. My position is unique. I'm the only deity mentioned in the laws from the time-before-time. I must exist," Fate replied. "Do let me know if the fabric of space-time begins to melt. I'll try to do good deeds faster."

"How can you joke about something like this?" Death was frowning.

Fate said nothing. He was rarely serious with anyone, at least, not outwardly. Emotions were vulnerabilities someone else might exploit, so he never displayed them. He sipped cold water from his glass and lowered his bleeding hand from its awkward position extended above his head. He was starting to feel tired, another human experience he'd never felt before. He had certainly never looked forward to being voluntarily unconscious for eight hours.

"You can't treat this like a game like you do the Futures of everyone around you," Gabriel warned.

"I don't consider the Future of anyone a game," Fate replied.

"You went off to play polo when I was getting ready to destroy the world."

"Because I can't possibly control the Future from a polo match?"

"Dude, seriously."

"You misunderstand what my duty is. I won't interfere with free will. I will ensure you don't destroy the world, but I won't take your choices from you."

"That's not true. You've done it. I've seen it." Gabriel fell quiet as their food was brought to them.

They waited until the waitress had left their side of the restaurant before resuming.

"You forget – I know how you worked for thousands of years to trap my predecessor," Gabriel finished somewhat angrily.

"How is Past-Death?" Fate asked.

"Well." The skin around Gabriel's eyes softened when he spoke of his mate. "Still adjusting to not being in charge."

Fate snorted.

"You interfere when you feel like it. You manipulate everyone. Maybe your karmic debt isn't meant to be paid in good deeds. Maybe you need to learn not to fuck with people like you do."

"Because fucking with people can never be for a good cause," Fate replied in open mockery. "Did you stop to think there might be a bigger picture? Another reason why I do what I do?"

"Yep. But I also think you're so fucking bored, you like to fuck with people, too."

It was true. Fate did have a reputation for playing games with people. He generally kept his games aimed at deities, who were almost always playing games with him and others as well. Gabriel was too new, too honorable, of a deity to understand he, too, would one day be involved in the complicated politics inherently involved in interactions among those powerful beings who ruled across multiple realms.

"Maybe I should view this as a vacation," Fate said. "One that might end with snuffing out life as we know it."

Gabriel shook his head. "Where is Karma? Does she know what she's doing?"

"She's wilder now than she was before her imprisonment."

"I'll find her and talk some sense into her."

"Good luck." Fate hid his smile. He could rely on Gabriel to help him without losing any of the favors owed him. He had a feeling he'd be cashing in a great many favors from his debtors before this experience was over.

Gabriel scarfed down his pie. "So … what's this about Ancients in town?" he asked. "Who was here?"

"Kiki and another Immortal. They were looking for someone."

"Demons?"

"Not quiet. Apparently, Wynn has an eighth child. Half human."

Death leaned forward in interest. "Half-Immortal, half-human? How is it possible no one knew?"

"I don't know, but they were convinced she was legit."

"She. Rhyn has a half-breed sister." Gabriel smiled slowly, referring to his best friend and exiled son of Wynn. The other half-breed in the family, Rhyn was half-Immortal, half-demon.

"Allegedly."

"What's her … specialty?"

Fate considered the answer. He hadn't spent enough time with her to know for certain. Each son of Wynn had a special talent, a reason he'd bred with the mother in the first place. Rhyn's was unparalleled power so strong, he'd been sentenced to Hell, the only place that could contain him, for hundreds of years before meeting his mate.

Deities often knew the secretive talents of the rest of the Council members, even if they tended to keep their abilities hidden from the rest of the Immortal society.

What struck him as odd: there was no benefit for Wynn to breed with a human, and Wynn didn't do something without a reason. The mystery of Stephanie deepened whenever he thought about her.

"Karma said she was a zombie," Fate said.

"Zombie?" Gabriel snorted. "Define zombie."

"She has some interesting traits, namely no future and no karmic load at all. We weren't able to figure out what that meant or how it was possible for someone not to have either of those things," Fate explained. "When I asked her, she said she'd had strange issues her whole life. Animals avoid her. People react strangely to her. Karma made the joke she's a zombie."

"Reanimated corpses are identical to the humans or Immortals they used to be. At least, when I bring them back from the dead, they are," Gabriel said, pensive. Fate guessed he was exploring the histories of his predecessors, some of which would be passed down as memories to him when he assumed his title of Death. "What you're describing isn't possible."

"You've heard of something like this?"

"I'm Death. I should know a thing or two about zombies, shouldn't I?" he joked darkly. "There's only one kind of being who fits this bill, but there's never been a human or Immortal like this from what I can see in the histories. She's not a deity?"

"Absolutely not. I met her before Karma stripped my powers."

Death appeared troubled briefly.

"What is she?" Fate leaned forward, utterly intrigued by the discovery of something that had never existed before now.

"The secondary definition for zombie," Gabriel gave a small smile. "A body without a soul. By nature, some deities give up their souls when they assume their duties, because it's considered a conflict of interest. But even deities are born with them. Everyone is born with one. What you're saying is that this woman was born without one. I can't find any insight into how that's remotely possible."

Fate lost all sense of where he was for a moment, too shocked to respond. "You're saying she's a half-breed, born without a soul?"

"Yeah. The first ever in existence." Gabriel shoved a large bite of pie into his mouth. "Pretty weird."

"You're certain?"

"I'd have to meet her to be sure, but what you're describing fits."

"It's impossible."

"It should be." Gabriel shrugged. "My view of what is possible and not changed when I became Death."

It can't be. Fate had taken every precaution possible to stop the one event in his own future he wasn't willing to face. He was still, silent. His mind was too quiet, and the world around him seemed to stop, as if time itself were holding its breath like he was.

"What's wrong?" Gabriel studied him. "What can be worse than you telling me the world will end if you don't get your power back?"

"I never thought I'd say these words, but I think I've made a mistake," Fate murmured.

"*You* made a mistake?" Gabriel asked. "How can someone who can see the Future make a mistake?"

Because this was supposed to be impossible. Fate pulled out his wallet and calmly pulled enough money out to cover the food and tip. Setting it down, he rose. "Fate is not all knowing," he replied. "Sometimes, Fate's a little blind."

Death followed him out of the diner. Fate's mind worked quickly. He was torn between staying where he was until he'd repaid his karmic debt and going after *her*. Leaning against the railing overlooking the beach, he found his thoughts drifting down darker paths, such as those he'd joked about with Gabriel.

He was serious about the destiny of life in general resting on his shoulders. The weight of such reality wasn't any heavier than usual; he'd been born knowing his role in the sacred trinity of laws from the time-before-time. But *this* ... her ... now ...

Her appearance had the ability to reset the board in some regards and explain how he, and Karma, became entangled in the destinies of the Immortals.

"I think I know what's worse than the world ending," Gabriel said suddenly. "Is this woman your mate?"

Fate was silent.

"Holy fuck." Gabriel faced him. "And you turned her over to Wynn."

"I don't exactly have any power to protect her from demons right now," Fate replied. For the first time in a few centuries, he was losing his cool. "Fuck!" He paced away from the railing and back. "This can't be happening."

"It happens to all of us," Gabriel said, entertained.

"I took precautions!" Fate retorted. "It's not possible for her to exist."

"Precautions? How can you prevent your mate from appearing?"

Fate shook his head, not about to recount the manipulating and deals he'd had to make to prevent his own future from happening. He definitely wasn't going to alienate his only ally by admitting what he'd done to the soul of his intended mate. As the appointed Guardian and Keeper of Souls, Gabriel took his duties seriously.

"Mates, blood, fate," he repeated. "Destiny is not set. I should have been able to affect this."

"Well you didn't," Gabriel said. "What makes you so sure it's her?"

"Long story and not one I'm going to repeat," Fate replied firmly. "Can you confirm if she has a soul?"

"Yeah." Gabriel started to smile. "Are you asking me for a favor?"

"I'd think a zombie rates your attention, no matter who's interested."

"Don't fuck with me. You want to know if she's got a soul. I want to know, too, but if I find out tonight or in a few years, I don't care."

Fate was starting not to like being human. He had fewer

bargaining chips to make anyone do anything. "Do it tonight, and I'll void one of the favors you owe me," he said.

"Deal. I'll be back in five." Gabriel strode away and opened a portal, disappearing into it.

Fate waited, not at all satisfied with the discovery. The unsettled feeling inside him was the most unpleasant sensation he'd ever experienced. Deities tended to have watered down emotions at best. But this, this was ... awful. His stomach felt like it was twisting and his chest was almost too tight for him to take a full breath.

He was being crushed by something that wasn't physical. It was a feeling or perhaps, several, ganging up on him. He'd never wanted a mate and taken great precautions to ensure she never was born. His parents left him no warm memories of relationships. As Fate, he enjoyed the freedom to change his world and his mind and future at a whim, to try out different realms, sleep with any woman who interested him and then move on when he grew bored.

Freedom, independence, free will ... he was fiercely in agreement with humans. Destiny should never become an unavoidable destination one barreled towards no matter what, but a culmination of choices and chains of events that changed the eventual outcome.

Confined by his duty, he wanted the same freedom in his own life. Yet somehow, against all odds, the woman meant to become his mate had been born without the soul he disposed of. Even worse, she was not only half-human, but the half-breed daughter of Wynn.

She was caught up with an Ancient whose definition of demonstrating mercy towards his children was either to exile or kill them. She was the worst-case scenario, appearing at the worst opportunity, in the worst circumstances.

Which means she needs my help. The idea of a mate, though, made him want to never cross paths with her again, until he recalled the unusual attraction he'd experienced upon meeting her and the odd energy that passed between them when they touched.

Every deity only had one chance at a mate. He hadn't wanted his anytime soon, but neither was he willing to rule out a time in the far-flung future when he might enjoy companionship. Eternity was a long time to be alone. He appreciated having his sister back, even if she usually got into some kind of trouble he had to help her out of. He never minded because she was a distraction from his boredom.

While the exact meaning of the *mates, blood, fate* bonds had been debated among deities for a million years, if not more, it was generally accepted that one had to claim his or her mate upon discovery. Even the Dark One had sought his and trapped her in Hell.

Fate's eyes went to the fog hanging overhead. He had made the mistaken assumption that balancing his karma load was meant to be easy: a vacation consisting of a series of good deeds, of living like a good human, for as long as it took.

He hadn't considered it might be *hard* to regain his position as a deity. He knew he'd have to be careful of those he crossed but not that he'd have to do what he always did – manipulate the board – without his powers. With the life of someone else, someone innocent, now entangled with his, he innately knew his chances at balancing his karma were likely tied to his decision about whether or not to claim his mate.

Fate was not used to being short sighted.

"You got that right," Gabriel said, walking back through a portal yawning open beside the diner. "No soul. It's amazing, really."

"I wouldn't go that far," Fate replied.

"You're stuck here being good and she's in the clutches of Wynn." Gabriel leaned against the railing beside him.

Did he risk losing his one shot at a companion by not acting? His life by stepping into a game when he had no power?

He did have thousands of years worth of knowledge, hundreds of favors and at least one ally. He'd worked with less before.

But did he really want this? If she were to die-dead at Wynn's hands, could he live with never having a partner? After all, he'd always have Karma.

Mates, blood, fate. What if his karmic balancing, and return to his position, required him to do something he didn't really want to do?

CHAPTER FIVE

STEPHANIE STUDIED THE SLENDER MAN WITH MIDNIGHT SKIN AND brilliant eyes awaiting her in a large study that smelled of books and sunshine. He didn't appear anywhere near old enough to be her father. His youthful features were offset by flaxen hair. Kiki, who seemed displeased at having a half-sister, had left her in the doorway without a word to the alleged head of the family.

Wynn didn't look a day older than he had in the one surviving picture Stephanie's mother had hidden in an old diary twenty-three years ago. Handsome with a near-regal appearance, he was the stoic man her mother snapped about whenever Stephanie asked about her father. Her mother always turned from warm and sweet to cold and dismissive when she discussed Stephanie's father.

It was a similar reaction to those of Kiki and Ileana, and Stephanie withheld judgment until she'd heard a good reason why no one seemed to like her father. She was in part excited to know her search for him was over – but uncertain how to talk to him.

Wynn leaned against the desk behind him and considered her for a long moment. She felt like she was in the principal's office, not meeting her father for the first time. He didn't seem appreciative of finding a long lost daughter.

"Your mother is Rachel Jennings?" he asked finally.

"Yes."

"You're a half breed."

Uncertain how to respond, Stephanie cleared her throat and looked around.

"What did she tell you about me?"

Stephanie shrugged. "Just that you ditched us soon after she got pregnant. She doesn't really like to talk about you."

"So you had no idea you were one of us?"

"Of course not."

He frowned. "Kiki confirmed your blood test," he said. "Do you have any tattoos?"

"Tattoos?" she echoed, confused. "This is the first time I'm meeting you in my life and you want to know if I have *tattoos*?"

"I'm not a normal father, and you're not a normal daughter. You'll learn when I ask a question, I expect an immediate answer," he chided.

"No. I don't have any tattoos. No birthmarks or scars or anything!"

"Good. Each of my sons has a particular gift inherited from his respective mother. Kiki is a math and science genius. My other son, Tamer, is a keeper of knowledge. He can read ancient writings and inscriptions in a way no one else in the worlds can. Do you – or did your mother – have any talents?"

"You knocked up my mom. Wouldn't you know?" Stephanie asked.

"I want to know what she told you."

"Nothing!" she exclaimed. "Do you even care how I spent my childhood or that she worked two jobs to raise me?"

"Had I known where to find you, I would've taken you with me. You don't belong in the human world. Your mother knows this."

This sent chills through her.

"Although, I don't know what use you'll have here, either," he added. "Fortunately for you, I'm three children short right now. There's room for the family to grow. You'll be treated with the respect your place in our society deserves."

"You say it like I'm staying," she said. "I don't have any idea what's going on, but I do know I'm not staying here."

"Of course you are. You're my daughter. Once it's public knowledge, you won't have anywhere else to go."

"What do you mean?"

"I have many enemies, the kind you don't ever want to meet. They'd likely use you or torture you to get to me."

She gasped. "You can't be serious."

"I'm very serious."

He was scaring her, and he hadn't moved from his spot on the desk or raised his voice in the five minutes that passed since she entered the study.

"You can't keep me here against my will," she said firmly. "I have rights."

"You're a half Immortal and the daughter of the primary Ancient, who happens to be the head of the Council That Was Seven. You have no rights but those I allow you to have. No one in their right mind would cross me," he replied with the same unflappable calm. "You're fortunate I want you here despite you having no unique talents and being a half-breed. The other half-breed in the family is in permanent exile."

I don't fit in anywhere. Stephanie wasn't certain how his statement could hurt her as much as it did. He was her *father* and he didn't think she was worthy of anything. How did this happen? More importantly, how had her mother ever fallen for an asshole like this?

Reeling from her latest introduction to the insane world, she couldn't get one word out of her mouth.

"I always did want a daughter," he added more softly. "Just not one that's a half-breed. But, I suppose that's my fault, not yours."

"Is every Immortal a total dick?" she snapped.

He raised an eyebrow in polite offense. "You'll need some polishing before I can introduce you to others outside the family. We're the Windsor's of the Immortals. You have a public responsibility to take on the roll I assign you. For your sake, you'll adapt to the politics of the family."

I'm not staying here, she swore silently.

"Your mother's life depends on you adjusting," he continued. "I'll suppress her identity but you can't be seen around your family. Kiki said you ran into demons already?"

She nodded.

"They aren't the only ones who will be after those you love."

She swallowed hard, an image of Olivia in her thoughts. "I'll call the police."

"And tell them what?" he challenged. "You're being chased by demons? Immortals? What will you tell your sister, who knows less of this world than you now do?"

Stephanie said nothing. He was right. Anyone who heard her story would lock her up.

Wynn gazed at her intently. "Something is very different about you."

Story of my life. "Aside from being told I'm a half breed Immortal princess?"

"Princess is fitting, albeit you're an illegitimate one," he said with a faint smile. "But there's something else. I spent enough of my second time in the mortal realm posing as a human to know you're not quite right."

"I've never fit in anywhere," she said with a sigh.

"It's a good thing. To be comfortable with where you are is to become vulnerable."

I really don't want to find out I fit in here, either.

"Did your mother ever share any insight into why you're special?"

"My mother wouldn't know. This is your world, not hers," Stephanie said, unable to understand his persistent questions about her perfectly normal mother.

"I guess I shouldn't be surprised." He glanced at his watch. "Kiki is going to coordinate a small dinner party for later this week where I'll announce you to the Immortals. I recommend you learn what you can about our society before then," Wynn added. "You're dismissed."

Ten minutes later, standing in the cavernous bedroom assigned to her, she was still running the bizarre meeting with her father through her head. When she was younger, she'd fantasized about what her father was like. He was the top neurosurgeon in the world, which meant he was going to be brilliant, dedicated to his job, compassionate towards others, saving lives every day and probably by this point, wealthy. Unless his heart was so good, he gave it all away to charity, which she'd secretly thought he would.

The only thing I got right was his money. She wasn't just disappointed by the revelation of what her father actually was – she was devastated. Her mother's reluctance and iciness to discuss him made sense.

Exhausted to the point of delirious after her day, Stephanie crossed to the mammoth bed with its four posters and heavy curtains neatly captured at each post. The headboard and furniture of the chamber were antique wood, the colors neutrals. Her room included an ultra-modern bathroom with jetted tub, small living space, and balcony overlooking an endless sea of green trees and mountains.

It was very unlike the series of two-bedroom apartments she'd lived in with her mother and sister. Wynn didn't appear to be the kind to move often, unlike her family did. A new town every year or two, a new school.

The décor of the bedchamber was elegant and simple but clearly expensive. Clothing with tags was in the wardrobe. She checked the sizes, a little closer to snapping when she saw they were hers. The clothing was conservative in shades of blue, gray and black, the dresses and skirts mid-calf in length and the slacks ironed within an inch of their lives. Even the designer, dark-washed jeans had been ironed.

"What kind of nut irons jeans?" Her hand fell from the clothing. She was trembling, and her insides were cold. A nightmare this real wasn't possible yet neither was she able to process what she'd learned – that she was a half breed Immortal princess.

Then why wasn't she panicking? Trying to get home?

Because this world feels real for the first time in my life. She wasn't able to deny the existence of the creatures that killed Olivia any more than her trip through a tear in the fabric of the universe that left her across the world. Her own quasi-acceptance of both surprised her more than learning she was one of these strange people.

Stephanie locked herself in the bathroom and sank down with her back to the door, hugging her legs to her chest. She tried to meditate or at least, soothe her frayed nerves, using the relaxation techniques Olivia had showed her. Grounding herself with great effort, she rested her head against her knee and listened to the rhythm of her breathing.

She was smart and capable and had always been at the top of her class. If she could make it through the male-dominated engineering classes at school, she could handle this strange new reality. After all, she'd finally found her father after years of looking. He was a jerk, but he was still her father.

As for the talk about Immortals …

Her breathing grew uneven, and she refocused quickly on what positives she could pull from this experience. She had a nice bedchamber, and …

Olivia.

Stephanie squeezed her eyes closed, unable to dismiss the sight of her roommate being killed. Tears leaked and traveled down her face. She lifted her head and sucked in deep breaths. It was the worst moment for her to lose it. She needed to think.

She stripped out of her clothing and took a long, hot shower, unable to relax on her own. When she was finished, she snuggled into a plush robe and looked around for her clothes.

They were gone. She hadn't heard or seen anyone enter to grab them and the door was still locked.

Stephanie drew a breath and let it out with a hiss. "Just ... go with it," she ordered herself. "It's just Immortal weirdness." But she felt like crying again.

She left the bathroom and lay down on the bed to gaze at the thirty-foot high ceiling. Struggling to find a way not to end up screaming, she decided to pretend she was at an exclusive hotel, and soon, she'd be back home with her mom and sister with the craziest stories to tell them.

Of all the thoughts in her head, she returned to the claim by her father that she couldn't go home because she'd be in danger. She began to think she'd be in as much danger from him pursuing her as anyone else. She'd have to convince her mother and sister to move, to go into hiding, all because some Immortal creatures were going to be after them.

There was no scenario she could create where the conversation played out how she wanted it to. How did she convince normal people about this strange sub-world hidden within their own? She'd barely tolerated Olivia's nonsense about souls and destiny; she'd have laughed off the idea of demons and deities if she hadn't met them.

Deities. How on earth was the guy she met a god? Why hadn't he wanted to tell anyone who he was? And why did she keep thinking about him and his mesmerizing eyes?

He helped rescue her, but he hadn't been able to help Olivia, and he'd been the first to speak utter nonsense to her. No matter how attractive he was, his appearance marked the point where her life plummeted into the gutter.

Restless, Stephanie dug out pajamas, not caring that it was midmorning in the Alps. It was bedtime where she was from, and she was too fatigued to take another moment of this nonsense. Perhaps, when she awoke, she'd be back home, and Olivia would have a wild explanation for what happened.

Recalling someone had slipped into her room to grab her clothing, she returned to the bathroom to change. Stephanie dropped the robe and tugged on underwear and a soft t-shirt. She bent to swipe the robe off the floor and froze.

"What the hell?" She twisted to get a better look at her lower back. Skin peeked through the gap between her shirt and underwear. She bore a marking of some sort at the small of her back. Tugging up her shirt, she stared over her shoulder at the bizarre tattoo that hadn't been there in the morning when she ventured to the book festival.

The letters *S H A I* were inked in blocky letters with a distinctly gothic feel and surrounded by geometric symbols. The tattoo was dark maroon.

When had she gotten a tattoo? She rubbed it. The markings were raised – and part of her. It wasn't drawn on, and it wasn't new.

Wynn had asked her about tattoos. Was this why? Did Immortals automatically get tattoos when they entered the society?

She lowered the t-shirt then lifted it once more. The tattoo remained.

Her heart was racing once more. She left the bathroom and pulled on a pair of jeans, preparing to leave, when a knock sounded at the door.

She went to it and cracked it open cautiously, uncertain what she'd find on the other side.

Kiki was outside her door. He handed her an iPad. "I put the meal times and instructions on how to get to the dining hall on the schedule. Orientation sheets are under the folder marked *Orientation and contact information* –"

"Yeah, hi, Kiki. Nice to meet you after all these years," she interrupted.

He gazed at her for a long moment before glancing both ways down the hall. "Can I come in?"

She pushed the door open and stepped aside. He went to the chairs before the hearth and sat down. She joined him.

"It's not an easy adjustment," he began.

"How would you know?"

He drew a breath. "Look, you definitely have the temperament to be my sister, but if you want to survive our father, you'll want to tone it down around him," he advised. "Just play along. Even if you don't know what game you're playing. It's safer that way."

She frowned, puzzled. "Is he that bad? I mean, he made it clear what he thinks about having a half-breed daughter but … shit. What's wrong with him? With all of you? With this place?"

"We've been in a state of transition," Kiki replied. "Leadership has changed hands multiple times within the family. Every brother that's died-dead has died within the past two years, and the ongoing battle between Immortals and demons has destroyed over sixty percent of the Immortal population. After a very long period of stability, it's been chaos."

"I feel like I'm in a movie with a really complicated plot," she said. *Except this still feels real.*

He smiled. "There are a couple of things to remember. Our father is feared by Immortals, demons and deities alike. But he loves his family in what way he really can. He mourned those who died, and he feels the loss of the others who are, well, away right now."

"How does he care about someone and exile them?"

"He exiles because he does care. If they weren't family, they'd be dead-dead."

She shivered.

"So you know he'll protect his family, no matter how shitily he treats you in the meantime."

"It's not just me?"

"Absolutely not. If anything, you got off easy. The only one of us kids he actually likes is Andre, the eldest, who you haven't met yet because he's kind of got something else going on."

"I can't imagine what that means," she said with a sign and rubbed her face. "None of this makes sense. I have seven brothers, a father who makes tyrants look like Disney princesses and am not allowed to go home because he fears people will use me against him."

Kiki nodded.

"Okay. So … my brothers. Tell me about them," she said.

A shadow crossed his face. "Kris was our leader for the longest time. He, Erik – who lived in seclusion in Siberia, and Sasha – who betrayed us to the Dark One – are all dead-dead. Andre is alive again but transformed into a deity. Tamer lived in Egypt until he decided to become a death dealer for Gabriel, and Rhyn, the half-demon, is in exile with his family. Then there's me providing the stability element during the transition the past two years. And now you."

Dark One. Dead-dead. Alive again. Death Dealer. Half-demon.

Stephanie dwelt on the otherworldly explanation that rolled off his tongue as if this was all normal. Unable to hold it together anymore, she began to laugh. She laughed until tears streamed down her face and she couldn't breathe then doubled over, holding her abs.

Exhaustion was the only reason she stopped, and she sagged in her chair.

Kiki was surfing on his iPad. He set it aside when she calmed.

"Questions?" Kiki asked. "I'll stick around as much as I can to help you adjust."

"Will you answer something truthfully?"

"Depends. What's the question?"

"If I go home, am I really putting my mother and sister in danger?"

"Absolutely."

She rubbed her face. "I don't want that to be true."

"I understand," he replied. "But it's a reality for now. Perhaps later, when you learn more about our society and your abilities, you'll be able to return without drawing attention."

"Hey – Wynn asked me about tattoos. Do you know why?"

Kiki hesitated for the first time since they'd met.

"Is it bad?" she asked, sitting up straight. "Like if they magically appear?"

His gaze sharpened. "Did one magically appear?"

She debated not telling him but stood finally, turned and pulled up her shirt to display the writing across her lower back.

"Shai," he read aloud, sounding puzzled.

"Yeah. Is it bad?" she asked again, returning to her seat.

"Not necessarily."

"I hear a *but* in your voice."

"I'm going to call Tamer. He's the historian in the family. He'll know what it means," Kiki said. "I think you need some sleep?"

She nodded.

He rose and started towards the door. "Just, uh, don't tell Wynn about the markings, okay?"

"He'll exile me?"

"Honestly I wish he'd exile *me*. I'd rather be at home in Tokyo than here dealing with this shit. No such luck yet. He'll be more likely to manipulate you if he knows you've got a marking. You want him to think you're of little use to him," Kiki advised. "Maybe he'll let you go. He can't know about the marking or he won't."

She watched him leave then crossed to the door to lock it. One hand went to her lower back, and she rubbed the raised tattoo through her shirt. How would a tattoo change Wynn's mind about her? Why did she have the feeling Kiki knew more than he was saying?

CHAPTER SIX

STILL BROODING SEVERAL DAYS LATER, DEBATING WHETHER OR NOT he wanted anything to do with a mate, Fate returned from a bike ride to the bed and breakfast. While she had no concept of the worth of money, Karma had paid for his room for six months. Coupled with the accounts, properties and stashes of money and fine art he had in the mortal world, he had a plan for surviving as long as required to work off his debt.

Normally invigorated by exercise, he was once again dissatisfied. He felt good physically but hadn't been able to take his mind off the issue. For the first time in his life, he had the uninterrupted time and mind to contemplate his own future – and he wasn't liking the down time at all.

He returned to his room and stripped off his shirt to cool down before hopping in the shower. He checked his form as he had every day to ensure he wasn't losing the body he'd so carefully crafted over the millennia. His skin was golden, his toned frame covered in lean muscle. Aside from the bruising around his ribs from the scuffle with demons, he looked every bit like he was supposed to.

After a quick shower, he left the bathroom to change when he noticed a letter on the nightstand where none had been before. He plucked it up curiously, appreciating the expensive linen paper and raised writing. A man of luxury, he knew high quality when he saw it.

He slid the card from the envelope and read it with interest. Unease stirred within him when he finished.

With some mirth, he realized he was fighting his own destiny.

The cool breeze of the place-between-places tickled the back of his neck.

"Do you wanna go?" Karma asked.

"You knew."

"Knew what, brother?" she asked innocently.

He faced her, eyebrow raised.

She rolled her eyes. "I suspected. I didn't know," she said. "Wynn's invited several deities and all the important Immortals for his newfound daughter's debutante dinner."

"I don't fit into either of those categories." He tossed the invitation on the bed and dressed quickly.

"You're telling me you don't want to go or you won't go?"

"I'm telling you I have no reason to be there."

Karma was quiet.

Fate tossed himself onto his back on the bed, listening to his muscles. He'd be sore again today, another experience he wasn't used to. It was also intriguing for him to learn about his body, to understand how each muscle worked and ached and why. Deities weren't as sensitive to the physical world.

"Okay, so did you miss the part where she's your mate?" Karma asked.

"No."

"I don't understand."

"I value my freedom over a mate."

"But what about her?"

"What about her?" he challenged.

"She's a human."

"She's an Immortal by their Codes. Anyone with any sort of Immortal blood belongs to their society."

The bed sank beneath Karma's weight as she sat beside him. She appeared genuinely puzzled. "Don't you *have* to claim your mate?"

"I'm Fate. I don't *have* to do anything," he countered with a faint smile.

"We only get one mate, one chance at true love."

"You've been watching too many movies."

"There has to be something to love if there are so many movies about it," she reasoned. "What if Wynn kills her or the demons eat her?"

"Demons won't touch someone without a soul. She's relatively safe on that front."

"You're avoiding the topic! Stop talking around it!" she snapped, hair rippling with colors mirrored in her eyes.

"I don't view a mate as positive," he said, amused. "I view any sort of obligation that limits my life as something I don't want."

"I limit your life."

"You entertain me," he replied with a wink. "And you're my family."

"She is, too."

"This is different." Fate's eyes shifted to the ceiling. The discussion with Karma was one he'd been having with himself for four days. He hadn't been able to rule out companionship with certainty, even if he wasn't convinced it was something he wanted either. But he could rule out destroying the universe. He'd always answered the call of his duties first.

"Is this ... are you trying to manipulate me into giving you something so you'll go?" she asked cautiously. Far more oblivious, if not naïve, to the political game among deities, Karma was glaring at him.

"You know I'm always open to negotiating," he teased. "You set all this up, or at least, had an inkling when you ditched me here of all places. You clearly want me to go tonight. But you didn't think this through, Karma. When manipulating a god, you don't leave anything up to Fate to decide."

"It's not fair," she mumbled.

"You started it. What's it worth to you for me to agree?"

She was quiet. He waited, unconcerned with how long it'd take for her to fold when he knew she would.

"Someone told me your power is not the ability to change the Future but to *know* the Future," she mused.

"It's true. My deity power is based on the ability to access knowledge. I'm quite harmless."

"Bullshit!" she snapped.

He laughed.

"This person said you were the most dangerous of everyone because of the knowledge you can access."

"It's not the knowledge that's important. It's what I do with it," he replied.

"You have an eternity of knowledge stored up. So, even without your power, if you wanted to, you could find a way to help your mate, right?"

"If I felt like it."

She slapped him on the stomach. "Then you need to feel like it!"

"You're my sister, but this time, I'm treating you like a fellow deity. If you want me to go so badly, you better be willing to cough up something I want," he replied.

Frustrated with him, she got up and paced, her hair and eyes turning wildly different colors as she thought hard. Fate watched her. He'd protected her from deities since they were young, and he began to think she needed to learn a few lessons herself about surviving the political landscape of the gods without being eaten alive by someone like him.

Even now, he was being kind, because she was his sister.

"I'll limit your karmic debt to six months," she said reluctantly.

"Not enough."

"You shouldn't get off easy because you're my brother!"

He laughed again and rolled onto his stomach, watching her stress out. "Try again."

"Four months and I won't balance you again for a thousand years."

"Closer."

"I won't balance you again for a hundred thousand years."

He pretended to consider. "I'm listening."

She gave a noisy sigh. "What do you want?"

"The most powerful form of currency to a deity."

Light dawned on her features. "A favor."

"Exactly."

Karma studied him.

"How badly do you want me there?" he asked and held out his hand to seal a formal deal in the tradition of deities.

"Okay," she said. "I agree." She tapped her fist to his. A flash of cold energy tore through him, sealing the deal, making it irrevocable.

"A word of advice, don't ever cough up that much shit to anyone ever again," he said and sat up.

"But it's important."

"You can't let the person you're negotiating with know that. There's no room for honesty when dealing with someone like me."

"At least you're going."

"I planned on attending anyway," he said.

Karma stared at him.

Fate winked. "Pick me up an hour after it starts. We can't be early."

"You're an asshole!" Furious, she summoned a portal and marched away into the place-between-places. The portal closed, and

Fate retrieved the invitation from his bed. His power had always stemmed from his ability to manipulate, along with the subtle threat others felt knowing he could change their futures if he wanted to. He'd rarely taken such steps, though, and relied on deals with others, common interests and goals with regards to limiting the influence of other deities, and the general knowledge he had all of eternity to achieve his ends.

He hadn't completely lost what made him dangerous, and he considered this as he tapped the invitation. If he viewed the mate challenge as a distraction, rather than an obligation that might limit his life, and kept his emotions separated from the rest of the world, he might just find this to be the ultimate adventure.

And then there's her. He was as unclear what to do about the woman meant to be at his side as he was clear about how to help her. What he knew for certain: he didn't lose once he decided to enter the game.

"I make a good human," he said. "Constantly lost and confused."

Despite the novelty of pretending to be a human, he was close to finished with the experience already.

He and Karma arrived at Wynn's chalet in the French Alps precisely an hour into the pre-dinner hoer d'oevres. Fate's attention was immediately drawn to the trays of food and the hearty scents rolling out of the dining hall next to the parlor where the guests were gathered.

Karma's eyes sparkled as she took in everyone. He could almost see her calculating who she wanted to balance next. Her brilliant fuchsia dress contrasted with her light green eyes and strawberry blonde hair. She was behaving – or trying to. Her eyes intermittently flashed different colors.

No one challenged deities, even the Ancient Immortal greeting everyone at the door. Kiki met his gaze and frowned. It wasn't an unusual reaction when Fate showed up. The Immortal son of Wynn said nothing more than a *good evening* before they swept through the door into a bustling room filled with light, warmth and people. French doors leading onto a balcony had been flung open to counter the heat of those gathered within.

Fate's heart was beating faster than normal despite his intention of not letting the event become more than what it was. He was cautious about starting a new game without his power, and he hated not being able to peek at the answers when he wanted to.

"This is amazing," Karma breathed.

"Remember – don't interact with the Ancients," he warned her. "Ever."

She sighed noisily.

"You have whole worlds to balance. Skip them for now," he said with a smile.

She nodded.

Fate wasn't impressed by fetes of this sort. He'd been to enough in his lifetime. Wynn knew how to throw a good party, and he'd invited the right people, but Fate was unusually disinterested in a few hours of entertainment. Karma wandered off almost immediately, following a woman in a brilliant teal dress.

Fate went to the open bar and ordered cognac on the rocks. He stood to the side, content to watch the Immortals and deities this night. He spotted Wynn near the balcony. The Ancient was mingling, politely greeting everyone with a quick smile and cold eyes, before introducing them to the woman he was officially claiming as his daughter.

Stephanie was radiant in a sapphire dress that clung to her curves and magnified the hue of her eyes. Standing beside one another, the similarities of father and daughter were evident: the same eyes, high cheekbones and naturally regal features. Slender and tall, Stephanie's subtle beauty held a quiet allure. She was gorgeous and approachable, her gaze direct yet her air one of uncertainty. She barely looked at Wynn, which led Fate to believe the relationship between them was tense, and rightly so. Stephanie didn't appear comfortable on display while Wynn was in his element.

Fate let his eyes linger on the woman he didn't know if he wanted in his life. His confusion ran deep, and without the ability to see into the Future, he was lost in the darkness of indecision once more. She was beautiful and strong – and some of his resistance to a mate vanished upon seeing her.

Wynn wouldn't hesitate to seize the chance to manipulate a deity through his daughter.

Wynn wouldn't knock up a human, either. Fate hadn't had the chance to dig around for information about Stephanie's mother before Karma balanced him, but he had observed Wynn long enough to understand the Immortal made no mistakes, especially when selecting the mothers of his children. With no soul for deities to read, Stephanie was a blank spot to anyone trying to solve the mystery of her mother.

The rumor of him having a mate would put his reputation at risk, as would his ability to stay one step ahead of the Dark One, who had become his chief opponent on the chessboard the past few millennia. Too much was at risk, both to himself and the rest of the world.

But walking completely away didn't feel like an option, either, as if some part of him accepted his place in her life. That piece of him was buried too deeply for him to determine exactly why he had decided to attend tonight instead of staying in Carmel.

"Can I get you anything?" Kiki asked, joining him.

"No, thanks," Fate replied.

"Mind if I join you?"

"As you will." Fate glanced at him. His instincts, honed over the course of a lifetime, understood Kiki wasn't there to chit chat. The business-oriented member of Wynn's clan had been the lowest of the

Ancients on Fate's radar for this reason. He wasn't erratic or prone to power plays like the others.

"We weren't introduced the other day," Kiki said.

"I know who you are."

"Usually when people introduce themselves, they both give their names."

"Hmm."

The Immortal shook his head. "Look, I'm not Wynn. I think she's in danger being here. Whatever game you guys are playing, take some poor human out of the middle."

"I'm afraid I don't know what you're talking about," Fate replied, sipping his drink. "If you'll excuse me, I'm going to check on my sister." He started away, irritated Kiki knew enough to suspect why he was there. Had he given it away? Had Karma said something when she shouldn't have?

"Shai," Kiki called after him.

Fate stopped in his tracks. He faced the Immortal, his lightheartedness gone, and returned to Kiki. "I haven't heard that name in quite some time," he said. "I wasn't aware anyone knew it."

Kiki cleared his throat. "I'm not trying to cause any issues. We just need to talk."

"You have my attention." Fate stood aside. "Let's talk."

Kiki nodded and led him through the crowd, out of the chalet and into the dark, cool night. Fate breathed in the scent of pine trees and sky, marveling at how strong the smells were as a human.

Laughter and light spilled out from the balcony four stories above them. Kiki's gaze flickered up to the windows of the party before he focused on Fate.

"What makes you think I can help her?" Fate asked before Kiki could speak.

"No Immortal is going to do it," Kiki replied. "And you're in the right position."

"Meaning ..."

"I saw the mating mark, and my brother deciphered whose name it is. By Immortal Code –"

"Immortal Code does not govern the doings of deities."

There was a pause, then, "You have to claim your mate. I don't care who you are. She needs your protection."

"I'm not in a position to protect her."

"You're a fucking deity!" Kiki exclaimed. "Wynn called this party tonight for the sole purpose of seeing what Immortal ended up preordained to take her as a mate. Do you have any idea what he'll do when he figures out it's not just an Immortal he can manipulate but a god?" Kiki ran a hand through his hair. "He's hoping her mate turns out to be from another Immortal family, an influential one he intends to crush after taking their money."

"The dealings of Immortals are not my business."

"But *she* is!"

Fate was quiet. He didn't care to openly admit to anyone, especially Wynn's son, that there was more involved than Stephanie at the moment.

"I knew your kind were trouble," Kiki muttered angrily.

"Most people know better than to insult a deity," Fate said, unable to help his amusement. He studied Kiki. The Immortal was in distress, pacing and clenching his hands. "There's something else going on here, isn't there?"

For a long moment, Kiki was quiet. "Wynn's up to something," he said at last. "I don't know what, but I know finding her now isn't a coincidence."

"You think he knew about his daughter."

"I'd wager my soul to a demon he did. No one knew he existed before a year ago. He's been planning something. It's what he does."

Fate listened. Wynn's reappearance, after being dead-dead for thousand of years, hadn't surprised him. In the complicated maneuverings of deities, he'd run across the chain of events that led to Wynn's return more than once and worked with Past-Death, his former adversary, often enough to suspect what she was doing in the background.

If she were half-human, Stephanie would hold no power that could help Wynn. Fate once again wondered what Wynn was truly after and what secret he and Stephanie were both hiding about who she really was.

"Will you consider getting her out of here for awhile?" Kiki asked.

"What does she know of her Immortal abilities?"

"Nothing yet. I told her she needs to become as useless as possible to Wynn."

"Wise. Why have you not turned her over to Andre?"

"He's missing."

"Missing or dead-dead?"

Kiki shrugged. "Wynn won't tell me. I know they met a few weeks ago, and Andre vanished."

"There aren't many places where a deity can be kept without anyone noticing."

"There's one I know of."

"The preferred place of exile for Wynn's sons," Fate mused, thoughts on how two of Wynn's sons had served stints in Hell, one voluntarily while the other was exiled. "A deity-son imprisoned by the Dark One and a daughter he suddenly acknowledges. Wynn is up to something."

"You're the only one who knows what."

"Not at the moment," Fate said carefully. "I'm on vacation."

Kiki scowled. "Then go back to work!"

Fate offered a distracted smile, thoughts on Stephanie. At first an inconvenient complication, her appearance was beginning to appear a little less random.

With turmoil in his breast, Fate realized he was going to have to enter this game after all. It meant he was also about to be at odds with Wynn – without the aid of his power.

There was a time near the beginning of his reign when he'd had to use more than wits to win. He'd never truly forgotten what it meant to fight, even if he'd moved away from physical altercations in favor of long-term manipulation to keep others in check. It was during this period he checked his future daily – and when he'd first seen the dual chain of events he first thought unlikely but which now seemed inevitable. Wynn was going to destroy the Immortals in his quest, and Fate was about to claim his mate.

"Does she know what the marking means?" he asked and swirled what remained of his drink.

"No. I told her to keep it a secret."

A shriek pierced the night, and both of them looked up in time to see one of Wynn's guests being thrown off the balcony by a man-sized creature with fangs and wings.

"Demons," Kiki breathed. He bolted.

What is Wynn up to? Wynn and the fortress held special magics to keep the demons out. For demons to appear in the middle of Wynn's party …

It wasn't an accident. Fate tossed the glass and ran after Kiki. They raced through the chalet towards the sounds of screams. Immortal warriors scrambled to react, and guests began pouring out of the massive chamber.

Kiki stopped and snatched one warrior, barking orders and gesticulating wildly. Fate fought the flow of panicked Immortals, eyes searching the crowd for signs of Karma or the mate he didn't want.

He shoved his way into the parlor and ducked out of the flow of traffic. Several demons were rampaging the parlor, killing and destroying everything in their paths.

"Brother!" Karma tripped and caught herself against the wall beside him. She appeared excited and sacred and grabbed his arm.

"The human. She's trapped!" She pointed.

"Get to safety," he said and pushed her in the direction of the other fleeing guests.

Without stopping to debate the wisdom of his actions, Fate worked his way through the guests until he came to a point where he could see exactly what was going on. Wynn was absent, and the bodies of several other Immortals littered the floor. Five rampaging demons were chewing and clawing a path through the guests. Blood sprayed the walls and ceiling and anyone near, including the frozen figure of Stephanie at the center of the drama.

His breath caught. As before, his insides seized as if crushed by an invisible hand. His instincts, the ones he normally silenced with peeks at the future, were screaming at the thought of her in danger. The intensity of his reaction startled him, reminded him there was something else at work here, a magic carried over from the time-before-time that not even he was immune to.

I never had a choice, he admitted.

Stephanie's eyes were squeezed closed and her chest heaving as if she were struggling not to panic.

One demon drew near, sniffed at her, and then swept by her.

The demons either couldn't sense her or weren't interested in a creature without a soul.

The shouts of Immortal warriors in the hallway, trying to get by the panicked guests, drew the focus of two beasts, who began chasing the fleeing Immortals.

Fate gauged the speed and movement of those that remained, capable of calculating the most likely actions after years of challenging himself to do so without the aid of his power.

He waited for his opportunity and strode confidently into the middle of the mess. Side stepping demons and over bodies, with his sensitive human senses trained on the world, he kept his focus on Stephanie. Whether or not he intended to, he'd just entered the game, and he was going to play it with the same methodology he used to plot the futures of billions of people: discipline, focus and the grim knowledge that losing meant the end of life everywhere. There was no room for error in what he did, ever.

As he drew near her, he saw the figure of Wynn in the balcony, shrouded by the night. The Ancient Immortal was smiling faintly, watching him.

Vaguely, in the depths of his mind, Fate realized this was Wynn's doing, to flush out the mate of his daughter. Fate's gaze was drawn to a demon and then quickly back to the balcony.

Wynn was gone. However, the feeling Fate was walking into a trap of some kind stirred, along with dread powerful enough, his stomach hurt.

CHAPTER SEVEN

STEPHANIE HAD BEEN ENJOYING THE DINNER PARTY AS MUCH AS possible. Everyone she met was especially nice, the food fantastic and the event a distraction from the fact she'd left her old life behind several days before. If anything, people seemed warmer towards her than they were Wynn. She hadn't expected such a welcome from complete strangers after never fitting in anywhere in her life. It was a pleasant experience.

Until the monsters came. She'd started to run then been cut off and watched several guests attacked. Unable to cope with the sight, she'd simply closed her eyes and waited to die. Somehow, the monsters hadn't gotten to her yet, despite the screams and sounds of bodies hitting the ground around her. She waited, trying hard not to panic and even harder not to run. She wasn't getting far in her dressy shoes and she preferred a quick death to a slow one.

"Hey, gorgeous." Warm hands rested on her forearms, and she flinched. "This party's gone to hell. You ready to get out of here?"

Her eyes flew open at the familiar voice, and she looked up into the mesmerizing gaze of the enigmatic stranger she'd met in Carmel. He smiled, seemingly unaffected by the massacre occurring around them. He wore a suit of light grey fitted to his athletic form. His shirt was open at the neck to reveal the golden skin of his chest, and his warmth countered the chill creeping in from the open balcony. His light brown hair was mussed fashionably. His direct gaze jarred her out of the cycle of inner panic.

Was he this incredible looking when they first met? Enough for her to forget the monsters around them?

"Y...yes," she whispered.

"Let's go." He held out a hand.

She took it, looking around feverishly at the demons he didn't seem to notice. The bodies were piling up, and she froze, unable to move. Visions of Olivia were in her thoughts again.

"Head up." He lifted her chin. "Ready?"

She didn't respond.

The man casually unbuttoned the jacket of his suit and began walking towards one monster. He tugged her when she hesitated, and she sucked in a breath, waiting for it to see them and attack.

It didn't. Their timing was perfect, and they reached the spot it was the second after it had leapt to attack someone else.

Stephanie didn't let herself look at who it was attacking. She gripped his hand in both of hers, hanging onto him for dear life as he seemed to follow an invisible path through the mayhem and monsters. Once, she was certain a monster was headed towards them only to be cut off by one of the soldiers that lived in the castle.

The stranger glanced over his shoulder to give her a quick smile of reassurance at odds with the steely determination in his gaze and continued the confident walk through the madness without slowing or stopping once.

Stephanie's amazement grew after another near miss, and she crowded him, going so far as to hug his arm so he didn't accidentally leave her behind. The cries of dying Immortals were soon joined by the pain-filled roars of monsters. She squeezed her eyes closed, close to panicking, and prayed with all her might for the stranger to lead them both to safety.

The sounds of mayhem grew fainter as he led her into the hallway and away from the people. She didn't release him then or when they turned a corner. It was all she could do to keep from collapsing into a screaming puddle of uselessness, the kind likely to get them killed if any rogue monster escaped the soldiers into the castle.

He stopped and drew her into his body. One of his arms wrapped around her back, the other around her shoulders so his hand rested on her head. He tucked her securely against him.

Stephanie struggled to block the sounds, the memories, the feel of blood splashing her skin. The man's body was strong, solid and warm. He grounded her when she thought for sure she had finally snapped. A few days pretending to lay low, to accept the insanity of a world she didn't know existed, had nonetheless been filled with enough angst and anxiety about her fate and that of her family that she'd spent every night crying herself to sleep. She'd been unable to leave and unwilling to try after another warning from Kiki. The sense of helplessness hit her again in the middle of the banquet hall, where she'd found herself almost grateful something was going to end the nightmare.

In the strangers arm, away from the mayhem, she shook hard enough she couldn't stand on her own. Instead of dwelling on how she was cowering in someone's arms, she focused instead on his faint scent – sandalwood and brown sugar – and pulling her senses and emotions back from the brink. The stranger didn't speak, for which she was grateful. Slowly, her mind left the banquet hall and returned to her. She clutched at the stranger's suit and opened her eyes. His heartbeat was steady and strong, and the warmth of his body bled through his shirt, assuring her at least he was real. The physical connection, the heat of his frame with the warm energy he gave off, soothed her.

Like this world, being in his arms felt too natural, too right, for her not to belong.

"I have a feeling what happens next is going to be equally unpleasant." He spoke in a low, calm voice.

She lifted her head to see his face. His enthralling eyes studied her features. Realizing she was intimately pressed to the body of a complete stranger, she stiffened and shifted away until they no longer touched. He released her readily, and they gazed at one another long enough for the moment to become awkward. The attraction was stronger this meeting than last, and she struggled against the urge to return to his embrace.

"I want to leave," she said hoarsely. "Now."

"The situation's complicated."

"It's easy. We just go."

"Has anything about the Immortal world been easy?" he challenged. "Your father isn't going to be so quick to free you."

"That asshole is not a father." She swiped at tears in her eyes. "I don't care. You can come or not." The moment she said the words, she wished she hadn't. She sounded like she was *asking* a complete stranger to accompany her, and her face flamed with heat. "I mean … I'm leaving." She spun away and started down the hallway in the opposite direction of the banquet halls.

She tripped on the heels and cursed, pausing to take them off so she could run without worrying about breaking her neck. Stephanie quickened her step, overly aware of the handsome man following her. His brown sugar scent lingered, and she found herself lost between the images of people dying in the banquet hall and how it felt to be in his arms.

Had she ever felt stripped so bare to the world? She focused on leaving the castle of the man who should never have been a father to anyone. Kiki's map had the exits marked and she sought to recall which direction would take her out of the madness. She reached the stairwell located in each corner of the castle and hurried down the cool stone steps.

"You don't have to come," she said over her shoulder.

"On the contrary, I do."

I'm not asking why. Something about the man always compelled her closer when she needed to run away. She reached the landing to the third floor and continued. By the time she was at the ground floor, she heard the sound of boots on stone as several people followed them. Fueled by fear of discovery, she reached the ground floor to join the rest of the guests who had been evacuated from the banquet hall. Grateful for the masses to hide in, Stephanie wove through the Immortals in the direction she thought the exit was.

Reaching an intersection, she started to the left, when the stranger touched her arm.

"This way," he said, indicating the right hallway.

She gazed at him briefly, uncertain what his motivation was for helping her when he was certainly one of these people.

"Trust me." His wink sent a surge of heat through her. He strode down the hall.

"Not a chance in hell," she muttered under her breath.

A stir went up among the guests behind her, and she risked a look over her shoulder. The Immortal guards were searching the women, checking everyone's face before moving on.

Her heart flew, and she hurried after the stranger. She ran down the hallway and turned a corner, pulling him with her just as the first of the Immortal guards called out to them.

She stopped in the middle of the hallway, hearing the clamor of more guards coming from the other direction. She'd managed not to panic with the monsters, but the idea of being trapped here or worse, imprisoned once she was discovered to have tried to escape, left her desperate.

Whether or not she belonged - she wasn't staying here. It was too crazy. Her mind raced with a solution to being discovered. No doors lined the hallway, and there was nowhere to hide. After a split second of thought, she whirled.

"Give me your jacket!"

The stranger studied her but obeyed, peeling it off his lean upper body. He handed it to her, and she swung it around her shoulders before reaching up to tug her long hair out of the French roll it had been so carefully tucked into. She tossed her shoes at her feet without putting them on and gripped the stranger by the lapels of his shirt.

Putting her back to the wall, she met his gaze. "Kiss me."

He started to smile.

"Fast! It always works on TV!"

A flicker of something – amusement? – went through his gaze. "As you will," he replied. He eased into her and wrapped one arm around her while the other hand cupped her cheek.

Before she could talk herself out of what she was doing, she circled his neck with her arms and lifted her face to him. Even after ordering him to kiss her, she found herself surprised by his confident touch – and thrilled by the sensation of his frame against hers.

A tremor of heated electricity tore through her as their lips met. The stranger pressed her to the wall and within seconds, the kiss turned from her idea into his. The pressure of his warm, full lips gently guided her, prodding her when she froze up and deepening the kiss. His tongue slid between her lips. She opened to him out of instinct. Their danger was forgotten the moment she tasted his sandalwood-brown sugar flavor. Any resistance she had to making out with a stranger melted under the combination of his scent, flavor and intensity.

Being in his arms had felt natural but this ... this was something else entirely. Primal need awoke within her, bringing with it yearning unlike anything she'd ever experienced. A resounding acknowledgement of her place in his arms warmed her from the inside out until she felt fevered and so aware of every inch of his body, she forgot the monsters and Immortals and Olivia's death – everything but the feel of his lips, his scent and taste.

In the arms of the man whose name she didn't know was the only place she'd ever belonged.

Lost in the moment, she pressed herself the length of him, needing more, wanting to experience every part of him.

He lifted his head too soon, and she opened her eyes, breathless and dazed.

"It worked," he whispered, gazing down at her.

Out of her peripheral, she saw the guards vanish around a corner.

"What ... oh. Good." Awareness crept into her once more, this time accompanied by embarrassment. She rarely dated, and the few times she'd kissed someone had been nothing like this. Did he think her naïve or stupid? Because she definitely felt that way.

Stephanie released her grip on him and stepped away, wobbled, and caught her balance against the wall. Her knees were weak, the hollow between her legs aching to the point she struggled to keep her thighs together and walk straight. Her hands quivered, and her thoughts were scattered by the fevered anticipation of her body.

Her plight returned to her but even her previous desperation wasn't able to displace the exhilarating connection with a stranger. She didn't dare look at him, certain he was laughing at a little kiss when she was full on staggering in public.

Shaking her head, she reached the corner and peered both ways before choosing to go right this time.

"Other way." His tone was huskier, low – and laughing.

She flushed and spun, heading to the left. Invigorated by the kiss, exhilarated by the idea of a second, she rushed down the hallway until she felt the cool breeze of an open door on her warm cheeks. Stephanie raced to the door and outside, stopping to breathe deeply.

"You have a part two to this plan?" the stranger asked, trailing her into the darkness outside the castle.

She faced him, grateful for the night to hide how red her cheeks were and for his calm when she was ready to freak out again. Tilting her head back, she stepped away when he drew too close. Even in the dark the draw was unreal.

"Car? Jet? Other?" he prodded, a faint smile on his handsome features.

She caught herself staring, breathing deeper to catch a taste of his scent, and blinked out of the spell. "Who the fuck are you?" *And where did you learn to kiss like that?*

He chuckled. "There's no right time to answer that question."

"Now would be appropriate," came a voice from the darkness. Wynn slid from the shadows, followed by a frowning Kiki with several other Immortal warriors behind him.

Stephanie whirled to face the direction from which they came. Between the stranger and Wynn, she'd take her chances with the man who could kiss her breathless. She moved closer to him, until she felt the warmth of his body at her back.

"She's going to find out eventually," Wynn added.

I'm sorry, Kiki mouthed the words to her.

"Show me the mark, daughter," Wynn ordered her.

"Um, no," she replied.

"Do it," the stranger whispered.

"You all want me to strip right here?" she snapped.

"I wouldn't mind," he said in a low, husky voice.

Desire and heat flared to life within her once more, flooding her with awareness and baffling sexual attraction towards a stranger she didn't even know if she could or should trust.

"You can do it on your own or I can have the soldiers help you," Wynn replied.

Stephanie glared at him. He waved two of his soldiers forward.

"I'll do it!" she snapped. She slung the jacket coat back at the stranger and stretched down. Tugging the dress over her head, she was grateful she'd worn a matching bra and underwear. She covered the front of her body with the dress and showed Wynn her back.

"Show him," Wynn said, calming.

With a frustrated sigh, she turned around.

"You have any doubts about what this is?" Wynn asked him.

"None," the stranger said.

Stephanie snatched the jacket from his arms, too embarrassed to meet the eye of anyone. "So what?" she demanded. She yanked the jacket on.

"Tell her, or I will," Wynn ordered.

Stephanie glanced from her unfriendly father to the stranger whose appearance in her life caused chaos. For once, the stranger didn't appear aloof, pleased or amused. The dark edge was back.

"There's no easy way to say this," the stranger said. "My name is Shai. I'm the deity known as Fate. Fun fact. The ancient Egyptians named a god after me. Maybe you've heard of me from them?"

"What?" Her brow furrowed. "Fate, as in the future?"

"Exactly."

"Are you shitting me?" Stephanie stared at him. "You're the god of the Future."

"He is," Kiki said.

"In the Immortal and deity societies, mates are preordained," Fate continued, his look softening when he met her gaze. "The name of the Immortal or deity appears on the mate he is meant to be with. Think of it as an ancient matchmaking service where the universe chooses who you marry. Usually, the name of the higher ranking being appears on the lower ranking being's body. For example, being a deity, my name would appear on you since you're an Immortal-human hybrid."

"The bond is unbreakable," Wynn added, sounding satisfied.

She felt the raised tattoo on her back. "Wait a minute. Are you telling me ... you and I ... we're *married?*" she asked in disbelief.

"Bonded is a better term," Fate said. "Vows can be broken. What we have cannot."

That's why I want to drop my clothes every time we meet. "I'm involuntarily married ... *bonded* to the god of the future." Tunnel vision was beginning to form. "This is beyond insane. Monsters, Immortals, magic tattoos ... No. Just ... no!"

The latest chapter of her adventure made her feel panicked, sick and delirious all at once. Before she could offer any sort of denial, she felt herself sliding to the ground. Grass tickled her cheek, and her eyes closed. A father she didn't want was one thing, but for them to tell her she had no choice in her life partner ...

When I wake up, this nightmare better be over.

CHAPTER EIGHT

Despite the traumatizing night, Fate slept well. It was the benefit of being human he liked most. His brain shut off at night, and he slept like the world was perfect.

But in a perfect world there wouldn't be six guards outside the door to his spacious bedchamber. His breakfast wouldn't be brought by a deaf mute incapable of answering his questions and he wouldn't be counting down the minutes until Wynn decided to act out one of the chain of events he'd seen many, many times before. If he had his power, would it be clearer how he arrived to this point, now that he'd met his mate?

Looking back at the week, it became obvious how, every once in a while, there was something greater than Fate at work in the world or perhaps, someone who managed to outmaneuver him with the help of every other deity in existence. Because that's what it'd take for him to be here, for his mate to be alive, for this chain of events to unfold.

His mind was not all on the dark days he knew were coming. He'd fallen asleep recalling what it was like to kiss his mate – how much more incredible it was than anything he'd ever experienced. And he began to understand why deities chose to give up a life of freedom to be with the one person who truly made them feel.

One kiss made him reconsider his future. What would a night with her be like?

He'd had to pretend like he didn't care when she fell, but his insides had seized uncomfortably. The physical reaction to an event that didn't touch him intrigued him. Wynn was too smart to let something like affection, or the appearance of it, pass. He may never harm his own daughter, but he'd use her and destroy her mate, if it served his purposes.

Fate stood at the window overlooking the expansive forests of the Alps, waiting for his own future to befall him and wishing he could save the woman who shouldn't exist.

The sound of scuffling came from outside his door, and he turned to face it. A moment later, the door opened and two women slid in: Stephanie and a pretty blonde.

Dark circles were beneath Stephanie's eyes, and she paused several feet into his chamber, staring at him with deep confusion in her gaze. He found himself recalling how she'd felt in his arms. He'd thought her pretty when they first met, beautiful the night of the dinner and today, too compelling to look away from.

"You probably shouldn't be here," he said quietly.

She drew nearer. "Hannah is helping me leave," she said.

He glanced at the blonde woman. He didn't recognize her. Without his power, he had no way of knowing if she were about to lead Stephanie into a trap. "You're certain you can trust her?"

Stephanie frowned. "I don't trust any of you people. But she hates Wynn for banishing her sister and can open a portal."

"As long as you determine the destination when you step through."

She hesitated. "How?"

"Picture the place you want to be in your mind. Focus only on it. One of the doors will glow. Walk through it."

Stephanie gazed up at him. He resisted the urge to touch her, uncertain where such an instinct originated in the first place.

"You want me to leave?" she asked.

"Yes and quickly."

Her wariness turned to confusion.

"I imagine everyone has told you an Immortal mate acts differently?" he asked.

She nodded. "Not that I believe that shit."

"My name's on your back."

She cleared her throat and stepped away, pacing a short distance. One hand went to the small of her back.

"In any case, I happen to know what comes next," he said. "And I know you should be as far from here as possible when it does."

"Because you're Fate." The words were hushed. She didn't appear ready to pass out this time.

"Because I'm Fate."

"Then why are you here? Why didn't you know to avoid Wynn's party?"

"Two reasons. One, my sister stripped my deity powers temporarily, rendering my Sight inoperable. Two, obviously I'm here for you."

"You can really see the Future?"

"See, control, change, manipulate. However, I tend to err on the side of free will," he answered.

She appeared to be trying to digest the answer.

"I need to tell you something else before you leave," he said with some reluctance. "You may want to sit down for this."

"I don't think anything can be worse than last night."

"It's about why you're so different from other humans and Immortals. I feel like I owe you an explanation."

She gazed at him for a minute before seating herself on the small sofa in the living space. He sat beside her, their knees almost touching, once more drawn to touch her. At one point, she started to reach for him and snatched her hand back.

Whatever this was, it affected both of them.

"Many, many years ago, I took precautions," he started. "Because I can see the Future, I knew you would enter my life one day and decided I wanted to control when that was. That meant ensuring you weren't born before I was ready."

She listened intently.

"The reason you don't get along with animals or people generally, and why the demons last night weren't interested in you, is simple. I hid your soul. You don't currently have one, which makes you an anomaly, someone who never should've been born. Even demons have –"

"What?" she asked. "Did you say you hid my *soul*?"

"Yes."

"You just … Buried it? Put it in the attic or something?"

"Not the attic," he replied with a smile. "I wanted to control my own future, to include if or when my mate was born. But … on occasion, I'm outmaneuvered. You were born despite the odds."

"And despite the fact you didn't want me to be," she finished.

Hearing her tone, he didn't respond.

"I have no soul," she said, a baffled look crossing her features.

"You have a soul. It's just not in your body."

Stephanie gazed at him in complete silence, unmoving. Finally, she released the breath she was holding and slapped him.

Fate wasn't surprised by the reaction. If anything, it was milder than what he expected. His cheek stung.

"You stole *my* soul. You didn't want me to be born!" she snapped. "What gave you the right to determine if I should exist?"

"Self interest."

Hurt crossed her features, and he debated the wisdom behind absolute honesty with someone who wasn't yet prepared for what she needed to know.

"I was going to ask you to come with me but after hearing this …" She rose and stared into space briefly. "You know what? Fuck you. I don't care what your rules are. I'm not your mate, not now or ever!"

"That part cannot be changed," he warned and stood as well. "What I can promise you is I'll do everything in my power to protect you from afar. Go home. Live your life. If I can't keep you safe, I'll come for you."

"Don't even bother!" she strode towards the door. "And don't ever come near my family!"

"Do you want to know where your soul is?" he called.

She froze without turning. She was tense enough he understood she was struggling again with everything new she'd learned.

Fate crossed to her and paused behind her. He breathed in her scent and admired the color of her hair before resting his hands lightly on her arms. A faint tingle of energy, of primal recognition, floated through him. The need to wrap her in his arms, to claim his mate roared. The foreignness of such an emotion disturbed him.

Her breathing was uneven. He was too aware of her shapely figure and heat, of the kiss they'd shared that may have doomed him when he was delusional enough to think he still had a chance to fight his destiny.

"What else did you do to me?" she whispered, stricken. "Why can't I just walk away from you?"

"I believe it's the nature of our bond," he replied. "We are destined to be together."

"Says the man who stole my soul."

"Would an apology help?" he teased.

"It'd piss me off more!" She sighed, affected by his calmness. The tension dropped from her shoulders, the stiffness from her stance. She leaned back against him lightly and shuddered as their bodies met.

The delicious sensation sparked a fire within him. Fate wrapped an arm around her and lowered his mouth to her ear, in case anyone was listening.

"When you're ready, summon Deidre. Tell her I left something with her. She'll know what it is. But, I'd recommend you don't do this until I'm there with you. Where she's from, you don't do favors without a deal," he said. "Without a soul, you're safe from many of the unsavory elements in the Immortal realms."

"Only you can make being soul-less not sound horrible," Stephanie grumbled.

"Stay safe. Leave quickly and stay away," he added and dropped his hands. "I'll do what I can to keep the Immortals away from you."

"I thought you said you have no power." She turned to face him. Her emotions had quieted, though her eyes darted to his lips.

"I have my charm," he said and winked. He wasn't going to admit the truth: that they were both in danger, and he was already fucked.

She hesitated.

"Go on." He glanced towards Hannah.

"What will happen to you?" Stephanie asked a little uncertainly.

"Nothing I can't handle."

She gave him a long look then turned away. Hannah opened the door to the chamber, and Stephanie followed her out into the hallway. She paused once more to look back at him before sliding out the door.

Of all the emotions Fate experienced, he didn't expect to feel relieved. With Stephanie out of Wynn's grip, she wasn't going to be used against him. Further, he'd have the opportunity to manipulate those he needed to on his end to keep his promise of protecting her without putting her in the crosshairs.

And ... the woman currently confusing him was gone. He had too much time to think when it came to being a human and not enough where she was involved. His fingertips tingled from where he'd touched her arms, and his blood was racing with heat. He had never been possessive about anything, even the Future, never felt drawn to fight the flow of life and the universe and take a real stand.

A tiny shift inside him, a tiny voice, yearned for his mate. This concerned him more than what Wynn planned to do to him. A mate left him vulnerable to manipulation and threatened his freedom.

And he began to think he really didn't care, not if giving Stephanie up for good meant he lost the unusual connection they shared before he'd had a chance to understand it. His life had been planned so as to eliminate the chance of regrets. He knew with no uncertainty that he'd regret losing her if he didn't have a chance to explore the appeal of a mate.

CHAPTER NINE

A WEEK PASSED. THEN TWO, THREE, FOUR, FIVE. BY THE SIXTH, the shock of Olivia's death and her introduction to the Immortal society had faded. All that remained were Stephanie's nightmares and the tattoo.

And bills. She sifted through the stack on the kitchen table she'd shared with Olivia. The apartment was quiet. At the very least, her rent was paid through the end of the year by Olivia's parents, who hadn't wanted to throw out their late daughter's friend after the trauma of Carmel.

"There's a baseball bat in every room of the house," her sister, Sammy, said, jarring her out of her thoughts. The blonde kickboxing champion entered the kitchen with a grin. "They're metal, too."

"But, remember, don't confront someone if you don't have to," their mother added. "Just run and call the police."

"Don't let them kidnap you though if they catch you."

"Sammy, these people are really bad. She'd just make things worse fighting them. It's what the police said. Run, get somewhere safe, and call."

"But what if –"

"Omigod. I'll be fine," Stephanie said and rolled her eyes.

They both looked at her, neither willing to call her bluff.

Unable to discuss what happened that night or where she'd gone, Stephanie let herself be swept away in the assumptions of others. Her mother thought she was suffering post traumatic stress syndrome from seeing her roommate killed and being kidnapped while others assumed she was in the middle of a breakdown. She didn't care what they thought, so long as they gave her some space and no one asked too many questions.

Stephanie expected to remain traumatized after leaving the castle, to become the basket case everyone else thought she was.

Her state of mind, however, was far from traumatized. The real world seemed less solid, less hers, and she found herself almost … bored. Waiting for something magical to happen when she turned the corner at the grocery store. She'd almost been special among the Immortals. Worse, as fucked up as their world was, she *felt* like she belonged, like her lifetime of not understanding how she fit into the human world suddenly made sense. The real world, the human world, was back to confusing her, to making her feel like life held no meaning and she was stuck on the fringes.

Not that she wanted anything to do with her father, but she had liked Kiki and …

Fate. Whenever she thought of him, of how ludicrous it was to marry a god, her heartbeat accelerated, and she smelled brown sugar. He'd somehow kept his promise. No Immortal or demon or anything else had shown up in her house in six weeks. Stunning in appearance, enigmatic and intelligent enough to scare her, Fate left her dumbfounded whenever she thought of him and their short conversations. She stretched back to touch the tattoo. If not for the markings, she would've dismissed the entire adventure as a psychotic break after witnessing Olivia's murder.

Realizing her family was staring at her, she shook off her thoughts and stood from the table. "I'm sure the bats are amazing, Sammy," she said with a snort. "And yes, Mom, I'll run."

"I'm going to make sure your windows are locked before we go." Sammy left the kitchen.

Rachel Jennings was studying her closely. "Someday, when you're ready, I really want to know what happened."

"I know."

"It's important."

Not a chance in hell. Stephanie smiled instead of speaking. "I'm okay, Mom, really." She hugged her mom. "They aren't coming back to get me."

"I wish I could believe that." Her mother sounded sad. "I wish I'd kept you safer."

"I'm twenty three. I can take care of myself."

"You'll always be my baby."

Stephanie smiled, happy to feel her mother's worry after the stint with the Immortals. "I love you, Mom. Kisses!" She started kissing her mother's hair the way she did when she was little.

Rachel laughed and tried to wriggle away. Smaller than either daughter, she was soon trapped when Sammy wrapped her arms around her, too, and both assaulted her with kisses.

Stephanie laughed for the first time in weeks. She released her, and Sammy did as well.

"My silly babies." Her mother's face was glowing. "I don't know what I'd do if something happened to you."

"Nothing's going to happen to us," Sammy said with a sigh. "I'm too tough, and Steph is too smart. We're good, Mom." She turned to Stephanie. "I meant to ask you last week. When did you get a tattoo?"

Stephanie froze then caught herself. Normal people didn't know what the tattoo meant. She tugged her shirt down over the hem of her jeans. "You saw that."

"It's gorgeous. I always thought I'd be the one to get one first." Sammy indicated for her to turn around. "Look, Mom. Isn't this cool?"

Stephanie lifted her shirt, aware neither of them had any clue what it meant.

"Who or what is Shai?" Sammy asked.

"Ancient Egyptian god of fate," their mother answered, a hushed note in her voice.

"How'd you know that?" Steph asked and faced them. Sammy, too, appeared surprised by their mother's obscure knowledge. A strange sense passed over Stephanie, one that made her wonder if her mom knew something more about Wynn than she'd ever revealed.

She dismissed the idea, not about to suspect her sweet mother of having that deep of an involvement with Wynn and his fucked up world.

Rachel was frowning. "I read it somewhere," she murmured. She stared hard at Stephanie. "I think we need to have that talk sooner than later."

"Not now," Stephanie pleaded. "Just give me a little more time."

Before her mother could insist, a knock sounded at the door. Stephanie fled the kitchen and opened it to find Olivia's younger brother in the hallway.

"Hey," he said. "I came to get another box or two."

"Yeah, sure." Stephanie led him into the living room, where she'd stacked the boxes of Olivia's things. Her brother dropped by when he was in the neighborhood, about once a week, to pick up another load.

"We're going to head out!" Sammy called.

"Call me when you're done!" her mother insisted.

"Okay," Stephanie said, though she had no intention of following through.

"I'm serious!"

"I heard you!"

Rachel continued to frown as she left the apartment with Sammy. Olivia's brother grabbed one box without a word and left the apartment. Stephanie did the same, gritting her teeth under the weight of the journals she'd found stacked in Olivia's closet. Stephanie walked down the narrow stairs and out the lobby doors to the Smart car parked in front of the building. Olivia's brother maneuvered his box into the passenger seat then took the journals from her.

She stepped back, breathing in the sea and pine trees surrounding the cozy town of Newport, Oregon. "You want me to get another box?" she asked.

Olivia's brother stood back and evaluated the space. "Nah. Not this time. I'll be back next week," he said.

She stepped onto the curb and shielded her eyes against the midday sun. Movement across the street caught her attention. A tall man with dark hair stood staring at her. At her look, he began walking.

Stephanie watched him. Uneasiness drifted through her. She'd grown wary, if not paranoid, about her surroundings since Carmel. She had no way of knowing if he was one of *them,* but she also didn't doubt he could be. He was creepy enough.

"See you next week!" Olivia's brother said and hopped into his car.

"Yeah," she replied, distracted.

The figure disappeared around a corner, and she stepped back from the curb. Stephanie folded her arms and retraced her path to her apartment. She'd left the door open and sighed, irritated with herself for not being more careful now that she knew monsters were real.

She closed and locked the door and started to return to the kitchen table to ruminate over how she was going to pay the utility bills when she had no job. A faint sound came from the living room, and she froze.

"Hello?"

No response.

Stephanie stretched for the bat Sammy had placed inside the kitchen. Her protective sister had been more than willing to help her feel safe again after the presumed kidnapping. Her heartbeat filled her ears and adrenaline lit her blood. She gripped the bat tightly and entered the living room.

A man sat on her couch, tossing magazines off the coffee table in disgust. He was well over six feet, muscular, with Middle Eastern features and a scowl. His eyes were amber enough to be gold. At first glance, he appeared normal, until she saw the weapons lining his belt. Normal people didn't carry weirdly shaped knives.

"What do you want?" she demanded, lifting the bat.

"First, to know why your magazines suck," he replied and tossed the last on the floor. Unconcerned with her, he stood. His gaze scoured the living area with disdain rather than interest. "This whole place sucks."

"Who the fuck are you?" she snapped.

He glanced at her. "One of your brothers. You know how hard it was to find you?"

"I didn't exactly want to be found."

"With a family as fucked up as ours, I don't blame you."

Something about his delivery reassured her he wasn't a demon or other kind of monster. She lowered the bat to her side.

"But ... you are family," he added, gaze settling on her. He held out a hand. "I'm Tamer."

She recognized the name from her talks with Kiki. Against her better judgment, she shook his hand and then stepped away quickly.

"I've been trying to find you for the past few weeks. Kiki won't leave me the fuck alone about making sure your life went back to normal."

"That's not possible."

"I told him the same fucking thing." Tamer crossed to the

photographs displayed on one wall. "Your mother is the only one that survived our father. He killed the rest of ours after they gave birth. I'm guessing she outsmarted him. Is she an Immortal? Doesn't look like an Immortal." He was quiet. "What the fuck do I know?"

She didn't feel as alarmed this time by the revelation Wynn had murdered seven women after they bore his sons. She'd kept her distance from her family since returning as well, as if a part of her knew her stint with the Immortals wasn't over yet.

"So what're you doing here?" she asked.

"Someone found you."

"Who?"

"Demons."

Oh, god. They were in her nightmares at least three times a week, either in their human forms with huge fangs or as monsters.

"Go pack. Time to move," he added.

Stephanie studied him before obeying. Her hands shook as she pulled a small suitcase from the closet and began tossing in the essentials. Was she horrified to be dragged back to their world or relieved to leave her boring one?

"Can I ask where we're going?" she called.

"Not Wynn's."

"Good enough." She tucked a picture of her family in the suitcase and zipped it. "How is Kiki and ... uh ..." She stopped herself.

"Your mate?"

"He's not my mate."

"Yeah. Get over it." He sounded amused. "Kiki is his normal, boring, organized self. Last I heard, Fate wasn't doing too good. Almost made the list."

"What list?"

"Death's list."

Her breath caught. Stephanie dropped the suitcase and returned to the living area. "He's not dead."

"Not yet. Close. My boss is freaking out about it."

"Your boss is … Death." She'd spent much of her time writing down everything she learned about the Immortals as a way of sorting through the overwhelming experience.

"Yup."

Stephanie absorbed the information. A sense of panic fluttered deep inside her. She barely knew the man and certainly didn't consider him a husband, even if the Immortals assumed that was the case. But … he'd helped her twice and promised to do what he could to protect her, despite being a prisoner of Wynn's. It was more effort than anyone else in their weird world had made.

"But he's not dead, right?" she prodded once more, uncertain why the thought made her start to panic.

"Nope. Boss says he can't die-dead or the world ends."

"Oh. That's … good, I guess. Wynn won't destroy the world, will he?"

"To get what he wants? Yeah."

"What does he want?"

"No one knows."

She shook her head, confused already, and grabbed her suitcase. "Can I … should I … uh, do something?" she asked awkwardly. She felt the answer but didn't want to acknowledge it.

"Come with me. It's all you can do."

A chilly, damp breeze touched the back of her neck, and she shivered.

"No!" cried a familiar female voice.

Stephanie spun. Fate's sister walked from a portal in her bedroom into the living area. Her eyes were wild, flickering rapidly between every color of the rainbow. Her hair rippled with unnatural hues as well, and her features were flushed.

Overwhelmed by her wired energy, Stephanie backed away.

Tamer eyed her. "Karma, I presume."

"Death dealer."

"Karma, as in *the* karma?" Stephanie asked.

"Yes," said the woman. She stepped between them. "And if you want her, you have to go through me."

"We're not enemies, godling," Tamer snarled. "My boss wants your brother alive as much as you do!"

"My brother is dying as we speak! He needs her!"

"If you have an ounce of sense, you'll know you can't fuck with Wynn without a plan!"

"Or … a third option. We can eliminate both of you and take her with us."

The two fell silent at the third voice. Three men in black, all with fangs, emerged from the kitchen.

Stephanie shifted to grab her bat once more.

"Oh, no. That won't happen." Karma stepped boldly up to the first. Her hair and eyes were black. She knocked aside his attempt to strike her and snatched him by the neck, lifting him off the ground with superhuman strength.

Stephanie watched. Just when she thought the Immortals couldn't surprise her any more, she saw the goddess Karma draining the life from a demon. The creature wriggled in her grasp without being able to escape. His skin began to shrivel and cling to his bones while blood streamed out of every orifice.

She stumbled away, not about to be an inch closer to Karma or the demons.

Tamer waved her towards him. She dropped the carrier of her suitcase and clambered over the couch to reach him. A portal yawned open, and she crowded him, ready to run.

"No!" Karma's cry came a split second before Stephanie was tackled to the ground by Fate's sister. Energy smashed into her, rattling her to her teeth like lightning. Stephanie lay still, gasping for air and uncertain what the hell was going on.

Karma and Tamer were fighting each other when not murdering demons. Stephanie barely escaped being trampled by the factions warring in her tiny living room and hauled herself up onto a side table, displacing the lamp that was there. Her gaze fell to the portal, and Fate's instructions returned to her.

More demons were streaming through the front door.

Stephanie bolted into the portal. When she stood in the cool depths with fog clinging to her ankles, she cleared her mind as much as possible. No image of where she wanted to go formed, for there was nowhere she knew to run.

"Somewhere safe," she whispered. "Wherever that may be."

One of the doors glowed in response. This one was a black door, unlike the yellowish doors lining the rest of the cave. She approached it, aware of the melee in the apartment behind her. Did she trust a magic door or take her chances with Karma and a bunch of demons?

"Can't believe I have to think about that," she muttered and stepped through the doorway.

Silence fell as she left the human world behind. A beautiful, petite, blonde woman in a Grecian style black dress stood several feet before her. The stone walls, ceiling and floor around her were black.

"I've been waiting for you," the woman said almost shyly. She smiled, revealing tiny fangs.

That's not good. Stephanie glanced over her shoulder to find the portal had already closed.

"Come on. It won't take them long to figure out where you are." The blonde began walking down a long, dark hallway whose lamps rendered it light enough to see but not clearly. *Darkyn* was written across her shoulders, once in maroon in a similar style to Stephanie's mating mark, the second time in black.

Stephanie swallowed hard, heart pounding. Wherever she was, she instinctively knew it wasn't anywhere in the human realm.

"You don't want my mate finding you either," called the blonde.

"Who's your mate?"

"The Dark One."

This was sounding worse by the second. Stephanie hurried to follow her. "Why are you helping me?" she asked, drawing abreast of the blonde. "Maybe I should ask … *are* you helping me?"

The blonde gave her a warm look. "I am. Sometimes good people get dropped into bad circumstances. This isn't for Fate, by the way. This is for you."

"Not many of you Immortal people get along well," Stephanie murmured.

"No, they don't." She smiled. "I'm Deidre."

Stephanie gasped. "The Deidre? Who has my soul?"

"Nice of him to tell you," she said with disapproval. "Yes, but you can't have it back. Not yet. Not here."

"Not where?"

"Hell."

Stephanie glanced around and shivered.

"Darkyn, my mate, will sense you if you have a soul. You're a blind spot to demons without it."

"But you knew I was coming."

"I'm not your average demoness. You'll be safe here for now."

If she stopped to think about the reassurance, Stephanie would snap. Instead, she focused on what she needed to think to survive. "Is that why the demons were at my apartment? Because you sent them?"

"No. My mate is looking for you, too. Which is why you can't leave your chamber unless I'm with you."

"Being mated to an immortal or deity doesn't mean you always get along," Stephanie observed.

"It's like any relationship. The universe puts you together. You have to make it work."

"You're a human like me."

"I was, up until a few months ago."

"And you're stuck with the devil? Why don't you just tell them all to go to hell and leave?"

Deidre smiled. "You'll see."

Compared to the devil, Fate didn't seem so bad. Stephanie kept quiet and hugged herself, not at all impressed by her latest jaunt into the world of immortals.

Deidre led her into a chamber whose walls were as black as the hallways. Even the sickly fire burned black.

Stephanie gazed around, not comfortable in the small, dark space.

"There's magic here," Deidre said and crossed to the nightstand beside the bed. On top of it was a round turntable. "When you're hungry and thirsty, tell the room what you want, and it'll appear here." She tapped the round table.

Stephanie said nothing.

"Are you okay to talk?" Deidre asked.

Stephanie was surprised to feel she was. Her thoughts weren't scrambled after the encounter in her apartment the way they had been when she was first introduced to the Immortal world.

"It'd be nice to talk to someone normal for once," Deidre added.

Hoping the only other near-human she'd met wasn't going to fuck her over, Stephanie nodded. Fate had warned her not to negotiate with Deidre even if the woman did have her soul, but talking sounded innocent enough.

Deidre went to the black rug before the hearth and sat. Stephanie did the same, and they gazed at one another.

"I can go first. Want to hear the wildest story in the universe?" Deidre asked with a laugh.

Hours later, when Deidre had finished, Stephanie sat in stunned silence.

"I can't even ..." She wasn't able to wrap her head around the tale

Deidre told her involving a human-turned-deity named Gabriel, Past-Death, Fate, and a slew of other people. "This is insane. After you left the Underworld, did you give Hell back to Darkyn?"

"What do you think?" Deidre laughed and rose, crossing to the magic tray table. She ordered food and seconds later, two plates with cheeseburgers and fries appeared. Bringing them back to the hearth, she handed one to Stephanie, who was recovering from the latest immortal weirdness.

"And you're happy?" she pressed.

"Yeah." Deidre nibbled on a fry. "There's definitely an adjustment period."

Stephanie shook her head. "It makes no sense."

"Darkyn wanted a mate. I think your struggle is different. Fate is … complicated." Deidre's expression grew puzzled. "The longer a deity has been around, the more potential enemies he has, too. He comes across as not caring but he picks fights with the strongest deities for a reason. He was an enemy of my twin and of Darkyn. But then again, none of the deities are ever at peace, unless they're working against someone else. It's this complex system of checks and balances. I don't know if it's a good thing for you or not that Fate's so good at it."

"Wynn isn't a deity but he's a heavyweight, right?"

Deidre's expression grew shuttered. "Yeah. He's in deep with a lot of powerful people."

"Sorry. I didn't mean to bring him up."

"You don't want to mention to anyone he's your father," she advised. "Or that Fate is your mate."

"Easy. He's not."

"Okay." Deidre giggled. "But seriously. Down to business."

Stephanie looked up from the last fry on her plate. "Business."

"You need to learn a few things quick to increase your chances of surviving this. The mate of a deity can make deals on his behalf. He has no magic at the moment, but you do."

She tilted her head, listening.

"Anything you promise anyone else, he's obligated to follow through with it. So ... promise carefully," Deidre said. "Among deities, these oaths form their complicated network of alliances and checks and balances. Oh, and never, ever make a deal with a demon. Hell runs off deals, and demons don't normally lose."

"You're telling me this because ..."

"We need to make a deal." Deidre smiled. "For your soul."

Stephanie's mouth went dry. "Couldn't start with something a little less terrifying?"

"I'm not my husband or Fate or anyone else. And, since this is your first deal, I'm not going to screw you over. Your soul is already in Hell."

"This is so fucked up."

"Just remember – you have control over your own life. It doesn't feel that way now, but trust me, you do. You're the daughter of Wynn and the mate of Fate. You have more potential power than almost anyone else I know."

Stephanie felt the tension in her belly uncoil some at the warm reassurance.

"And so you know, your soul is safe here with me. I took an oath to Fate to protect it, to protect *you*. I can't return it until the timing is right. But I will return it, if you're willing to make a deal with me."

Do I really have a choice? "Okay. What is it?"

"Wynn."

Stephanie waited.

"As the leader of the Immortals, he's dangerous. He needs to be replaced."

"Killed?" Stephanie whispered, stricken.

"Replaced. How it's done is not my concern. For your sake, you want to keep a deal as general as possible. No timeframes, no specifics that limit your wiggle room."

Stephanie deliberated before speaking again. "Is this a demon speaking who wants him out of the way so the demons can raid humanity?"

Deidre shook her head. "This is the human side of me speaking. Humanity stands a better chance against my mate without Wynn in control. Wynn's goal is power not protection."

Stephanie drew a deep breath. "Okay. I agree."

"The last thing you need to remember to do is stipulate there are no unwritten terms and conditions. Demons love to trip you up with small print."

"In exchange for my soul, I'll find a way to replace Wynn," Stephanie said. "No unwritten terms and conditions.

"Good enough. Fate will know how to follow through." Deidre held out her hand. "Fist bump."

Stephanie did so, and a streak of coldness shot through her.

"It's now irrevocable," Deidre said. She rose. "I'll leave you to rest. You're safe here. Just don't leave the room, okay?"

Stephanie nodded.

"Bathroom's over there." Deidre pointed. "Clothing in the wardrobe. I'll check in on you in the morning."

With no clocks or windows, Stephanie had no idea what time it was. She was full but not tired, too freaked out by the idea of sitting in Hell to want to sleep. Crossing to the bed, she sat with her back to the wall and stared at the door. She didn't need Deidre's reminder not to leave the room. She had no intention of wandering through Hell and running into demons or anything else her imagination could create.

She was, however, fascinated by the magic turntable.

"Organic chocolate cake with caramel icing made with no processed foods whatsoever," she said, testing the magic of Hell.

It appeared instantly. She eyed it, a little leery of eating food in

Hell, before she leaned over and grabbed it.

Her Hell cake was the best food she'd ever tasted. She scarfed it down and ordered warm milk next. Drowsy after the snack, she rested on her side without going so far as to commit to crawling under the blankets and drifted to sleep facing the door.

CHAPTER TEN

WYNN WAS PACING IN FRUSTRATION.

It was Fate's only comfort in the dungeon of the chalet. Blood dribbled off him from too many wounds to count, often times further tormenting the delicate skin around injuries that had already begun to heal. He gazed at the stone ceiling above him, unable to move. Spread eagled and naked on his back with his limbs tied tightly a little too far from one another to increase his misery, he was in one piece. Wynn had ordered him tortured but all of his appendages remained accounted for.

For now.

Wynn's first demand came as no surprise but his second, revealed today, had Fate wondering if his favorite appendage was going to survive the Immortal.

He'd been able to neatly avoid the sensation of pain for tens of thousands of years, an advantage of being able to See the future. The feeling shocked him at first. Similar to his first kiss as a human-ish being, he wasn't accustomed to how intense humans experienced their world. But in the six weeks since this mess in Wynn's basement first began, he'd begun to categorize the kinds of pain and soreness to keep his mind occupied on his misery and not wandering into worry.

Warm pain, hot pain, agony, anguish. Slow, creeping pain … bright, sudden pain … He'd ranked them from bad to worst and was currently debating whether the initial pain from broken bones or that from fire held the number one spot for worst pain ever.

"It's simple," Wynn said, calming. He sat once more in the chair beside Fate's suspended form. "I will get what I want from you."

Fate said nothing. He was enjoying the breather too much. A tremor of concern went through him. He'd been awake for multiple days straight, too long for him to recall when he'd last called in a favor from a fellow deity to extend the tenuous protection he arranged for Stephanie. He dared not waste a favor by calling it in too soon, but if his human mind was too confused to know for certain, he risked exposing her to everyone who was looking for her by not acting.

He tried again to count how many days it'd been. There was a blank spot in his mind where he had no idea how much time had passed.

"One favor from Fate. Just one," Wynn continued. "Don't you think your life is worth one favor?"

Fate had no intention of cracking. He surprised himself with his resolve. He hadn't been physically tested in millennia. His normal game was mental, and he was pleased he made it this far.

"Try the second request," Wynn's chief tormenter, an Immortal with one eye, said from the corner. "He blinked when you mentioned her."

Ah. He caught that. Fate's physical weakness and exhaustion were wearing on his mental sharpness, which was what Wynn intended. People under physical duress were easier to manipulate than those who weren't, a technique Fate had used countless times.

"It's not a request," Wynn replied. "It's an order."

"You can't order me not to claim my mate," Fate said, amused despite his pain. "Your Code forbids anyone from interfering."

"If you choose to abandon her, it's not me interfering," Wynn responded acidly. "What does a deity know of selflessness? Of love?"

"What do *you* know of either?" Fate tugged at one of his bonds restlessly. The human experience was starting to get old, but he only began to worry when he realized he had no idea of he was succeeding in giving Stephanie her life back.

He didn't even know if she was alive. The stark limitations of a human's mind had begun to fuck with his thinking and knowledge of the world. Wynn wasn't going to let anything happen to her before he got what he wanted, yet the uncertainty, the fear for his mate, remained.

"You look down upon Immortals and humans alike but it is you who is not worthy of us," Wynn added. "You think I'll turn *my* daughter over to a creature like you? You have no value for life."

"You've never cared for any of your children let alone a daughter you only just met." Fate grimaced.

"I care for all my children."

"You're not after her," Fate ventured. "But something she can offer you. What?"

New pain, this one stemming from a slap with a barbed whip by the one-eyed tormenter, flashed through him.

"Is this vengeance … or something else?" he gasped.

"Vengeance is a good start. There are six of you I have particular plans for," Wynn replied.

"Hurting me will hurt your daughter."

"Perhaps. But it'll hurt you more." Wynn rose and motioned to the tormentor. "Put him on the wheel for the night."

Damn. Fate didn't particularly care to be tortured but the wheel was his least favorite. The medieval contraption meant he neither slept nor was able to heal, not when he was being inflicted with new wounds for a solid eight hours in a row.

"And so you know, I wouldn't object to her being mated to a

deity. I object to her being mated to *you*," Wynn added from his position standing at the door.

"Because I had a hand in killing you."

"Because you don't know how to do anything but manipulate and lie. You'd trade her to the demons for a favor."

Wynn left, slamming the door open on his way out.

The words resonated within Fate. Would he view a mate as nothing more than an additional tool in his toolbox to manipulate? Everyone in his life had a purpose and a role, and not one of them was present out of a sense of friendship or loyalty. Fate didn't know the meaning of fidelity to anything, except for Karma, who he still planned to use when needed.

His fatigue, coupled with the incessant pain preventing him from real rest, was wearing down more than his resistance to Wynn. His own perception of the past millennia had begun to shift in a timespan not worth remembering given the extent of his lifetime.

For once, his focus wasn't on the great game, on what hobby he wanted to master next, on the drama among deities and Immortals that kept him entertained. His mind was on the one thing he'd never put much thought into – how he filled his life with hobbies, politics and games because there was nothing else to fill it with. Time, living and the Future had lost their value to him. His existence had become a series of distractions, one after the next.

Alone with his thoughts – or strapped to the wheel, experiencing pain as a human – he began to notice how, when the distractions were stripped away, his life was filled with nothingness. Tons of it.

The tormentor brought in two more of his thugs to lift Fate from his position and carry him into the room next door, where the wooden wheel awaited him. At each of four points was some tool of torture. The wheel dragged him through water at its lowest point, fire at its highest, razorblades on the eastern point and feathers on the west.

After several nights on the wheel, he dreaded the feathers the most.

Pain radiated through him, distracting him from his thoughts. They strapped him to the wheel, face down tonight, and stepped aside to move the torture devices in place.

Fate rested his cheek against the wooden wheel and steeled himself for hours of agony.

Without the distractions, what was there? Further, who was *he* if we wasn't searching for distractions? Was this what Karma had meant about him losing himself?

He had no answers, and this disturbed him more than hearing the motor of the wheel rumble to life.

"You shouldn't be here," he whispered, sensing Karma.

His sister had visited often in the past few days. Her hair and eyes were black, and she was wringing her hands.

"I can't find her," she said, distraught. "I had her and then ..."

"Is she safe?"

She nodded. "She was but then she was just gone. Brother, if I could just talk to the Ancient, I could -"

"Absolutely not. I've warned you many times. You do not do business with them." Concern made Fate lift his head. "If you want to help me, find her, Karma. Please."

His sister nodded, and the wheel began to turn.

CHAPTER ELEVEN

"TRY AGAIN," DEIDRE URGED.

Stephanie drew a breath, calmed her nerves and killed the logical part of her that freaked out at the idea of tearing a hole in the fabric of the world. Of the many lessons Deidre had been teaching her the past two days, this was the one she struggled with most.

The tide ran closer to their feet the longer they spent on the beach beneath a dark sky and full moon. The familiar sound and scent of the ocean helped her nerves.

She willed the portal to appear.

It opened, and she stepped back.

"It's getting easier," she reported. "Still freaky though."

"You get used to it. It's so much better than dealing with TSA at the airport."

Stephanie laughed. "For a demoness, you're kind of cool."

Deidre smiled.

"Am I interrupting?" a low male voice came from behind them.

Stephanie turned and had the urge to hide behind the demoness. The muscular man behind her towered taller and wider than Tamer. His features were hard, his dark eyes moving from her to Deidre. He wore a black trench coat, and the glimmer of weapons lining the interior caught the light of the moon.

"Gabriel, this is Stephanie." Deidre's smile was warm.

"We've been looking for you," he said with a grim expression. "You've been hiding in Hell?"

"It's not like she can go to the Underworld without a soul," Deidre pointed out.

Stephanie's alarm grew. She hadn't wanted to meet the figure known as Death under any circumstance let alone on a dark night.

"I figured you wouldn't mind her coming to our monthly meeting for former humans."

Gabriel gazed at Stephanie hard enough for her heart to race before he gave a brisk nod. "Welcome to our world," he said.

"You guys meet monthly?" Stephanie asked, brow furrowing.

"We made a deal," Deidre replied. "To help us remember what it means to be human. It's easy to get lost among the Immortals, to forget the value of life when you've got an eternity to live."

Eternity. Stephanie hadn't considered living forever. "Do I have an eternity?" she asked.

"You do," Gabriel said and swung his trench coat off. He rested it on the beach then sat down, elbows on knees. "If you want it. You're half-Immortal."

"I'm not so sure," Stephanie murmured. "I've yet to see anything that makes me want to live longer than I have to among you people."

Gabriel gazed at her quizzically.

"They're having issues," Deidre whispered.

"There is no *they*," Stephanie corrected her.

"Good luck with that," Gabriel said. "Although I don't blame you. Deities have a much different view of the world than even Immortals. And Fate?" He shook his head. "Yeah. Good luck."

"Why are you looking for me?" Stephanie asked and sat a few feet from him.

"Right now there's one way for Fate to survive Wynn. If you return to your father."

Stephanie grimaced.

"You have a better chance of freeing Fate if you're there," Gabriel said.

"I don't know if I want to free him," she retorted.

Deidre ducked her head, smiling.

"Okay, I'll make this simple," Gabriel said, unfazed by her refusal. "There are three laws that govern deities."

"Deidre told me."

"Good. So you know if Fate dies at Wynn's hands, life as we know it ends."

Stephanie was quiet. She'd manage to rationalize away any notion of being stuck – for *eternity!* – with a stranger if the people around her didn't continue to bulldoze through her denial.

"Fate's a fan of free will. You choose," Gabriel added.

"That's so not fair!" she exclaimed. "You're putting the world on me?"

"I am."

"There's no choice. I can't snuff out existence because I'm afraid of Wynn or feeling completely overwhelmed. But, how does anyone just accept being assigned a spouse?"

Gabriel snorted without answering.

"We're not saying it makes sense," Deidre replied. "Maybe just focus on Wynn. Who knows? Maybe you'll be the first mate to walk away from the man the universe chose for you."

"No one walks away," Gabriel said.

"You're not helping!"

"How is a demoness the good guy in this conversation?"

Deidre rolled her eyes at him.

Stephanie watched them interact, sensing the depth of their friendship. "Is it safe to guess you want something from me, too?" she asked Death.

"You made a deal?" Gabriel asked Deidre.

She nodded.

"Don't make deals with demons," he grumbled. "I want to help you, Stephanie. Fate is an ally of sorts but more importantly, he needs to make it through this. What I … what *we* think will work is for you to work from the inside."

"Like a spy," she said.

"Yeah. Like a spy. One who should know going in what Wynn does to traitors."

She held her breath, waiting for him to tell her something worse than she'd seen yet.

"I imagine he'd exile you somewhere unpleasant, like Hell," Gabriel said. "Don't get caught before you have backup."

"Where do I find backup?" she whispered, unwilling to think about what Hell would be like if she were sent there by Wynn.

"Two options: Rhyn and Andre, your brothers. Rhyn is off the map, because Wynn has it out for him and his family. He was managing the Council just fine before Wynn manipulated him out of the position. I'll keep looking. As for Andre … you'll need to find that out from Wynn," Gabriel said grimly. "He's not dead-dead. That much I know."

Deidre cleared her throat. "I know where Andre is."

Stephanie listened. How did she feel responsible or loyal to brothers she'd never met?

"Wynn traded him to Darkyn," Deidre said quietly.

"Fuck," Gabriel muttered. "How?"

"I don't know the details," she admitted. "But I know he's in Hell and Darkyn brought him there."

"You can't get him out."

She smiled without answering.

"You *won't* get him out," he corrected himself.

"Because no one wants to piss off the Dark One, even his mate," Stephanie said. "I'm picking this shit up slowly."

They fell quiet. She found herself brainstorming the issues of a world and strangers she didn't know existed before a few weeks ago.

"What if ... what if I got him out?" she asked. "Is it possible? I mean, assuming we can't find Rhyn."

"No way," Gabriel said. "You wouldn't survive a deal with Darkyn. Even Fate works around him."

Deidre, however, was quiet.

"If demons ignore me because I have no soul, then can I just walk in and ... I don't know, unlock his jail cell?" Stephanie asked.

"Yes," Deidre said.

"No," Gabriel replied simultaneously. "You know the danger, Deidre. She's not invisible. There's one way into Hell, unless you're a demon or with one. If anyone saw her go through the portal, she'd be killed, soul or no soul."

"She *can* do it. I'm not saying she should. Death dealers cross through Hell all the time," Deidre reasoned. "Send Tamer and have him bring her with him. Death dealers know the layout relatively well."

"Things have been tense for a few months," Gabriel said. "Darkyn's limited our access to once a day."

"But if I went with Tamer, and then maybe met him once I'd freed Andre, he could take us all out, right?" Stephanie pressed.

"Darkyn's going to know who tipped us off," Gabriel said, eyes on Deidre. "Unless ..." He gazed at Stephanie thoughtfully. "I have an idea. As a mate of a deity, you can access the Oracle's records at the Sanctuary. You can see most of what Fate can see. If you go there first, you can find out the details of the deal Wynn made. Deidre and I can't be officially linked to this. Deities don't fuck with another's domain. Well, they claim not to anyways."

"Okay. So, I go back to Wynn and pretend I want to be there then secretly sneak out with Tamer and try to free Andre. Then, he can help me free Fate. Right?"

The two were frowning.

"It's dangerous," Deidre said.

Gabriel stiffened and twisted to see behind him.

Stephanie leaned around him.

A portal yawned open, and Karma stepped through. "Finally!" she breathed, eyes on Stephanie.

"That's our cue to go," Gabriel said and stood.

Deidre rose as well.

"Wait!" Stephanie scrambled to her feet. "That's it? You're leaving? Do we even have a plan?"

"Ssshhh," Deidre said and moved closer, until certain only she could hear. "We aren't supposed to help one another like this. Gabe and I are doing it because we know what it's like to be a human in an Immortal's world. We can't openly help you or it disrupts the balance."

"This is politics," Stephanie said.

"Remember what I told you about deals. Be careful who you trust. The alliances among these people shift with the winds. You can summon Tamer the way I taught you to summon me, okay?" The blonde gave her another quick smile and turned away, disappearing into a different portal than that which Death took.

Stephanie watched them both go. Karma drew abreast of her, radiating agitated energy.

"I've been looking for you," Karma said. "We have to save my brother."

"Yeah, I know." Stephanie faced her.

Karma's hair and eyes were the same color brown.

"There's a plan, but it's really fucked up."

Karma brightened. "You're going to help him?"

"Well …" Stephanie cleared her throat. "I'm going to do

something. We'll leave it at that."

"I need to help!" Karma exclaimed. "Please, please, please!"

"Yeah, totally. I think initially you need to keep out of the way."

Karma frowned, and her hair turned silver.

Sensing the deity was going to be a handful to work with, Stephanie sought another task to give her to keep her out of the way. It was going to be hard enough to convince Wynn she wanted to be his daughter without worrying about Karma shorting out.

"I mean, you'll be out of the way, because you have a very special role," Stephanie added. "You have to let me handle the Immortals."

"Because you are an Immortal."

"Um, yeah. Whatever. Anyway, you need to find Rhyn."

Karma appeared pensive.

"He's missing. And I need his help in order to free Fate."

"Hmmm. Okay. I can find him. What do I do when I find him?"

"I guess bring him to me."

"I'll start looking now." Karma whirled and summoned a portal, her hair flashing white as she strode away.

Stephanie waited until the goddess was gone before she shook her head. She felt like she was herding cats who had magical powers to fall back on if they didn't want to play fair.

After a moment of debate on the best way to proceed, she called her own portal and stepped into its dark depths. "Oracle on the Sanctuary." She repeated Gabriel's words without understanding where or what the words meant.

A yellow door pulsed in response. Feeling a little more confident after her time with Deidre, she crossed to it and stepped through.

Warm, humid night air washed over her, smelling of the ocean and sand. She oriented herself to the tiny room lit by lamplight. Wind swept in through the windows, and she heard the distant crash of waves on the shore. The stone structure reminded her of Wynn's castle, and a wooden door was cracked to display a darkened hallway beyond.

On a lectern opposite her was a book whose words were being written by an invisible hand before her eyes.

Stephanie approached it, watching in intrigue as the words appeared on the pages. What kind of ghost could write?

She gazed around. As in Hell, magic rendered the air charged. "Um, I need to see the deals. There's one with Wynn and Darkyn or … something." Her cheeks grew warm.

The book flipped its pages before her and settled on one covered in the geometric writing of the Immortals. Stephanie was about to ask for a translation when the letters appeared to leap off the page before her and landed back on the page, this time in a language she could read.

"Ancient Immortal Wynn repays debt to DO. Peace volunteers in Immortal's place." She puzzled over the sentence. "So why did Peace agree to go?"

The pages flipped again and more writing raced across its surface.

"Peace granted Ancient Immortal Wynn one favor in deal to spare Ancient Immortal Rhyn." She sucked in a breath, recalling Fate's warning about the power of a favor. Wynn had used his children to manipulate Peace into Hell. "What a sick bastard." She chewed on her lower lip, rethinking the idea of becoming a spy in the home of a man who had threatened to kill one son to extort a favor from his eldest son – then sent him to Hell.

If what Deidre said was true, Wynn had the potential to extort the mate of Fate as well. She'd have to be careful and do as Deidre said – deal carefully.

"Am I really the mate of Fate?" she whispered to the Oracle, uncertain what kind of reply to expect or even if she wanted one.

This time when the words leapt off the page, they formed scenes captured in bubbles. One popped up in front of her, then another and another and another. She was soon surrounded by visions unlike any she'd ever seen before. It was like being in a multiplex movie theatre with hundreds of screens, all playing at once.

The bubbles began to pass through her, imprinting in her thoughts, and she froze, horrified to realize each one was a window into the life of a complete stranger's tomorrow. Reunions, work, birthday parties, commutes, family life mixed with street crime, desperation, financial strain, hospital stays.

The potential tomorrows of dozens of people played through her mind as they passed through her body. She witnessed a boy graduate high school and end up hit by a car, a woman fall at a concert and her future husband help her up, the starving children in an impoverished country breathe their last breaths, the lottery winner realizing his number had been chosen ...

Each vision contained the raw emotion of the person experiencing whatever happened.

Stephanie staggered, unable to fend off the emotions that felt like hers – but weren't. She dropped to her knees and struggled to keep up with the whirling emotions left behind by lightning quick visions.

At long last, they stopped and receded to the pages of the Oracle, leaving her with the emotional hangover of hundreds of people. She was panting and sweating profusely despite the cool night breeze off the ocean.

Is this what Fate lived with on a daily basis? There were billions of people. How did he cope with the emotions, with knowing how much pain and suffering there was in the world?

Too caught off guard about her circumstances, she'd never thought twice about what he experienced as a deity. He came across as unflappably amused by everyone and everything around him and not at all like the destinies of billions rested on his shoulders. Immortals and deities alike viewed his every action with suspicion, and he had been ousted as manipulative – if not a liar – by everyone she'd met.

Stephanie shivered, but not from cold. Five minutes with the lives of a few dozen people, and she was in tears on the floor, weeping for strangers she'd never meet. How could anyone do this every day and night for thousands of years and not end up twisted, warped or crazy?

What if he were those things or worse?

Regaining her composure, she returned to the book on the lectern. "I want to know what he's like," she told the Oracle.

The writing paused before another surge of images lit up her surroundings.

Stephanie stepped back and knelt, afraid of being overwhelmed once more. This time, the images were of the Past, of Fate guiding, cajoling or out right manipulating the Futures of Immortals and humans alike. She watched in some confusion as he seemed to operate out of selfish reasons sometimes and other times, to help those he crossed avoid early deaths or misery. Nudging those who needed it one moment, he turned and bartered with deities over the lives of others the next.

The book was able to show his actions but not his motives. Stephanie watched the images, struggling to piece together a better picture of Fate's personality by the lives he touched.

What became clear from the dizzying images, Fate had a method to his madness, and he operated alone. Always. And it wasn't because no one reached out to him or held out a hand or peace offering. She saw him rebuff such efforts early on in his position until people no longer offered. He was a one-man machine evaluating the destiny of the universe as a whole and tweaking it as needed for a vision she wasn't able to interpret from his actions.

He was generally benevolent, if not kind, towards humans. The immense power he potentially wielded was kept in check by the fact he rarely ever needed to use it.

The more she watched, the less she understood.

She had the sudden sense of not knowing Fate at all. The man in search of amusement held a much deeper, darker side which seemed to guide his interference with the lives of others. He alone was privileged with the knowledge of who would have a reason to rejoice or who would die tomorrow. How could he seem so unaffected by anything when he was privy to the greatest despairs and triumphs of tomorrow awaiting the people around him? How had he done this alone for so long?

Even watching him in action, she wasn't able to get a better understanding of his mind. How could he hide himself so well?

Her shaking ceased as the emotions of others faded. Stephanie wiped her features and glanced up at the book before she stood.

She had what she came for – an excuse as to why she knew Andre was in Hell so as not to get Deidre in trouble. The insight she sought about Fate only left her less certain about him, about what motivated him and how he chose when to interfere and not. His actions weren't random, and each was measured so he only did what was absolutely necessary to spur a new chain of events or alter and existing one.

"Thank you," she said to the book. "Can you show me where he is now? If he's okay?"

The multitude of images around her coalesced into one, and she gasped.

Fate was strapped face down on the ground, suspended by his arms and legs above a puddle of blood. A man whose face she couldn't see was peeling strips of skin off his back and swelling, but this wasn't the only source of blood. At least one limb was broke by its awkward angle, and scratches, burns, bruises and other signs of torture covered his body.

His head sagged as she watched. The man motioned to another, who stabbed his arm with a needle.

Fate's body jerked, and his head snapped back up. The man torturing him went back to ripping skin off his back in long strips.

"Stop!" she cried and covered her eyes. "Stop, stop, stop!"

She'd never seen anything like this, never imagined anyone was capable of hurting another to this extent. Her stomach was in her throat, and she swallowed hard a few times to keep from vomiting. The reaction was bone deep, far worse than what she'd experienced when Olivia died.

This was her fault. She'd left him behind without understanding what kind of monster her father was.

Gabriel had a reason to be concerned. No one could handle such torture, and Fate had been stuck with Wynn for over six weeks!

"What happens if he dies?"

The room filled with countless images. Bubbles filled with the lives of thousands upon thousands stacked up on top of one another until the noise and colors were too much for her to identify individual lives and stories.

Just as suddenly, all the visions turned black. They stayed dark and then faded away.

"So they weren't being overdramatic," she said. *I have to do something.* Her thoughts went to Wynn, who she began to regard with even more distaste. If anyone knew how to stop what Wynn was doing to Fate, it'd be Kiki.

This world was beginning to feel more and more concrete. The idea of prearranged matches was no less baffling than before, but the Immortals, the politics, the people she'd met …

"I belong here," she whispered, gazing around. And it made no sense why her instincts agreed.

Calming once more, unconcerned with how she looked, she concentrated on summoning a portal. It yawned open on the side of the room opposite the Oracle. She envisioned her chamber in the castle, and one of the doors before her glowed in response.

Stephanie entered her room once more. It had been tidied up from her stay. She collected her thoughts then went to the bathroom to wash her face and prepare to face Wynn. Changing out of her clothing into those that had been chosen for her, she left the bedroom with trembling hands and began wandering through the castle.

Wynn and Kiki had taken her to rooms on the first floor, so she descended to the ground level. She walked until she found one of the two men she sought, relieved when she saw it was Kiki. He was in a massive, modern gym tucked in one corner of the bottom floor, on a treadmill.

By his pace and the sweat covering his body, he was running from something or someone. She could guess who. She circled the treadmill and waved to him.

He tugged ear buds from his ears and turned off the machine, snatching a towel as he hopped off. "What're you doing here?" he demanded.

"I'm here to do whatever it is Immortals do."

He lifted an eyebrow.

Stephanie cursed herself. If Kiki didn't believe her, Wynn never would. "Okay. I'm here to free Fate. Wynn's going to kill him."

A shadow crossed Kiki's gaze. He glanced around, as if worried someone would overhear them, then waved for her to follow him. He led her into a waiting area at the front of a spacious locker room and disappeared into the men's section. Ten minutes later, he reappeared, bathed and dressed.

He sat down across from her. "You sure you want to do this?"

She nodded.

"Fate's alive, which means Wynn wants something from him. He won't tell me what."

"Do you think I can get him out of here without Wynn noticing?"

"Nope," Kiki replied. "But I think you can negotiate with Wynn. He wants you here where you belong. You have some power."

"So you think I should just outright ask him."

"I think you haven't been around long enough to fool him."

Stephanie nodded, silently agreeing. Spying on Wynn was one thing. Manipulating him or rescuing Fate without him knowing was another entirely. "Where is he?"

"You ready to face him now?"

"I don't have a choice."

"Study."

Stephanie rose. "Thanks. Hopefully, I'll see you later."

"Be smart. Don't try to take him on. Just tell him what you want and see if he'll negotiate."

Stephanie said nothing and left the locker area. Anxiety made her grateful she'd skipped lunch. The images of Fate being tortured were forefront in her mind. It hadn't touched her like the other bubbles of people's lives, but she still felt pain on his behalf.

She made her way through the castle to the study and paused outside the foreboding doors stretching from floor to ceiling. She reviewed everything she'd learned from the people she'd met since entering this nightmare. A few months ago, if someone told her what kind of person her father was, she wouldn't believe it was possible for anyone like him to exist.

She tapped on the door.

"Enter," came Wynn's muffled voice.

Stephanie took a deep breath and pushed the door open. Her father sat at the hearth, reading, as if he were comfortable knowing someone was having his skin stripped off in his basement. His gaze flickered over her, and he set the book aside.

"I wasn't expecting to see you," he said.

"I'm figuring things out," she replied.

"Such as?" He motioned to the chair across from his.

"How I didn't belong in the human world. How I'm special for a reason," she replied truthfully. Stephanie sat down and clenched her hands together to keep them from quivering. "How I had no idea people could be so depraved."

"Depravity is a matter of perspective. One could say manipulating the Future to serve one's purpose is depraved."

She bit back her response, knowing she needed him to work with her. Stephanie debated what exactly to say before going with Kiki's advice.

"What will it take for you to let him go?" she whispered. "I know what you're doing to him. It's not right."

"When he gives me what I want, he's free to go."

"What do you want?"

Wynn studied her.

"If it's something I can do or if it's about me, I'll do it," she said. "I've learned how to negotiate and how the deities run on a system of oaths. I have his power, because I'm his mate. So if there's something you want from him that I can give you, I will, in exchange for you freeing him now."

Wynn started to smile. But it wasn't the smile of a predator like she expected. He wasn't gloating or triumphant. If anything, he seemed almost proud. "You're learning your power and beginning to accept your position," he observed. "No longer denying where you belong?"

"Kind of hard to come back from seeing demons eat people."

He snorted.

"Is that part of it?" she asked. "You want me to be an Immortal, whatever that entails?"

He was quiet for a moment, and she held her breath, afraid to say anything else until he was ready. "What I want from him is a favor."

"Blank check," she said. The kind he'd extorted from Andre and then used to send his eldest son to Hell. She clutched her hands harder.

"Correct."

"You'll let him go immediately, and never harm him again, if I make the deal?"

"I will." Wynn sat forward. "And yes, I do want you to take your place with your family. It doesn't need to be part of the deal we make, but I want your word you'll stay here and not try to return to the human world."

"I can do that, yes," she said.

"You're welcome to bring your mother and sister here," he added.

Her heart flipped over in her chest. "This is my place, not theirs. I won't put them in danger."

"You saw her recently?"

"Of course. She's my mother."

"She said nothing of me, of all this?" he pressed.

She gazed at him in confusion. "Why would she?" One of her instincts tingled, and she recalled how her mother had echoed Fate's words about his name. But no part of her was going to believe her mother had anything to do with this world, just because she knew some obscure trivia, no matter what the master manipulator before her tried to imply.

"As for the favor from Fate, you'll agree to grant it?" he asked.

"As long as you agree to free him now, alive, and never to harm him again," she replied carefully. "With no unwritten terms or conditions."

"Someone's been teaching you."

"It's necessary for my survival, I think."

"Smart girl. Your mother was smart as well, which is why I haven't been able to find either of you in twenty three years. I admire those who can outsmart me."

She said nothing.

"I'll make the deal. He'll be free to go as of now." Wynn held out his hand.

Stephanie hesitated then touched hers to his. Cold fire tore through her. Wynn had agreed too quickly for her taste. Either he really wanted the favor, or she'd forgotten one of the lessons Deidre gave her. She went over the deal in her mind without finding any flaw.

If there was one, it was likely something Wynn knew and would use against her when the time came.

"Thank you," she said. "Can I see him before he leaves?"

"You may. Later today, after he's cleaned up."

She was ready to bolt, but he continued speaking.

"I'm not a typical father, and I know this," he began. "I never had much of a chance to know my five younger sons and of course, you. Even if I had, I'm not the kind of father to dote on children. I do want you to know I've always cherished my offspring in my own way. If you are ever in trouble, if you need assistance your mate cannot provide, I will."

"I'm sure it comes at a cost," she murmured. "Like everything else here."

"No cost. No strings," he replied. "I care for my children in what way I can."

"You're torturing your child's mate!"

"That's personal. Before you existed, Fate helped kill me the first time around. I think I deserve a little payback."

After her trip to the magic book, Stephanie knew enough about Fate's dealings not to push the topic. "You're saying if I need help, I can come to you? Like we're a normal father-daughter?" she asked skeptically.

"Yes."

She studied him. She didn't want to believe him, but he appeared sincere. She had often seen a glimmer of warmth in his gaze when he looked at her. But he was, in every way, a complete and total asshole who made the lives of everyone around her, especially his children's, nightmares. So why was she seriously considering his offer of support?

Did it have anything to do with wanting a father when she was younger? With the small hope inside her she'd one day meet him, and he'd not only be amazing but proud of her as well?

Incapable of true paternal instinct, Wynn was offering what he could.

"You sent Andre to Hell," she blurted out. "Why would I ever come to you for anything?"

"He's comfortable. I ensured Darkyn didn't toss him in a cell or into the depths of Hell. Besides," Wynn replied, "Andre can take care of himself. You cannot."

She wanted to get up and leave, slamming her door on the way out in defiance of the man who seemed to be a master of misery.

Instead, she was buying into whatever display this was, searching for some sign of deception in his features.

"When I was little, I used to dream about meeting you," she said.

"I'm nothing like what you expected."

"No. But it seems like I'm not what you expected either."

"You're brilliant, beautiful and brave. I'm pleased with how you turned out."

"For a half-breed."

"For my daughter."

She looked away. If this was part of his game, it was sick – and working. She doubted she'd ever feel warmth or kinship towards him, but some small part of her rejoiced at the acknowledgment from her father. It made her feel dirty.

Stephanie stood. "If you don't need anything else, I'll head to my room. Kiki gave me a lot reading material the first time around."

"Very well. I'll need you to begin your official duties tomorrow morning. Family dinner is at seven every night."

"Okay."

With calmness she didn't feel, she left the study and closed the door. Then she leaned against the wall and bent over at the waist, sucking in deep breaths to keep from panicking or throwing up. The simple exchange with Wynn had taken the rest of her energy and she felt sick to her stomach and heart.

Fate was free. She may never understand Wynn, but at least she'd saved the life of the person who could save the Future.

CHAPTER TWELVE

STEPHANIE SPENT THE DAY ALTERNATING BETWEEN ROAMING THE castle and hiding in her room. She navigated using the map Kiki created for her and found herself drawn more than once towards the wing of the castle where Kiki said Fate would be.

The third time she stood before his door, she knocked. Wynn hadn't given her the okay to see him yet but she was anxious to know he survived for reasons she couldn't fully define. It was a feeling, a need.

Realizing what she was doing, she stepped away from the door. Whatever Immortals believed about their mating rituals, she wanted nothing to do with it. So why was she knocking on the door of the man allegedly chosen by the universe for her?

"Come in," came the muffled voice from inside.

Stephanie clenched her fists, about to leave, when she felt compelled to do the opposite. She opened the door.

Fate stood in front of the French doors, back to her, dressed in a t-shirt that was snug across his shoulders and dark-washed jeans. His hands were clasped behind his back, and his hair appeared recently combed and damp around the edges.

The tug was stronger, and she scoured his body with her eyes, unable to help the flush of warmth emanating from the base of her belly.

"I, uh, wanted to make sure you're all right," she said somewhat awkwardly.

He turned at the sound of her voice. He appeared healed and healthy, albeit pale. His strong jaw bore a faint scar that ran down his neck, and his iridescent eyes flickered between hues.

My god he's stunning. And he was hers, if she wanted him. "How are you healed?" she asked.

"You sound disappointed." His warm, rich voice was the only rough part of him.

"No, that's not true. But I saw ..." Too aware of his intent gaze, she cleared her throat and glanced around a chamber much like hers. "Anyway, I'm glad you're alive."

"You returned voluntarily?"

She nodded.

"I don't recall you among my visitors in the catacombs," he said wryly. He moved towards her and paused a meter or so away.

"You know. News travels fast."

"Ah. So you just heard I was in danger and rushed back?" There was a mocking note in his tone.

"Yeah." She was gazing at him dreamily. "I mean, no. The magic book told me," she said with some embarrassment. "And I didn't rush back. Not straight back anyway."

"Magic ... the Oracle?"

"Yeah." He was just out of arm's reach and too close. She was overheating once more. "So I came back and had a heart to heart with daddy dearest and he let you go."

"Just like that?"

She nodded.

"Six weeks in the catacombs being tortured, because he wanted something from me, and he just lets me walk because you asked him."

Stephanie's face warmed. "Because I gave him what you wouldn't."

Silence. She looked up at him. Fate's jaw was clenched and his expression blank. The only sign of his agitation was his eyes, which flipped even faster between colors than usual. His aloof façade was gone.

"He would've destroyed the world," she added. "And you."

"There is a reason I don't grant many favors."

"Some things are more important than power," she replied. "Look, you don't have to agree with what I did. It was my choice."

"True, but I have to live with the consequences. You've figured out a few things," he started. "Do you understand why it's dangerous to give Wynn what he wants?"

"I do."

"But you did it anyway."

"So you're going to judge me for making a decision after declaring humans have free will. Oh, and after hiding my soul so I couldn't be born." She crossed her arms.

"I'm the last person to judge anyone."

She eyed him, suspecting he was toying with her.

"There are worse things than the world ending," he said.

"You can't be serious!"

"Next time, talk it over with me, before you make a deal with someone like Wynn," he said. "It is *my* power." The firm note in his tone was new, and the dark edge she often glimpsed was present.

"You would've preferred being skinned alive and the world ending," she said. "I'll keep that in mind next time!"

He considered her. How he had the nerve to be ungrateful after she'd saved his life, she didn't know, but his calm rejection of her good intentions infuriated her.

"You're welcome," she snapped. "You're also free to go." She wrenched the door open and stood to the side.

He glanced from her to the hallway and back. "And you?"

"It's none of your business what I do with my life."

"Wynn won't let you go. He's planning something, so I assume he manipulated you into staying."

"He didn't manipulate me. I volunteered."

"The best manipulators know how to make it seem like it was your idea when they're pulling the strings."

Some of her anger faded. Wynn had been too calm upon seeing her enter the study. "You'd know, wouldn't you?"

"Absolutely," Fate said without hesitation. "Just like I know you don't have the depravity for the type of manipulation men like us conduct on a daily basis."

She'd seen evidence of this already in what the Oracle showed her.

"He will do what it takes to get what he wants from you, too." Fate stepped towards the door. He pushed it closed. "Which is why I won't be leaving."

Her heart skipped a beat. Of all the reactions she expected from him, remaining here wasn't among them. "Don't stay for my sake," she said.

"There's no other reason to stay," he countered quietly. Standing too close again, he gazed down at her, his warmth and strength agitating her as much as it comforted her. "You won't face him alone."

"I don't need your help."

"You will not face him alone," he repeated more slowly. "You have no idea what you're up against. This is not your game and even if it were, you'd never survive facing someone with skills similar to mine."

Her breath caught at the open admittance of what he was. He held her gaze, and she glimpsed the type of steely determination she knew had to be present. The sense there was more to him, that she was only scratching the surface, returned, along with a flicker of fear. Compelled to him, scared of what he was, she stood her ground beneath his penetrating look.

"Got it?" he asked, a flicker of his playfulness back.

Stephanie found herself nodding.

"Good. We need to get a few more things straight." He motioned towards the sitting area before the hearth, simultaneously resting a hand on her.

The warm tingle of energy flashed through her once more. She shivered, moving away and hoping he didn't notice that she noticed.

"I kinda like it," Fate said and touched her arm.

She twisted away. He did it again, this time laughing huskily, as if he hadn't just threatened her.

"Are you, like, five?" she asked, bewildered by his ability to go from serious to fun.

"You're very grave. About everything," he replied. He zapped her again, and she swiped his hand away. "Things aren't that bad."

"You just got tortured and Wynn wants to blow up the world," she reminded him. "How is this – stop!"

The warm energy sizzled along her nerves and pooled in the base of her belly, making her too sensitive to her world again, enough so to notice his scent.

"You're okay with the world ending and saving a man from torture but not …" He zapped her once more, and she pushed him away. Tripping over the rug at her feet, she careened dangerously, only for Fate to catch her.

His arm snaked around her midsection, and he pulled her against him.

She shuddered once more at the energy as it seemed to flow between them, lighting her blood on fire as it did so. She marveled at the sensations of his hard, warm body, their weird energy exchange, his scent and the way he gazed at her.

The moment grew long and awkward. She didn't want to leave his touch but was too aware of how little she could trust him. He'd admitted to being the lying, manipulative god everyone thought he was. Then why was her heart racing in the arms of such a person? Why did she melt from a single searing look and yearn for him to do more than tease her? His eyes went to her lips.

"I like this even more," he admitted and met her gaze again. "What you did, making a deal with Wynn, was very brave. And insanely foolish." His arm tightened around her. "Don't ever do it again."

She saw more than determination on his features. For the first time since meeting him, she saw the threat others claimed he posed in the hardness of his eyes and face. Stephanie pressed her hands to his chest, confused by the combination of lust and fear.

"Please," he added, as if to soften the words. "My power is a very dangerous one in the hands of the wrong person. A favor does just that – puts my power at the mercy of another."

"I know," she said quietly. "I wanted to help you."

"Talk to me before you consider making another deal."

At his softer tone, she stopped pushing at him and rested against his frame, once more certain this was where she had always belonged without knowing it. She chewed her lower lip, debating for a moment. "The Oracle showed me a lot, including how my brother Andre got exiled to Hell when Wynn cashed in the favor he granted him. But after everything I saw ..." She trailed off, a little embarrassed by her rationale or perhaps, by her lack thereof.

Fate tilted her chin up. "What?"

"I had the Oracle show me what it was like to be you." Stephanie shivered, this time recalling the emotions of others. "I don't know how you do what you do. I don't know how you manage knowing the fates of everyone, experience all that emotion, all at once, alone. I saw you won't let anyone else help you, either. Ever. For any reason. I wasn't about to ask you if I could save your life after seeing that, even if it was your power. You needed help, and I was the only person who could help you. I'm not sorry for what I did, and I don't care how upset you are."

"You shouldn't have looked at my Past." His hand fell away from her face, and he considered her for a moment. His expression was unreadable, but if she had to guess, he wasn't happy with her declaration. "I can't involve anyone else in what I am and what I do." He released her.

Stephanie watched him turn and walk away. Her body mourned him while her mind was even more perplexed than before. One minute he wanted her to talk to him, the next he teased her and the next, he walked away. Was it possible for a deity to be confused?

"I don't think you have a choice." *And I shouldn't have said that.* "Anyway, I don't want to keep a secret about something else I did involving you. I'm not the kind of person to hold back information like hiding someone's soul from them."

Fate glanced at her, a glimmer of his calm amusement returning. He sat down in the chair near the hearth, eyes on her.

"I made a deal with Deidre for my soul," she said.

He leaned forward with interest. "What were your exact words?"

She told him, and he nodded. "She went easy on you."

"Would you?" she asked before she could stop herself, leery of the man no one trusted.

"Go easy on you?" he asked. A smile tugged up the corner of his full lips. "You tell me. Would I?"

"No." She had the sense of being on the wrong side of a science experiment, as if he were evaluating her from the inside out.

He didn't reply.

Jittery and fed up with the man she didn't want to leave and didn't remotely trust, she started towards the door.

"For the record, I wanted to save the world, and nothing you can say will make me think I made the wrong decision," she said with a flash of fire.

"Before you go."

She paused with her hand on the doorknob and turned to face him.

"When I hid your soul, I was relieved I wouldn't be stuck with a mate yet. I wanted nothing to do with one," he began. "After six weeks with nothing to do but think, stuck as a human no less, I think that was wrong of me to do."

"You should never hide anyone's soul," she snapped.

"Not the hiding part," he clarified with a chuckle. "The part about not wanting a mate. I've decided … you're mine. And I want you. That's why I'm staying."

Stephanie wrenched open the door and stormed out, slamming it behind her. The simple words sent her emotions into a frenzy, one she wasn't able to make sense of. Was she scared? Turned on? Ecstatic? All of the above? Her thoughts were torn between confusion after all the Oracle had shown her and the memory of the knee melting, heart stopping kiss she'd shared with Fate.

She was starting to feel eager about the idea of at least seeing what was possible between them. Unless … he was doing what he claimed Wynn had and purposely manipulating her.

She had no way of knowing for certain, not just about Fate, but about anyone she had met since the night Olivia died.

This reality depressed her.

CHAPTER THIRTEEN

Until they'd met again, Fate wasn't entirely certain he planned on pursuing a relationship with someone he hadn't wanted in his life at all. The latest interaction settled some of the uncertainty he experienced whenever he dwelt too long on his latest challenge. He wasn't able to pinpoint why, except the bond between them was stronger and ... he wanted something more than a mandatory companion.

As much as he despised people doing things for him, because they ultimately wanted something for him, he had a feeling she'd acted without malice or self-interest when she bargained away a precious favor to Wynn.

With no ability to seek insight from the Future, he was puzzled by Stephanie, by her intentions and her actions, and off balance by the idea of sharing power with anyone.

But he did know one thing with certainty. He wasn't going to be content until he'd claimed his mate completely. Their physical bond was too strong for him to turn away. Her beauty and spirit had ensnared him from their first meeting. The odd possessiveness he'd never before experienced no longer surprised him with its insistence, not when their every touch fed it, made it stronger.

Weakened from Wynn's torture, despite the healing favor he'd called in, Fate released a breath once Stephanie was gone. He hadn't wanted her to see he was in worse shape than he seemed. He needed rest and dropped onto his bed, eager to sleep the day away so he was ready for Wynn and his mate tomorrow.

The next morning, he sat in a chair along the wall in the small chamber where the Council met. The Council was woefully understaffed, with only three of Wynn's eight children present. Tamer appeared anxious to leave while Kiki's nose was in his iPad. Stephanie's discomfort reached him from across the room. She was fidgeting beneath the table. Wynn alone seemed pleased to be there.

Fate, the great observer, witnessed every glance, tell, and nervous tick in dispassion. His eyes fell to Stephanie more often than anyone. She was adjusting well to the role, feeding the instinct that there was more to her than he was able to make out. She wasn't happy but she was holding her own, which wouldn't be possible if she were half-human. He began to run the list of other options, including deities, through his head, trying to find clues in her personality as to who her mother was.

He sensed she was silently panicking at Wynn's latest task.

"You want me to pass judgment on petitioners?" she repeated.

"It's a duty of the Council – to hear the claims, disputes and other issues causing friction among Immortals," Wynn explained. "You'll listen to each circumstance and decide if recompense or another form of action is required. Many Immortals are submitting claims to the treasury for the stipends and wages of their recently deceased family members."

"A lot of them are lying bastards," Tamer added.

"And others want to curry favors in place of money. You're authorized to negotiate to an extent," Wynn seconded. "Kiki is on security detail this week. You'll swap duties next week."

"Wynn likes you to keep a list of people you think are trying to cheat us," Kiki said quietly.

"Those who try to take advantage receive my personal attention," Wynn said.

No one spoke, and Fate felt the tension among his three children grow thicker. Stephanie had gone rigid. Tamer rested a hand on the hilt of a knife and Kiki pushed aside his iPad.

"What makes you think I have any clue how to do this?" Stephanie asked.

"This is the best way to learn," Wynn replied. "I'm counting on your mate to teach you a thing or two about negotiations."

No one looked at Fate, as if to acknowledge him would draw the ire of Wynn. He presumed he had a task of his own after receiving an order to attend the meeting. Wynn did nothing without a reason. They were similar in this – men of vision, foresight and control.

"My pleasure," Fate said at Wynn's penetrating look.

"Dismissed," Wynn said and rose.

His three children reacted more slowly. Kiki slipped Stephanie a note before leaving. Tamer summoned a portal without speaking to anyone and disappeared.

Stephanie wasn't acknowledging him. She read Kiki's note then tucked it in her pocket and left the chamber. Fate trailed her, joining her in the hallway when she paused to check her map.

"This way," he said and pointed.

"I don't need your help," she snapped.

He snatched her iPad. "What floor are we going to?" he asked pointedly.

She glared up at him, her gorgeous features already tinted pink, and teal eyes suspicious.

He grazed her forearm with a finger, and she shivered at the delicious, warm shock of lust the simple touch sent through both of them. He loved this game and her reaction more.

"Stop it! Give me my iPad!" she ordered.

"Just admit you don't know and I will."

She reached for it instead, and he zapped her again, holding the tablet over her head and away.

"Is everything a game to you?" she demanded. She pushed at his shoulder to turn him and reached once more for the iPad.

He zapped her again, entertained by her exasperated sigh in response. "You could use some games in your life. You're too tense."

"I'm tense because I'm freaked out and you're not helping!" She tried to snatch the iPad once more.

"Then let me help." He caught her around the waist, secretly satisfied to feel her body pressed to his once more. "I happen to know a thing or two about dealing with manipulative petitioners."

Her breath hitched audibly at the clash of their bodies. She gazed at him for a moment. Her pupils were dilating by the extended touch. "Fine."

He released her. "This way," he said again and started down the corridor towards the stairs.

She followed him, drawing close enough to snatch her iPad back. Fate smiled to himself, amused by the differences in their personalities. If he knew anything about Wynn, the Ancient had likely made this first test of his daughter brutal. He had little mercy for his children and none for others.

They reached the office on the ground floor outside of which the petitioners had already formed a queue.

"Holy shit. This is worse than the DMV," Stephanie breathed, staring at the line that ran for a hundred meters.

Fate glanced at her. She was gaping, and he sensed the silent panic once more.

"You're not alone." He nudged her forward. She went reluctantly, cutting through the line of people to the table where two staff members sat to record the results of the meetings. Stephanie sat in the seat marked by a high back, intricately carved. Fate took up a position within her line of sight, seated at a smaller waiting table nearby.

Her gaze lingered on him before one of the staff members waved the first petitioning Immortal forward. An older woman with a cane approached the table and began speaking to Stephanie, who was trying hard not to appear overwhelmed.

Fate listened to the sob story told by the woman.

Stephanie was buying everything, not even blinking at the price the petitioner claimed was necessary to make up for the incomes of her sons killed in battle with the demons.

Fate signaled her and shook his head once, subtly, when she looked his way.

Stephanie stared at him and shifted in her chair. He knew she was debating who to trust in that moment. She made a few notes on her notepad then spoke hesitantly.

"That's too high."

"My five sons die, and a living wage is too high?" boomed the old woman loud enough for those in line to hear.

Fate smiled faintly at Stephanie's bewildered look, which was accompanied by a flush of red. "I'm sorry. I didn't mean …" She cleared her throat and glanced at him once more.

Stay strong, he willed her. The woman in his life had to be capable of the type of shrewd negotiations and decisions he routinely made, which included dealing with people who approached them for favors and requests to alter or access the Future.

"If you give me their names, I'll put the request in," she said the petitioner and lifted her pen to write.

Good girl.

"Who?" asked the petitioner.

"Your sons," Stephanie replied and looked up from her paper.

There was a pause.

Picking up on the hesitation, Stephanie leaned back. "You know Wynn deals personally with those people who aren't truthful to me. I don't want to have to give him your name in the daily report."

It was the petitioner's turn to be caught off guard. "I had one son," she admitted.

"Would you care to revise your settlement amount?"

The petitioner bit off her response.

Fate realized with no small amount of satisfaction Stephanie trusted him enough to take his recommendation. She was fighting the bond as much as he had, but it was only a matter of time before she folded.

Stephanie proved a quick learner, shrewd enough to see through emotions and compassionate enough not to outright challenge anyone in a way that left someone pissed or vengeful. Fate observed her as well as the petitioners as the day progressed, signaling to her whenever she looked his way. People were generally easy for him to read, more so when they paid no attention to him from his position. He could watch without them knowing. While she adapted to the duty well, Stephanie at no point appeared comfortable with passing judgment on anyone's case.

Kiki arrived in the afternoon and paused beside Fate. "How's she doing?"

"Good," Fate answered.

"Wynn wants you to report to him."

Fate considered the order. "When this is over," he replied.

"He said now."

"Then he can come here. I'm busy."

Kiki's sigh was much like Stephanie's, and Fate began to wonder what other traits she had in common with her brothers.

"He said it's about Steph."

"What about her?" Fate asked casually.

"Dude, seriously." Kiki yanked out a chair and sat. "Can you play along with him?"

"I spent six weeks in the dungeon. What do you think?" Fate replied.

"I think we don't know what's going on, what Wynn's planning, and if you get kicked out of here, she's got no one to help her."

"She has you."

Kiki shook his head. "My sole mission in life has become preventing the Immortals' infrastructure from collapsing. If you think I have time for drama, you aren't paying attention to how bad things are."

Fate met his gaze for the first time since Kiki approached him.

"Forget I said that," Kiki said, awareness on his features.

"This is the first thing you've said of interest to me," Fate replied with a smile. "How bad is it?"

"It's none of your business. If you don't go see Wynn, he'll kick you out." Kiki rose, irritated. "I can't watch over my newfound sister and keep the Immortals afloat." He strode away.

Fate stood and approached the table. He leaned down, lips brushing Stephanie's ear to send another spark of need through them both. "I need to check in with Wynn. If you get stuck, wait for me."

"I can handle it," she replied tersely.

He zapped her.

Stephanie elbowed him in response.

Fate left the audience chamber and went to the study, where he assumed Wynn would be waiting.

The Ancient Immortal didn't disappoint him. Fate walked in and closed the door. Wynn sat on the edge of his desk, legs crossed at the ankles and brilliant eyes hard.

"You look well," Wynn said.

"Called in a favor," Fate replied with a shrug.

"My daughter no doubt told you how she freed you."

"She did."

Wynn was pleased, if not secretly gleeful, and Fate felt a flicker of true annoyance. He could overlook being a virtual prisoner in favor of staying close to his mate, but Wynn's quiet triumph angered him.

"I have a mild problem you may be able to help me with," Wynn said.

"You're calling in your favor already?"

"Not quite. More along the lines of us having a common goal."

"Such as?"

"Darkyn."

"I'm listening."

"He's been quiet lately. Our spy network is much compromised after the past couple of years, but we've started to hear rumors. He's seeking souls again for his Army of Souls," Wynn said.

"He's been building it for thousands of years," Fate countered. "This isn't news."

"Then perhaps this is. Through whatever means, he's been made aware of Stephanie. No human or immortal has ever been born soulless and managed to survive. As you can imagine, Darkyn is overly interested in my daughter."

Fate didn't say what he wanted to, that he was pretty certain Wynn had probably told Darkyn about Stephanie's unusual circumstances. Fate trusted Deidre to keep a secret from Darkyn more than Stephanie's father.

"He can't reach her, as long as she's here," Fate said. "Assuming you don't let another round of demons in."

Wynn studied him. "I had to know who her mate was."

"At the expense of what? Twelve Immortals?" Fate shrugged. "None of my business, but you're running out of Immortals as it is."

"Which is none of your concern," Wynn snapped. "What happened to her soul is a mystery, even to me. What should concern you: She's become a target for Darkyn."

"Convenient timing," Fate murmured. "She's a target when I

have no power and you hold all the cards."

"Motivation to play nice with others, which you don't usually do."

"Is it wise to make your daughter the target of Darkyn? From what I understand, the Immortals aren't in a position to take another hit from the demons," Fate said.

"Like you, Darkyn's always willing to negotiate."

Fate hid his rising uneasiness, not liking the idea of Wynn controlling Stephanie's future. "You said we had a common goal. I've yet to hear what it is."

"Protecting Stephanie, of course."

"Of course." He managed to can his sarcasm.

"Encourage her to stay here, where it's safe. If she leaves, Darkyn will grab her, and I won't stop him."

"You should know better than to make a deal with the Dark One," Fate warned. In just under four months, when he had his powers, he could protect Stephanie from Darkyn. But now … Wynn was playing a dangerous game with dangerous deities.

"I have an out," Wynn replied. "Namely a favor from you."

"Everyone wins," Fate said. "Except me."

"Exactly. I knew you'd understand."

"Effective plan. Short sighted but effective," Fate allowed. "Lucky for you, I have nowhere else I'd rather be right now."

"Good. It's in your best interest to keep her here." Wynn circled his desk to sit behind it. "I hope that doesn't interfere with your love of *free will*."

"I'm learning free will and mates don't exactly go hand in hand."

Wynn chuckled, amusement in his gaze. "No. They don't."

Once again, Fate had the sense Wynn wanted something from Stephanie, something he was willing to make a deal with the one deity no one ever wanted to deal with. He hated not knowing, hated the idea she was in danger, and he had no way to stop whatever might be headed her way.

"How are the petitions going?" Wynn asked.

"She's a natural."

Wynn appeared pleased by the news. "Perhaps this half-breed will turn out better than the last."

More anger stirred. Fate didn't reply. He had the sudden urge to hide Stephanie away from Wynn.

"Dismissed," Wynn said, focus on his laptop.

Fate left and walked through the chalet, mind on Wynn's subtle threat. To negotiate with Darkyn then use the deal against him was smart, except he wasn't the sole determining factor in whether or not Stephanie stayed. She was too strong willed to remain somewhere she didn't want to.

Returning to the petition chamber, he resumed his seat and submerged himself once more in watching those around him while his mind skipped from thought to thought. Karma's timing was monumentally horrible. He'd wanted to experience what it was like to be a human, to live in the moment and fear the next, and he was being granted his wish. How bad this experiment was going to affect the world, he didn't even want to guess.

"How do you always know?"

Fate withdrew from his thoughts, barely aware of the last petitioner leaving. Stephanie stood before him, eyes lined with dark circles. "You figure it out over time," he replied. He reached out to her automatically and took her hand.

She gazed at their clasped hands but didn't move away. It was too hard, even for him, not to touch when they were so close. "But every time? You just *knew*."

"I'm that good," he said with a smile.

"At manipulating people."

"At everything." He winked and rose, stepping into her, until their bodies brushed. "You have plans this evening?"

She reached for him, stopped herself, and awkwardly shoved her hand in her pocket. "Plans? Like leaving this nightmare behind me?"

"I was thinking more like a date."

Her eyebrows rose.

"Our first one was interrupted," he reminded her.

"You go from being pissy with me for using your power to wanting a date?" She scrutinized him.

"I think we could use some us-time, don't you?" he asked and cupped her cheek with one hand. "You and me. Nothing formal. We can talk and ... whatever else."

Interest flared in her gaze, and she started to nuzzle his hand before yanking out of the spell threatening to mesmerize him as well. Stephanie stepped back, fighting the pull.

He zapped her, and she growled, slapping his hand. "Come on. Don't be scared," he teased and tipped her chin up.

Another zap and she ducked her head but not before he saw her smile starting to form. "You are such a jerk!"

"Ahhh. Knew that, too," he said and touched her again.

She batted his hand away. He caught her wrist and tugged her into him once more, satisfied to hear her breath catch at their contact.

"Date?" he prodded.

Stephanie gazed at him for a long moment, relaxing into his hold. "Okay," she said. "Date."

"Meet me on the front lawn in an hour? We can walk to the lake."

She nodded.

Fate released her once more. She hesitated then moved away, cheeks red. He watched her go, eyes roaming over her tall, trim frame in appreciation. The warm energy of her touch faded before she reached the door, and he grew concerned once more. He was going to have to warn her about not leaving the property, at least, not until he had his power back. Wynn had sent one son to Hell; he'd do it again. The Dark One never turned down the opportunity to cage a deity. But with Stephanie, Darkyn was likely to torture her or conduct science experiments to see why she was able to live without a soul.

Fate returned to a thought he hadn't wanted to acknowledge fully. Chances were, he'd have to approach Darkyn with a deal before this mess was over, which Wynn and Darkyn probably knew going into their deal. Darkyn would pursue Stephanie as he had others in the past. He was relentless, unstoppable. With or without his power, Fate was going to have to confront the Dark One to keep his mate safe.

Pensive, Fate returned to his room to get ready for his date. An hour after leaving her in the audience chamber, he went to her door and tapped.

There was no immediate response, so he opened the door.

The air smelled of a recent shower, and the drawers of her bureau were open.

But Stephanie wasn't present.

Uneasiness growing, he searched her room and determined she hadn't left long before he arrived. They didn't pass in the hallway, and he saw no sign she'd even put on shoes.

Someone had taken her.

For the first time since losing his power, Fate resented the lesson he was supposed to be learning. He had no idea what had happened, what would happen or even who took her. He was, for the first time in his life, completely blind.

CHAPTER FOURTEEN

ONE MINUTE, SHE WAS GETTING READY FOR HER FIRST REAL DATE in … well, ever. The next, she had a bag over her head, and someone slung her over his shoulder. She felt the cool mist of the place-between-places then heard the unmistakable sound of the ocean lapping shore. Seconds later, they went back into the misty portal, out, back through and out again. This occurred several more times, and she squirmed, only to have her captor's grip around her tighten.

She went still and waited.

A blast of cool air hit her, and she was lowered to the uneven ground.

Stephanie yanked off the hood and looked first at the tall figure with a shock of white-blond hair then at her surroundings. She was beside a lake surrounded by vibrant green trees.

At least I'm in the human world.

She climbed to her feet with an annoyed glance down. She'd gotten one shoe on before being kidnapped.

"I'm Kris."

Her gaze lifted. It took a moment for the handsome man's name to click. His eyes shifted from blue to amber as she watched. "Uh, aren't you supposed to be dead?" she asked.

"I was."

Stephanie sighed. She straightened and faced the latest of her brothers to barge into her life. Built like a cross between Tamer's bulk strength and Kiki's lean athleticism, Kris's blond hair stood out in stark contrast to his honey colored skin.

"You could've knocked instead of kidnapping me," she said.

"I had to take precautions."

If she had learned one thing about her brothers, it was they knew how to make an entrance. "Whatever. So ... where are we and why?"

"Come with me." He whirled and strode away, into the forest, towards a small cabin perched on the edge of the lake.

She snorted at the stiff order before recalling he'd been in charge of the Council for many years. With nowhere else to go, Stephanie followed him, stepping carefully so as not to injure her exposed foot.

Kris disappeared into the cabin and left the door open. She entered several steps behind him. The cozy, two room cabin was made of thick logs and featured a stone fireplace at its center. She liked it instantly and sat on the couch while Kris went to a minibar and poured them both whiskey.

He sat down across from her, giving her a look very much like one Wynn had issued her on many occasions.

"I hear I have a sister," he started and sipped his drink, eyes turning from amber to green.

"Yep. Half breed," she said. "Seriously, why didn't you just knock?"

He lowered the drink and swirled it, gazing at her briefly. "It's complicated."

"No shit. Try me."

He lifted an eyebrow. "Something about half-breeds ..." The disapproval was subtle. "In any case, our father can't know I'm here."

"Here or ... not dead?" she asked.

There was a pause, and he tilted his head. "Both."

"Is there something about me that just screams *tell me your secrets?* When will you people stop telling me things?"

"I'd say it's your gift."

She frowned. "Come again?"

"My father … *our* father doesn't make mistakes. He chose your mother like he chose the mothers of all of us," Kris replied. "There had to be something special about her in order for him to choose her."

"So I do have a gift?"

"Yeah."

"We just met. How do you know?"

"Because that's my gift," he said with a slow smile. "I just know."

"Okay. Then what is it? What's my magic power?" she asked, unable to help her curiosity. Would there ever become a day when she wasn't lured into a discussion with one of these people by her curiosity?

"Secrets."

"Meaning …"

"Ever notice how people tell you things? Randomly? Without you asking or even knowing their names?" Kris replied. "What did I say after 'something about half-breeds'?"

She chugged the whiskey and hissed as the heat tore down her throat. "This is just stupid. You said Wynn couldn't know you were here."

"Did you hear the words or know them?"

"Heard them. Because you said them."

"I didn't say them. You read them from my mind."

She reviewed their conversation mentally. "That makes no sense."

"My guess is you haven't been tuned into your gift. Each child of Wynn has one. Assuming your mother was human, you wouldn't inherit the gift from her. You probably got it from Wynn."

"Wynn knows everyone's secrets?"

"I'd say so. There's nothing else that explains his ability to manipulate as well as any deity with no real power to match. We've always known he was an incredibly powerful healer, but it never explained how he could get to people the way he does. I think you just confirmed he's got a secondary skill."

Stephanie absorbed the information. She'd always wondered why people told her such odd, personal things upon meeting. It never occurred to her that she might be reading the secrets out of their minds.

"That was easier than I expected." Kris rose and returned to the kitchen. "Now. I can't send you back, or Wynn will know."

"So if he can read secrets, and I can read secrets, do we cancel each other out?"

"Don't be ridiculous."

"I've never heard his secret."

"Wynn's gift has been a secret for a few hundred thousand years. He knows how to hide it."

"Then I can learn, too, and go back."

"Go back?" Kris faced her. "Why would you want to go back?"

Fate. She cleared her throat. "It's not that bad."

"You're not leaving." He gazed at her hard. "You're going to help me get rid of him for good. It's why I was brought back. Wynn is fucking up the world or will soon. He's running the Immortals into the ground. Pretty soon, we won't be able to defend ourselves against Darkyn let alone save humanity from the Dark One."

It was the first thing he'd said that made sense to her. Stephanie sat up straighter. "Everything seems fine there," she said, puzzled. "You're saying he's working to destroy everything in the background."

"He'll do whatever it takes to get what he wants."

"What does he want?"

"No one knows."

Stephanie chewed on her lower lip. No one knew what Wynn was after, and everyone feared he was going to drag the world down his obsessed trek with him.

"This was why he was rendered dead-dead in the first place," Kris added more quietly. "This is why I took over. He went mad, and he's about to do it again."

"That's good but … he's going to notice I went missing and follow."

"I took multiple portals through multiple places. He can't find us."

"Neither can Kiki. I can't leave Kiki alone."

"Why do you want to go back?" Kris demanded bluntly.

"I'm not saying I do."

They stared at one another.

"All right, fine! I was about to go on a date with someone who actually wanted to go out with me for the first time ever!" she exclaimed beneath his intent look.

"So the fate of the world is less important than fucking some idiot?"

Stephanie gripped a pillow on the couch, put it to her face and screamed into it, fed up with everything being on her shoulders and so overly dramatic, she was never going to say anything right to these people.

When she felt somewhat relieved, she lowered the pillow. "I'm going back. I won't tell anyone you're here, and you don't kidnap me the next time you want to talk to me."

"You can't leave. We have matters to discuss!"

She stood and accidentally knocked the pillow to the ground. "I've had it up to here with Immortals!" She lifted her hand to the level of her chin before bending over to snatch the pillow from the ground.

Kris caught her arm with lightning reflexes and whirled her to face the window. He pulled up her shirt with the other to see the tattoo at her back.

"Fate," he said, surprise in his voice for the first time. "How does a half-breed rate a deity?"

"I have a feeling we aren't going to get along," she snapped and yanked away. She shoved her shirt down.

This time, his long look was less dismissive. "I learned this lesson before. I'm not going to repeat my mistake." His eyes turned from orange to green once more. "I apologize. I shouldn't have underestimated you. But it's highly unusual for purebred deities to take on a half-breed or half-human mate."

Surprised, she faced him fully.

"Hear me out," he added. "Please." He poured another shot of whiskey and held it out to her.

Stephanie stepped forward and accepted the peace offering. She sat when he did, unable to shake the disappointment at standing up Fate, even if she'd been secretly panicking at what might happen between them if they went on a date.

"Tell me about you," Kris said. "And your family. Mother. Any siblings."

It was the first time she'd been asked about herself since stumbling into the Immortal society. So she gave him a brief rundown of her life. He appeared to listen to the relatively boring account of a normal human, and she sipped whiskey as she spoke, growing more relaxed with the second eldest brother in the family she'd never known existed.

When she was done, they both sat in quiet.

"So Fate has no power," he mused.

She gazed into her glass, unable to recall how many shots she'd drunk but starting to think it was too many. "None," she replied.

"This must all be a shock to you."

"Definitely. Learning my father is an Immortal monster, my brothers are half dead, and I'm supposed to be okay with being assigned a husband?" She shook her head.

"You're handling it well."

"Doesn't feel like it."

"What kind of man is Fate?"

She looked up, hearing his tone change. A stirring of wariness fluttered through her. What had she heard about Kris? Something about him being power hungry at one point? Her thoughts were too fuzzy for her to recall. "I think I've had enough to drink." She set her glass beside the half empty bottle of whiskey.

"Simple question," Kris said with a shrug. "I've never met him. Wouldn't you be curious?"

She was having trouble refuting his logic when her thoughts weren't able to stick in her mind for more than a few seconds. "He's hard to describe. Harder to understand," she said finally.

Kris waited for more. "The mating bond is … complicated," he said when she said nothing else. "No one, not even a bond, can tell you who to love, who to trust."

She gazed at him, sensing his sadness. "But it's a mandatory … thing, right?"

"It is. Unbreakable."

Her thoughts went to the small shock she received whenever Fate touched her and how he'd subtly guided her into knowing what petitioners were trying to trick her.

"Do you have a mate?" she asked.

"I do. I haven't told her I'm back from the dead-dead yet," he replied. "It's difficult to drag someone into this world, and she's been through so much already …" He drifted off.

Stephanie nodded, understanding his concern completely. She blinked – and her eyes stayed closed long enough she started to doze.

"Blankets."

She opened, realizing she'd been totally lost in her drunken thoughts. Kris held out an armful of blankets and a pillow. Stephanie accepted them and stretched out on the couch. He returned to the seat beside the fire.

"What about you?" she asked sleepily. "What's your story?"

"I guess we have time," he said with a glance at the clock over the hearth.

She cuddled up in a blanket and shifted to face him. Not soon after he began talking, she dropped into a deep slumber.

She awoke with a splitting headache the next morning to find a bottle of water and three painkillers on the table beside the couch. Staggering into a sit, she held her head until the worst of the pounding subsided. It took her a moment to recall where she was before she started to recount the discussions she'd had with Kris. He was nowhere in the cabin. Only when the painkillers began to work did she stand and double check.

In fact, there was no sign anyone else had been there. No whiskey bottle or dirty glasses, no fire in the hearth, no clothing or bedding in the tiny bedroom.

After a hot shower, Stephanie sat on the couch once more and downed another bottle of water. Kris hadn't returned, and she went through the cottage once more, puzzled as to how everything she'd seen the night before was gone.

The alcohol had certainly been real. She hadn't had a hangover like this one in some time. But why had he disappeared after insisting she stay if he planned on being gone when she awoke?

Stephanie left the cabin and paused beside the lake. The trail she'd walked the day before was present, but there was no boat or car or any sign either had been there recently.

"Weirder and weirder," she muttered and turned away. At least she knew how to summon a portal to get back to the castle.

"What the fuck are you doing out here?"

She turned at Kiki's irritated voice and saw him approaching from the direction of the forest, accompanied by Fate.

"I don't even know," she said, gazing around.

Fate studied her. Kiki appeared frustrated. "I covered for you with Wynn, but he's not gonna be happy if you aren't where you're supposed to be."

The sound of a falling tree crashed in the forest.

"We need to go," Fate said quietly. "Now."

Her eyes went to him then Kiki, who didn't appear as concerned. "I want to know how you got here first," her brother said.

"I was drinking. Maybe I wandered into a portal."

Another crash sounded, this one closer.

"Summon a portal, Kiki," Fate said.

"I will," she said, sensing his urgency. Stephanie calmed herself and focused on creating a hole in the world. One yawned open near her.

A familiar figure darted above the tops of the trees and ducked beneath the canopy of leaves once more. "Oh, no," she whispered. "Demons."

Fate took her hand and raced into the portal, Kiki at their heels. Warm energy tingled and energized her, and she gripped his hand tightly as they raced across the place-between-places towards a glowing portal.

They emerged into the foyer of the castle. The portal closed behind them, and Kiki muttered a few curses. "You're late," he snapped. "Go do the petitioners. We'll talk about where you went later." He strode away.

Fate waited until he was out of earshot to face her. "You went to great lengths to avoid our date," he said casually. "Kiki and I chased you across the world."

"Yeah, sorry," she murmured.

He tilted her chin up. "Considering you left with one shoe, I'm thinking something else happened."

Stephanie found herself starting to topple into his gaze as she often did. "Petitions," she said and withdrew. "Kiki's right." She started down the hallway.

"No," Fate said and caught her wrist. "Tell me."

She glanced down the hallway. "Not here."

He stepped aside to let her lead them elsewhere. Needing a change of clothing, she went back to her room. He closed the door behind them. She flung herself across her bed.

"My head!" she groaned and clutched it.

Fate stretched out beside her on his side, waiting for her to begin her tale. He didn't appear angry at being stood up or particularly concerned about what happened. She released her head and gazed up at the ceiling, suddenly aware of how close he was.

He rested a hand on her forehead. The warm shock eased some of her pain, and she sighed, closing her eyes.

"You're not upset?" she asked.

"That you stood me up? It's a first." He sounded amused.

"Didn't see it coming?" She couldn't help the barb.

"I figured you'd run."

Startled, she met his gaze. "What do you mean, run?"

"You're clearly in denial."

Stephanie propped herself up on one elbow to glare at him. His hand fell away from her forehead.

"Start talking, gorgeous," he said softly, the edge back in his features.

Her stomach fluttered with desire. A thrill worked through her system at the thought he'd actually missed her. "You are upset."

"I lost a bet." He shrugged.

"Can you be serious? Ever?" she snapped, uncertain why he couldn't just say what he felt.

His response was swift. Before she could fire off another round of angry questions, his hand cupped the back of her head, and he was kissing her. Unlike their first kiss, which had been a little awkward, this one was sure, deep and heated. If his touch enthralled her, his flavor turned her into a puddle. Surprised by her own surge of passion, Stephanie returned the kiss and felt herself beginning to slide at first then plummet into the primal lust demanding more and more from the man the universe chose for her.

As before, he lifted his head, breaking off the experience before she was ready, leaving her breathless and confused. Lying on her back, she was tucked against his side. He gazed down at her, eyes laughing, and traced a forefinger down the side of her features. The hot sparks left in its wake made her shiver.

"I don't think you're ready for me to be serious," he said huskily.

She silently warred with herself, afraid and curious to know where this led and certain she'd never quite be ready for a man like this. The idea sent a thrill through her.

"I met another brother," she said, gazing up at him. Her heart was racing. "One who's supposed to be dead."

His gaze sharpened. "Which one?"

"Kris."

Fate's eyes turned colors at a mesmerizing pace.

"I mean, I think I did," she added. "When I woke up, everything was gone and so was he."

"Then you probably did. Kris was widely respected if a little controversial. Wynn's leadership skills and control issues with none of the madness. He didn't like deities and wouldn't humor them."

"Not sure I blame him," she said beneath her breath. "Sorry I just disappeared. I didn't really have a choice."

"What did you discuss?"

She hesitated a moment too long, debating whether she should reveal her gift to anyone let alone someone she knew would use it.

Fate smiled. "Knew there was more." She didn't trust the gleam in his eyes. Wynn had spent his lifetime as an Immortal not revealing the skill. She had the sudden urge to hide it as well. "Start talking."

Rather than answer him, she took Fate's face in her hands and pulled him down for another deep kiss. His response was more demanding than before, and she understood the danger in trying to distract him too late. The draw between them was too strong, the strange, Immortal bond compelling strangers together a slippery slide she didn't think she alone could fight her way back to the top of.

"How far are you willing to go to distract me?" he whispered and pressed his lips to her jaw. He spread hot kisses along her jaw and down the sensitive skin of her neck.

"As far as I have to," she said.

"That's quite a sacrifice."

She laughed breathlessly, fevered and aching for him to the point she was nearly giddy. The second his hand slid beneath her shirt to rest on her abdomen, she bit back a moan. The idea of skin-on-skin contact with him, of his lean frame pressed to hers, crippled her reason and rendered her a hot mess of anticipation.

He pressed his mouth to hers once more, and she tasted him hungrily, her control turned to ash in the heat of her desire. Firmly and always in control, Fate guided her mouth and body.

A resounding knock jarred her. "Stephanie?" Wynn called.

Fate stiffened and lifted his head. Her rough breathing filled the air between them. Stephanie couldn't look away from him, from his striking beauty and the rare intensity in his gaze that seemed to be reserved solely for her.

He's mine. She'd never been so awed by any thought before.

"Never thought I'd worry about someone's daddy walking in," he said, gaze lingering on her lips.

Whether or not it should've been funny, she laughed.

"To be continued on our date tonight," he told her.

Exhilaration, mixed with some fear, flew through her. "Tonight," Stephanie breathed. Already images of the two of them naked in bed were in her head. She was going to need several cold showers before they met up later for their date.

He eased away from her. She sat and took a deep breath to steady the furnace raging inside her then crossed on wobbly legs to the door. Irritated at being interrupted, she wrenched the door open.

"What?" she snapped at Wynn.

He gave her a disapproving look. "You're late to start with the petitioners."

"Fine. I'll be down." She closed the door without waiting for him to say more.

"Careful," Fate said quietly. "Wynn is dangerous."

But I know his secret. Her eyes strayed to him and where he sat on the edge of the bed, the perfect specimen of male. Athletic, gorgeous, fun … He had an erection whose size left her blushing and aching even more to experience every part of him.

It was hard to think of him as a deity capable of changing the Future at his whim when all she wanted to do was leap into bed with him. Whenever she started to recall what he was beyond the person he pretended to be, her fear returned, and she had the urge to flee. If Kris could stay hidden by bouncing around through different portals, couldn't she? Run away from the madman Wynn, flee the deity she wanted desperately to strip her down and make love to her, escape from the Immortal world …

… and return to a world where she'd never been normal or comfortable to start off with.

"You've got that look again," Fate said, studying her. The wariness she glimpsed occasionally returned, a reminder he wasn't the laid back person he presented himself to be. He was a man accustomed to knowing, if not controlling, the Future, to predicting the actions of everyone around him and renegotiating future actions for a purpose he alone understood.

He was more dangerous than Wynn, or would be, once he regained his power.

"Just freaked out," she replied honestly.

Fate stood and approached her. "You're the one person anywhere who has no reason to fear me," he said.

"Are you sure?"

"Mostly."

How he did this, made her blood heat and then terrified her seconds later ... "I'm serious," she said and licked her lips nervously. "Are you gonna fuck me over when this is over? Should I be worried about what happens when my soul is returned and I do have a future and you decide you're done with this mate business, or I'm a liability to you, or I make a deal with the wrong person?"

"What are you asking?"

"I'm asking ..." She compiled her rambling thoughts into one. "I'm asking if I can trust you. *Really* trust you."

"Yes," he said without hesitation.

She gazed at him, mystified as to why she wanted to sink into his arms and believe him. "That's it."

"That's what you asked." He zapped her.

She swiped his hand away.

Fate's eyes twinkled, and he zapped her several more times, until she was laughing, and his arms were around her. "Now that I know you're ticklish ..." he murmured. He stilled his movement.

She rested against him to catch her breath, her back pressed to his chest, uncertain why she accepted the touch of a stranger so easily.

"You can trust me," he said, warm lips grazing her temple. "But you're the only one who can."

Her heart did a somersault, and she was momentarily awed by the quiet promise from a powerful deity. She rested her hands over his and breathed in his brown sugar scent. The sense of him being her home radiated through her, warmed her. Baffled her.

"But you stole my soul and hid it in Hell," she murmured. "That's not a great way to start a relationship. Definitely not a foundation for trust."

"Believe it or not, I actually understand your concern." He sounded somewhat proud of himself. "I wouldn't have before Karma made me human-ish."

She waited for more and then prompted him when he was quiet. "When a woman gives you a leading statement like that, you're supposed to reassure her."

"You're too strong to need coddling. What you need and respect is the truth. The truth is you can trust me. I may not always explain the game to you, but you are exempt from it and from … well, me. This is as confusing for me as it is to you, but I believe you are better left on the sidelines of routine political maneuvering."

It wasn't the reassurance she sought. If anything, his attempt at being supportive was downright terrifying. "I guess that's good."

Fate shifted forward to rest his cheek against hers. "Don't piss off Wynn," he advised. He squeezed her closer before releasing her. "And don't tell him you left the premises."

"Why?"

"Just trust me on that one." He winked.

Stephanie pursed her lips but didn't challenge him. Her skin was tingling from his touch, her lower belly blazing. She didn't think they'd make it the normal multiple dates before she was willing to whip off her clothes. But to trust him?

I don't think it's possible. Ever.

She changed clothes quickly, troubled by her latest interaction with her mate.

When she was ready, she walked to the door and paused. "Are you going with me?" she asked curiously and then rushed on. "You don't have to. I thought I'd ask."

"I'll be down," he replied. "I need to talk to someone about Kris."

"I don't think he wanted Wynn to know."

"I don't want Wynn to know either."

She nodded, gaze lingering on his chiseled features. "You know where I'll be." She left and went to the first floor and the large chamber filled already with petitioners.

Kiki sat at the table in her place. His eyes lit up when he saw her, and he leapt to his feet to leave.

"Thank god," he muttered, joining her.

"Does the new guy always get the shit job?" she responded.

"Don't even think of whining! I've been the one listening to petitioners for a *year*, Steph!" he snapped. "I fucking dream about these people."

If there was one thing to say about her new family, it was that they were truly the least friendly group of people she'd ever met. Groaning internally, she nonetheless took her seat and began to listen.

Until she saw a familiar figure pass the doorway.

Stephanie blinked and sat up, certain she'd imagined the woman. She stared for a moment then started to relax. She was hung over and high on desire.

Just as she looked down, the figure passed by the entrance again. Her head flew up, and she stood. This time, she was certain she'd seen Olivia. It wasn't possible, though.

Kris was dead, too. This thought made her gasp. "Excuse me," she said hastily and rushed away from the table. She darted into the hallway and paused, looking around wildly.

She spotted Olivia turning a corner and raced after her. "Olivia!"

Her former roommate didn't reappear, and Stephanie continued to run after her, through the halls of the bottom floor, always just missing her. She stopped at the entrance onto the back lawn to catch her breath and spotted Olivia disappearing into the forest on a trail she'd seen without knowing where it went.

There's something weird about this, she thought and hesitated.

Just then, Olivia turned and waved to her with a grin.

"Olivia, wait!" Stephanie called and started forward.

Olivia gestured for her to follow and took off at a run into the forest.

Stephanie slowed at the entrance to the woods. With a glance over her shoulder at the fortress where her dysfunctional family lived, she plunged into the forest after her friend. She caught glimpses of Olivia's red hair and followed until she reached a large lake whose flawless surface reflected the cloudless blue sky above.

Olivia was nowhere to be seen, and Stephanie sucked in deep breaths as she studied the gorgeous scene before her.

"Is there a human alive who will not fall for such deception?"

She whirled. Two men with dark eyes and fangs melted from the shadows of the forest. They were accompanied by Olivia.

Only, upon closer inspection, she could see how unlike Olivia the figure really was. The build of the smaller demon was wrong, and Olivia's features appeared almost … melted. The demons were smiling, armed – and blocking her escape route back to the fortress.

God, I hate demons! "You don't want to do this," she blurted out and began backing away.

"We won't kill you, morsel," one of them assured her. "Our dark lord would not approve."

Her heart felt like it dropped to her stomach. Even Deidre feared dealing with the Dark One, her mate. Stephanie thought about a return trip to Hell and made a quick decision.

She turned and bolted. She made it all of ten meters before one of the demons tackled her. Stephanie hit the ground hard enough to knock the air from her lungs. Incapacitated, she didn't fight him as the demon hauled her to her feet. The other two hung back, and she eyed the melting face of Olivia with a cross between horror and disgust.

"Breathe, human," the demon holding her growled. He landed a hard smack on her back, and she sucked in a breath and began to cough. The muscular creature held her in place and signaled the other two. He snatched her by the back of the neck and yanked her head up, peering at her features with riveting blue-green eyes. "The Dark One wants you in perfect condition. He has plans for you."

Stephanie steadied herself and pushed at him.

"Are you certain taking her is in your best interests?"

Her heart soared at Fate's voice.

The demon twisted to see who spoke, and the other two drew weapons. Spotting the deity, the three grew wary. Fate appeared perfectly at ease, dressed in designer jeans and a gray t-shirt. His eyes whirled with colors, and his chiseled features displayed a bored expression she was starting to realize hid the sharp, dangerous mind of the intelligent godling.

"Name yourself," ordered the demon holding her.

"Does it matter?" Fate returned. "Whatever I am, it is far more than what you are. Is she worth pissing off a deity?"

"Shut up. Open a portal," their leader ordered the others. The two hesitated, eyes on the unnamed deity whose casual challenge worked on them as well as it did her.

"Trayern, isn't it?" Fate asked.

The demon holding her stiffened.

"Back from the depths of Hell, I see. I thought Darkyn would've left you there after your previous failures."

"All the more reason not to fail this time!"

"He values you, so I'll do you the honor of explaining why you aren't going to take the human with you," Fate said with a smile. "If you do, you will start a war your lord does not want."

The demon Trayern didn't speak. His grip remained tight on her neck, and she gazed hard at Fate, willing him to win this deceptively simple battle of wills.

"Take him this message," Fate said, drawing near. Unarmed, powerless, he nonetheless portrayed the calm confidence of someone who had already won this round. "Tell him he has an appointment with destiny. Go now, if you like. I'll await his response right here."

"Trayern," one of the others warned. "The Dark One will not forgive disobedience."

"He will forgive you," Fate said, focus on Trayern. "He trusts you. Show him why his trust is well placed. Take my message back to him, and, if he rebukes you, you can take us both with you to Hell."

Stephanie's breath caught.

Whatever game he played, it worked. Trayern released her and stepped away.

"I'm leaving them," Trayern lifted his head towards the other two demons.

"Fine."

The wary demon summoned a portal and disappeared. Stephanie's gaze, however, was on Fate.

"Do you know what you're doing?" she asked quietly.

He winked.

She had the urge to wrap herself in his arms – or maybe run the opposite way. There was never a middle of the road reaction to him. She hugged herself, unable to help the stir of desire and fear his appearance always caused.

"Are you hurt?" Fate asked, searching her features briefly.

"No. Just freaked out." She glanced towards the remaining demons. "How ... did they steal Olivia's face?"

"It's a shapeshifter demoness," Fate explained. "Crudely effective and rarely able to hold their shapes for long."

"Right."

His gaze lingered on her, and his quick smile was warm. "You didn't play the mate card."

Stephanie had no idea how to respond. Fate and Wynn seemed to be universally distrusted. Would that have made her fate at the hands of the demons better or so much worse?

"You really should," he advised.

"You have no power!" she whispered.

"Because that's what's stopping you."

She rolled her eyes.

"At least you got out of listening to petitions," he added.

She started to laugh, stopped and then shook her head, uncertain what kind of reaction was appropriate while waiting for the Dark One to drag them to Hell. "You are ... amazing," she said finally. "And I don't think I mean that in a good way."

"When you've lived as long as I have, you never take a moment to smile or laugh for granted. Especially when you know you're about to make a deal with the Dark One."

The somber note in his voice drew her attention from the demons, and she studied him. She didn't sense self-pity or sorrow in the deity capable of experiencing the futures of billions. "I can't figure you out."

"Do you really want to?" he countered, gazing down at her. The rare intensity was displayed once more.

Her cheeks grew warm under his look. She didn't have an answer.

"You do," he said. "Good."

The cool breeze of a portal reached them, and she turned to see a smaller, leaner demon with youthful features and cold, black eyes leading Trayern out of the place-between-places.

"I need you to promise me something," Fate whispered.

"What?"

"If I miss our date tonight, you'll meet me Friday night, here, at eight in the evening."

Her brow furrowed.

"Agreed?" He held out his hand.

"Is an official deal really necessary?" she asked. "You don't think I'll show?"

"Agreed?"

Sensing he wasn't going to reveal anything he didn't want to – ever – she tapped her hand to his.

Before she could say anything more, the two demons were within earshot, and Fate stepped in front of her to greet them.

"Darkyn. Always a pleasure," he said smoothly.

Stephanie peered around him to see the demon, not expecting the Dark One to be so much smaller than those around him. Just under six feet tall with a honed frame and black stare, he was intimidating but not like Trayern, who was a head taller and one and a half times as wide.

Darkyn's gaze rested on her long enough for her to shrink back. He seemed to peer through her to her non-existent soul.

"I know your condition, Fate," the Dark One snapped. "And I know you are far from helpless even without your power."

"We both know Wynn allowed you to set foot on the Immortals' territory," Fate replied. "You want her. But I'm willing to bet you want me more. Or perhaps Wynn?"

"I have no quarrel with Wynn."

"Except he managed to elude your prison again. That's twice in a row this lifetime. You and I both know he should be in Hell."

The Dark One was quiet momentarily, his gaze going to Stephanie once more.

"I'm willing to negotiate," Fate added.

"This is business. It's also personal." The Dark One signaled to Trayern to leave them. "I will never forget how you fucked with my mate."

"Delivered her to you, I think you mean."

Stephanie shrank back, not certain she was ready to hear the types of secrets deities kept. Her thoughts went to Deidre, who had seemed content as the bride of the devil, but only after the trauma of her story. She hadn't mentioned Fate's role in the whole ordeal, and Stephanie had the sudden urge to ask her what exactly he meant by delivering a human into Hell to become the mate of the Dark One.

"We will negotiate in private," the Dark One said and stepped away.

Fate didn't leave his protective position between them as he trailed the demon.

Stephanie watched them, unable to stop the cold fear spiraling through her. Her eyes were glued to Fate, who appeared unconcerned, in control, as if his powers being gone was an inconvenience rather than the crippling situation she suspected it truly was.

The other two demons eyed her hungrily, and Trayern stood at rapt attention, focus on his master, in case things broke bad.

It was impossible to read either deity to understand how the negotiations were going or even what they were about. It was like watching two master poker players who had ironed out their tells. For all she knew, they were choosing where to eat for dinner.

The two spoke for a good thirty minutes before their heads lifted, and they touched hands to seal whatever deal they came to. The two approached, neither breaking the stoicism of their features.

"He's agreed to leave you alone for now," Fate said. "In exchange for the ability to ask you two questions and verify your condition."

"Meaning ..." she asked, backing away as the Dark One took a step towards her.

"Don't run," Darkyn said with a cold smile.

"You last longer if you don't fight a demon," Fate explained. "He won't hurt you."

She stared at him, recalling what demons had done to Olivia. Fate had stiffened at the Dark One's approach but made no move to stop him.

Trust me. He mouthed the words to her.

She sucked in a deep breath and nodded, heart hammering and palms clammy.

Darkyn snatched her neck. He made no attempt to be gentle and dragged her into him, staring into her eyes. He didn't blink, and she started to push at him, freaked out by the expanse of nothingness in his gaze.

Fate shook his head in warning.

She stopped. The Dark One pushed her back onto her feet without releasing her neck and circled her slowly. When he returned to his position facing her, he spoke.

"Describe in extensive detail, your skill, unique to the children of Wynn," he ordered her.

"I … I can hear or … I don't know … somehow know people's secrets," she said in a whisper.

Fate stepped closer in interest.

"It usually happens when I touch them. Always with humans, mostly with Immortals, not at all with deities," she continued. "When I first met Kiki and touched him, he was afraid to discover I was who he thought I was. Ileana didn't want me to pity her for having one hand. Wynn …" She drifted off, alarmed by the reaction of both deities at the mention of the Immortal.

The Dark One she expected to be predatory, but the sudden sharpness in Fate's colorful gaze left her thinking she was about to fall into a trap lain by both of them.

"Wynn what?" Fate asked.

"Wynn has this gift, too," she said in a hushed tone. "I couldn't read him but Kris believed him to have the ability to hide his gift."

"Kris," Darkyn hissed.

"Back from the dead-dead. One guess as to who brought him back," Fate said, his tension easing. "But Kris is only half right."

"These are not secrets you read in people," the Dark One said. "It's fear. You can sense what they fear most the moment you touch them."

"It's a critical advantage to someone as resolved as Wynn."

Fears. Suddenly, she pitied all the people whose hidden fears she'd inadvertently heard. She'd thought them strange for telling her random things, only to realize she alone was privy to something causing those she ran across so much suffering. It was a terrible privilege to be aware of someone else's deepest fears.

She began to understand why Wynn hadn't let anyone discover his gift in all the years of his life. Where she empathized with those alone with their fears, Wynn used them to manipulate people. The two deities before her wore similar expressions, and she could guess that they, too, would find such a skill useful.

Darkyn released her. "I'll save my second question for next time." He turned and strode towards Trayern.

She released her breath. "That wasn't so bad," she said and clenched her trembling hands.

"Not at all," Fate agreed. "I'm afraid I have to cancel our date tonight."

She frowned.

"When you're ready," Darkyn barked, standing before a portal.

Fate glanced towards him.

"What's going on?" Stephanie asked. "You're not going with him, are you?"

"I am."

"I don't understand."

"We have some business to conduct," he replied with a shrug.

"Stop lying to me." She searched his features. "You didn't make a deal with him, did you?"

"I guess you could say we made a pre-deal. He leaves you alone, so long as I'm down there with him."

Stephanie gasped. "You're joking!"

"It's temporary."

"Define temporary."

"You barely agreed to go on a date with me. You can't be concerned for my welfare," he teased.

Rationally, she wanted to agree, but the tiny voice inside her, the one that wanted a chance with him, that had already claimed him, refuted any notion he wasn't on some level important to her.

"Wynn wants you isolated, alone. As long as I'm here, I can help you," he said quietly. "But if I don't go, Darkyn takes you to Hell, and I won't allow that."

"You'd go to Hell for me?" she asked.

She saw the answer on his face. However aloof he was, however baffled she remained, she felt like she was truly seeing him for the first time. All his layers, all his jokes, hid something very good, however small that nugget of good was.

"If he's here for me, it's my choice," she said. "You can't do something like this for me, not after what you went through at Wynn's hands!"

"No," he said.

"Free will, remember?"

"No." His voice was soft, firm. "Sorry. No free will today."

"But it's not fair." Tears of frustration were in her eyes as she realized how perfectly Wynn had set them up.

Fate cupped her face in his hands, his touch calming her panic. Her eyes were riveted to his, her senses filled with him. The idea of losing him, when she'd just started to think she wanted to know more, disturbed her.

"I won't put you in that kind of danger," he said.

Stephanie stepped closer and pulled his head down to hers. She kissed him deeply without caring about the demons looking on. Fate looped an arm around her and held her against his hard body, his response as hungry as it had been in her room earlier.

What if this is the last time I see her? This time, she knew the words weren't spoken aloud, and they managed to yank her closer to the man she hadn't wanted to care about. She was reading his deepest fear – and it crushed her to learn it was about her.

He pulled away too soon and rested his forehead against hers.

"You don't have to do this," she whispered.

"I do," he replied firmly. "Listen carefully. There are two threats to you. Darkyn is one. Wynn is the other. Of the two, I alone can handle Darkyn. But that leaves you vulnerable to Wynn. Play along with him until you find Kris or Andre. They'll know how to handle him. But you must not challenge him alone."

It was the most serious he'd ever been since they'd met.

"Do you understand?"

She nodded. "You'll come back, won't you?"

He traced the pad of his thumb across her lips. "You do owe me a date," he said. "I figure I can't die before I collect, right?"

Stephanie was feeling nowhere near as confident. "I want you to come back," she whispered.

He kissed her on the forehead and stepped away. "Keep Karma out of trouble."

Seemingly at ease with being stuck in Hell, he joined the Dark One and disappeared into the portal. He was followed by the remaining three demons.

Stephanie waited until they all disappeared, overwhelmed once more and trying to figure out why she felt like she did the night she saw Olivia being attacked. She barely knew Fate, barely trusted him, and her insides were twisting and tearing.

Reviewing his parting words, she found herself rooted in place for another long minute, waiting for him to reappear. When he didn't, she faced the direction she'd come and began walking mechanically, too absorbed in deciphering what she was feeling to pay much attention to where she went. She walked in a daze until she reached the castle. Only then did she recall what Fate had said, what she was supposed to be doing.

She wanted to hate Wynn, to march into his study and tell him exactly what she thought of him, now that she knew he used people's deepest fears against them. Instead, she returned to the line of pissed off petitioners and began to hear their cases once more. Her mind was anywhere but there, and she began to consider how she was going to find Kris again or break into Hell to free Andre.

Hours later, she'd created a tentative plan.

"Kiki, can we talk?" After an awkward, quiet family dinner, Stephanie waited until Wynn had left the dining hall to approach her brother.

He glanced around as if to ensure they were alone. "Yeah. Come on." Leading her out of the dining hall, he headed towards the fourth floor, where their rooms were located, and entered his. Decorated much like hers, the main differences were the computers and desks upon which they sat lining the far wall. "We can talk here." He tossed his iPad onto his bed and motioned her to the seating area in front of the hearth.

"I'm not sure how to say this." She debated in silence for a moment. "I met Kris."

Kiki sat up straighter. "What?"

"That's why I disappeared last night. He grabbed me out of my room and dragged me through, like, a dozen portals. Apparently he was brought back from uh, being dead, or whatever, so he could get rid of Wynn again."

Kiki was listening closely, his eyes wide. "Tell me everything."

"That's pretty much it," she said with a shrug. "I guess he heard about me and wanted to meet me to see if I was real. He didn't want me coming back but then he saw the tattoo."

"Kris won't break the Code's laws about mates. Did he say where he was going?"

"Nope. He got me liquored up real good with whiskey so I barely remember half of what we talked about." *I'm not about to reveal my secret skill after seeing how Fate and the Dark One reacted.*

"Did you tell Fate?"

"Yeah. And …" She sighed. "The Dark One knows, too."

Kiki frowned.

Stephanie explained her encounter with the Dark One resulting in Fate going to Hell. She paused afterwards, trying once more to explore what she felt. Ever-present confusion, sorrow and … amazement. A man who barely knew her was taking her place in Hell. Drawn to his handsome features since their very first meeting, perplexed by his complicated personality, she'd never thought him capable of anything so selfless. She was starting to crave learning more about him, from the hard body to the center of his complex mind. If he could cease scaring her with deity talk long enough for her to feel at ease with him …

"We have to do something," she said at last. "He said to find Kris or Andre."

"We know where Andre is."

The same place Fate is. She pondered the idea of voluntarily breaking into Hell and the half-assed plan she'd made with Gabriel and Deidre before they were discovered by Karma. "I have an idea," she said slowly. "I think it's probably a really, really bad one."

"There's a good chance I've heard worse," Kiki said.

I really hope so.

CHAPTER FIFTEEN

FATE RESTED AGAINST THE BLACK WALL OF THE CELL, HIS NEW HOME for the time being. He hadn't wanted to worry Stephanie by telling her the truth. If he ever left Hell, there was a chance it was after a few hundred thousand years at Darkyn's mercy. He had no optimistic hope of surviving this trip, even if he ultimately needed to live in order to prevent the world from disappearing. Darkyn would likely test the limits of the rules remaining from the time-before-time.

Fate would do the same. He viewed these precious few moments as possibly the last downtime he ever experienced. Hell and the Underworld of Death held the oldest of magics capable of absorbing the power of a full deity. If he happened to spend his four months here working off his debt to Karma, he'd end up trapped even when his power returned.

So many times in his life, someone – usually another deity – had wanted to capture Fate, to control the godling master of the Future. He never dreamt he'd voluntarily enslave himself to anyone.

But the alternative, letting Stephanie learn the depths of darkness only Hell could contain, was not an option. He didn't know what to feel for his mate, but he wasn't going to fail to protect her from the world he had already experienced.

"What did you do?" the soft voice came from the cell door.

He twisted his head to look. He couldn't see out of the six by six box, unless someone was at his door. An invisible, magic door separated him from Deidre, who was frowning.

"You can't tell me you're not pleased to see me here," he said with a smile.

"I'm not. I was angry with you for a while but ... I mean, how could I stay angry? You did try to protect me."

"In what ways I could."

"In what ways you knew how to."

"Deities are not much in the empathy department." He chuckled. "Does Darkyn know you're here?"

"Of course," she replied. "I don't keep secrets from him."

"Except about your recent half-human visitor."

She eyed him. "Okay, so I do keep secrets. But he knows I do. He respects them."

"So he knows your secrets already and pretends like he doesn't."

"This isn't about me!" she snapped. "Why on earth did you agree to come down here?"

"The same reason Darkyn doesn't call you on your secrets."

Deidre was quiet. When he looked at her, he found her smiling. "Go ahead and gloat for now. When I'm rendered dead-dead, you can deliver the message to her," he said.

"If there's one thing I know about you, it's that you can take care of yourself."

"I'm not worried about me."

"Don't you start," she chided him. "You aren't gonna manipulate me!"

He laughed. "Very well. But I am only partially trying to extort your sympathy."

"You made a deal with Darkyn, didn't you?"

"I did."

"Then you don't need to worry about him hurting her," she reminded him.

I'm worried I won't get to see what having a mate feels like. He said nothing aloud. The thought was too private to share with anyone, and the idea he had a soft spot for the woman destined to become his mate was going to be used against him at every turn, if anyone knew. But he did have a soft spot. He had witnessed the shift in Stephanie's gaze when she realized what he'd done.

It touched him on a level he hadn't known existed. He'd made a decision to claim his mate, if only to keep her safe, and was finding it hard not to want there to be something more. A relationship, the kind he didn't normally have with people. This one would be mutual without expectation of something to gain. He'd also feel, really *feel* her, for the rest of eternity. He had dismissed such an idea long ago. How was *feeling* so venerated? It was crude, human physical science and nothing more.

And yet, whenever he kissed her, when her musk reached his nose and her fingers his skin, his whole world seemed to stop, to grow less important than sharing a moment with her.

"Are you happy with Darkyn? Truly happy?" he asked Deidre.

"I am."

"Good." He had originally pitied her for where she was headed. "You know I can't interfere, right?"

"I do," he replied. "But you can sit and talk to me, can't you? Eternity is a long time to spend here."

She sat beside his cell. "I'll be here."

"Talk to me. Tell me something new," he said and rested his head back against the cool stone wall.

Deidre began talking about her life in Hell. Fate half-listened, allowing his mind to dwell on the puzzle that was being mated to a stranger in between responses to her. She stayed with him for an hour or more, until her gaze strayed from him to someone approaching from down the hallway.

He didn't have to ask to know it was her mate. Deidre's features flushed pink, and her eyes sparkled. She stood and stepped to the side. Darkyn stopped beside her and peered into Fate's cell.

"I've been waiting a lifetime for this," he growled.

"Let's get started," Fate said and stood.

"Not so fast." Darkyn was entirely too pleased for Fate's comfort. "You have a long list of people clamoring for a shot at you while you're here."

"Brilliant, as always. I'm certain you're extorting favors left and right from them for a shot at Fate," he said ruefully.

"I have never seen so many deities eager to deal with me," the Dark One said, coldly amused.

Shit. This is gonna hurt. But Fate smiled, not about to appear weak or uneasy in front of anyone. "The circus is open for business."

Darkyn's smile was nothing short of terrifying.

CHAPTER SIXTEEN

"This is a terrible idea," Tamer whispered.
"If you aren't back by nine, I'm gonna have to tell Wynn," Kiki reminded her.
"Don't tell Wynn! Grow a backbone for once, Kiki!"
"I'm the only reason this entire fucking society hasn't crumbled." Tamer rolled his eyes. "Whatever. Come on, Steph."

Dressed all in black, certain she probably wasn't coming back at all, Stephanie swallowed hard. She gave Kiki a quick squeeze of his arm, not wanting him to be upset, and trailed Tamer into the forest.

"Remember. There's one way into and out of Hell." Tamer said for the zillionth time. He shrugged into a huge overcoat that covered him from neck to ankles. "I'm sneaking you in under my trench coat. Stand on my feet like you're four."

Stephanie obeyed and leaned back against him. She folded her arms across her chest. Tamer closed the coat around them both and buttoned it until she could see nothing. "It's hot," she complained.

"Shut up. This was your idea," he growled.

It's a horrible idea.

"Ready?"

"Sure," she said in a tight voice.

He grunted in response. Tamer took a few steps to make sure she didn't fall then opened up the coat. "This isn't going to work right." He jostled her aside and yanked off his belt, widening it until it was long enough to go around both of them.

"I can hear Wynn now," Kiki said from nearby. "He'll let you stay in Hell. You both know that, right?"

"I know, I know," Stephanie responded. "Wish us luck."

"I'll wish you quick deaths if caught."

Tamer snapped the belt around her midsection and replaced the overcoat. She was soon enclosed once more in the stifling heat. Her brother did several more test steps then opened a portal.

"Here we go," Tamer said.

Stephanie focused on keeping her feet on his. He moved in a slow lumber, and only the belt kept her from face planting. Even the chilly place-between-places didn't cool her down. She had no way of knowing where they were in the process of entering Hell until Tamer paused.

"Routine collections," he said briskly.

She held her breath, terrified of being discovered. But Tamer went unchallenged and was soon walking once more. She heard the muffled sound of a door close and silently begged him to hurry, about to hyperventilate without air in the thick coat.

A few moments later, he stopped again and unbuttoned the coat.

"Oh, my god!" she gasped and fumbled to unfasten the belt. She all but fell into the wall they faced.

"Quiet!" he hissed. "You're on your own. You have fifteen minutes before you have to meet me here. Got the map?"

She lifted her hand, where she'd redrawn the map he gave her, along with instructions.

"Go." He started the timer on his watch. "Don't get caught."

She did the same, turned and hurried down the black hallways lit by black torches. She paused at the first intersection to listen for sounds of anyone approaching from either direction before sliding around the corner to the left.

Convinced this was the single worst idea she'd ever had, she nonetheless felt familiar desperation, the kind that had been plaguing her since the night Olivia died and she was first introduced to this insane world. By all accounts, the eldest child of Wynn was also a deity and the only level headed, rational member of her dysfunctional family. If anyone could cancel out Wynn – and also help her free Fate – it was a deity who was also family. Andre was going to help her fix her life. He had to. She had no other option.

At least, this was what she told herself to keep from breaking down into a delirious, sobbing heap as she crept through the corridors of Hell. With some relief, she found Tamer's instructions to be exact down to the smallest distance. Twice she ran across demons and was forced to wait and watch precious seconds tick down on her watch. Once she was certain she was spotted but no one appeared to challenge her.

She was doubly grateful when she realized the instructions weren't taking her into the bowels of Hell, where she was likely to witness just how horrific this strange world was. Her brother was being kept in a quiet hallway with a dead end, off the beaten path.

"This is where it gets tricky," she murmured.

Four doors, four rooms. Tamer hadn't known which was Andre's.

After a brief hesitation, she went to the nearest and opened it.

"Empty." She sighed. The room was larger than hers had been during her brief stay in Hell. Tamer had said Darkyn was treating Andre as a guest, not a prisoner, and the size and layout of the dark room seemed to support this.

She closed it and went to the door across the hallway and opened it next. A man with white eyes and a shimmer of power marking him a deity stood before the fire and twisted to see her. For a moment she was stuck in place, gazing into the unusual gaze. He was tall and fit, pale of skin with jet-black hair and the penetrating stare of a predator. He moved with athletic grace unlike any she'd ever seen.

Another deity but definitely not Andre. By his look, she didn't want to know which one.

"Sorry. Just, uh, ignore me." She started to close the door.

With movement too fast for her to see, he was suddenly at the door with his hand jamming it open. He yanked it out of her hands, and she stepped back, alarmed.

"What are you?" he demanded.

"Just in the neighborhood. Sorry to disturb you. Maybe ... maybe you should just go back to your room," she said.

"You have freed me. I will not."

"I don't have time for this. Whatever. I gotta find someone and you're not him." She shifted away and went to the next door.

"You're not a demon."

"No."

"Yet you're in Hell." He trailed like a curious puppy.

She opened the third door and released her breath when she saw it, too, was empty. "It's a long story, okay? You're free. You don't have to hang around."

"Why would I leave when you're going to show me how to escape?"

Kiki had started to brief her on the hundreds of thousands of Immortal laws in either Code. Was freeing a random deity from Hell breaking one of them? Worse, which deity was this? A good one or one Kiki refused to talk about?

"I'll owe you a favor of your choice," the deity added.

She paused, hand on the doorknob to the final room. Fate had told her this was the ultimate currency to Immortals and deities. "As long as you don't get in the way," she said. "But I've got to save my brother first."

"I will be but a shadow."

She snorted and pushed the final door open. The handsome, night skinned man with aquiline features seated at the fire with a book had the most luxurious room on the block complete with his own miniature library and a bar.

Wynn's claim to have made a comfortable arrangement with Darkyn returned to her.

"Whoa," she said and looked around. "This is nicer than my room at the castle."

"Why do you rate this and I didn't?" the deity behind her grumbled.

"Shadow!" she snapped at him. "Go guard the hallway."

He did so.

Andre, the deity Peace, lowered his book with elegance and poise that made her think she should change into a dress and curtsey. His teal gaze settled on her, and he waited politely.

"Uh, hi," she started and took a deep breath. "This is a long story so I'll keep it short. I'm your long lost sister, Stephanie, a half-breed. I'm here to break you out so you can stop Wynn from being Wynn. I have no soul because my mate hid it, which means Darkyn can't sense me, but Tamer brought me and we have four minutes to make it back to the portal room before someone freaks out."

Andre rose as she spoke and set his book down. "It's a pleasure to meet you." He held out his hand. "I always thought our clan could use a sister."

She blinked, not expecting the tranquil response or warm smile. "Um, thanks." Something about him calmed her frantic thoughts.

"I look forward to hearing your story once we're free."

No smart ass remark like she'd hear from Tamer or Kiki, no cold plotting like she'd sense from Wynn, no games like she'd expect from Fate. Andre was genuine. Warm. Friendly.

"I don't even know you and I missed you!" she said and hugged him hard.

Andre chuckled. "Welcome to the family."

She released him, optimistic for the first time in weeks about her chances of surviving the Immortal disaster. "We have to hurry." She took his hand and pulled him into the hallway, pausing when she saw the deity awaiting them. She almost asked who he was or at least, whether or not he was going to fuck them over once they were free.

They had no time to talk about anything – just to run. Stephanie bolted forward once more. She led them through the corridors at a sprint, more concerned about reaching the portal before Tamer left them than whether or not she ran across any demons.

When she reached the spot they'd agreed to meet, she was gasping for air. Tamer greeted Andre with a nod before staring at the fourth member of their party.

"Who the fuck is that?" he demanded.

"Let's go!" Stephanie begged and gripped his arm, tugging him towards the portal room.

"You don't just pick up hitch hikers in Hell. There's a reason Darkyn captured him."

"Puh-leeeeeease, Tamer!"

"I can't get three of you out of here!"

"Don't concern yourselves. I can take it from here." The strange deity said and strode around the corner.

Tamer looked from him to Stephanie. "Do you have any idea what Darkyn will do if you freed the wrong person? What Gabriel will do to *me* once he figures out who was involved?"

"Yell at me later. Please!" she said and trailed the strange deity. She stayed at the corner until he disappeared into the portal room. Stephanie cringed, waiting to hear some horrific sounds of violence.

No noise came. Seconds later, the deity popped his head out of the door and grinned. "All clear!" He ducked back into the room.

"I hope he hasn't killed anyone," Andre said in disapproval.

Stephanie darted down the hallway, trailed by her two brothers, and entered the portal room.

She relaxed. No one was present except for the deity. "Oh. I thought there'd be someone guarding it."

"There was," Tamer said grimly. "There are six demons here at all times."

Her gaze settled on the deity. *I really hope I didn't fuck up the world by setting him loose.*

"Come quickly." The deity motioned to them from his place on the platform.

Tamer sighed and went to the control panel to open the portal. Seconds later, a cool breeze swept through the room, and a hole yawned open.

Stephanie had never been so glad to see the fabric of the universe torn. She bolted forward, followed by the others, and formed an image of the lake in her mind. One door glowed in response, and they rushed through it.

She burst into the cool night air of the human world and bent over, swallowing rapidly to keep from throwing up. The portal closed behind them, and she straightened. She wouldn't feel safe until she was at the castle, locked in her room, hiding in her bathroom or safely under the covers of her bed.

"I'm in so much fucking trouble," Tamer snarled. "I've gotta tell Gabe before Darkyn does." He strode through a portal and disappeared.

"Much obliged, soul-less one," the strange deity said and approached Stephanie. He held out his hand, and she accepted it, once more entranced by his eyes. "Until we meet again." He kissed her knuckles and then walked away.

"Wait," she called. "Who are you? How do I summon you for my favor?"

"I'll be in touch," he promised.

She shivered. "I really, really hate this world." When he'd

vanished, she faced the only brother she wanted to claim as such. "I'm sorry Wynn traded you to Hell."

"You grow accustomed to these types of deals," Andre said. "Although, you really can't adequately prepare for the outcomes."

She started to smile. "No. You can't."

"What's your plan?"

"This is as far as I've gotten," she admitted. "Fate said you and Kris were the only ones who could stop Wynn."

"Fate."

"Yeah." She cleared her throat. "He's kind of my mate. And kind of sitting in Hell right now."

"Perhaps we should start from the beginning." Andre offered her his arm. "I know a café near here that serves the best hot chocolate."

Stephanie nodded. Her throat was too tight for her to respond. Of everyone she'd met, Andre was the only person who seemed to care, understand and above all – have the wherewithal to figure out what the fuck she was supposed to do next. She rested her hand on his arm, and he summoned a portal.

CHAPTER SEVENTEEN

"You're strong to have gotten through all this."

The more time she spent with Andre, the better she felt. Her adrenaline had long since worn off since they began talking. Coupled with three cups of hot chocolate, she was craving a nap. Stephanie glanced at her watch and almost groaned. She was due to listen to petitioners in less than an hour.

"I have to go," she said and straightened in her seat. "But I don't know what to tell you to do next. Can you go somewhere safe?"

"Don't worry about me," Andre replied with a smile. "I'd recommend not telling Wynn about any of this. He'll find out soon enough I'm missing. If Darkyn tracks you down personally, don't deal with him. Summon me."

She nodded. "Where will you be? Or is it better I don't know?"

"I've got friends." Andre winked. "Focus on staying alive and off Wynn's radar. Fate is right – Wynn is the worst kind of dangerous. I'm going to find Kris and have a talk."

Stephanie rose. "I'm so happy I got to meet you," she said. "You're the only almost-normal person I've met."

"I'm as normal as Immortals come." He smiled. "I'll give Fate's position some thought. After recent dealings with Darkyn, I understand better why everyone says not to deal with him directly. There is a way to free your mate. We just have to find it."

Hope bubbled inside her. She feared dwelling too long on what Fate was going through and how horrible it had to be. When Andre explained the mating bond, their society and why things were so fucked up, her perspective began to shift from entrenched denial into consideration of a future most Immortals could only dream of.

Stephanie left Andre at the café and returned to the fortress through a portal. She had time for a quick shower and breakfast before she went to the audience chamber to listen to petitioners. The moment she sat down, she wanted either a quadruple shot of espresso or to run and hide in her room.

Kiki had texted, and she messaged him back between petitioners. She started to relax about her midnight adventure and assume she'd pulled it off. Darkyn and Wynn didn't confront her, and she made it to the evening family dinner in peace.

Kiki was late to dinner. With Wynn at the head of the table and no Kiki to ramble on about logistics, it was more awkward than any other night. Wynn didn't wait for her brother to join them but began eating.

Stephanie did as well, sneaking a peak at her cell phone to see if Kiki had texted. His last message came an hour before dinner.

"Kiki isn't joining us?" she asked finally.

"He is not," Wynn replied.

Stephanie waited for the second course to be served before the awkward silence between them grew unbearable.

"I saw sixty people today," she said.

"Good. How are you enjoying the work?"

"It's ... interesting."

Wynn leaned back. "There's no better way to learn the names and struggles of our people than to interact directly with them. Petitions maximize this opportunity."

"I'm definitely meeting a lot of people," she agreed.

"Tomorrow you can start working on the infrastructure issues."

"Kiki's job?"

He nodded.

She grinned. "I can't wait to tell him he's got petition duty. Or did you tell him?"

"I did not," Wynn said. "I'll leave that pleasure to you when he returns."

"Returns?"

"It seems Andre escaped from Hell, voiding my agreement with Darkyn. He demanded another child to replace him."

The fork fell from her hands and clattered against the plate. The sound jarred her but not as much as his words. Wynn appeared to be watching her, waiting for her reaction.

"Why … why him?" she managed finally. "He's running everything."

"Apparently your mate made a deal whereby Darkyn can't touch, talk or make deals with you," Wynn said. "I hope you can learn Kiki's job quickly. He was running everything and now, you are."

Stephanie said nothing, stunned. Of all the sons she'd met, Kiki was the least deserving of a stint in Hell. Did Wynn know of her involvement in Andre's escape?

Would the master manipulator tell her if he did?

She picked up her fork, uncertain what exactly to do. The warnings from Fate and Andre replayed in her head, and she didn't dare admit anything about her involvement in Andre's escape. The moment she left the dining hall, she was summoning Andre.

"Sorry I'm late." Kiki opened the doors and rushed in.

Stephanie stared at him then looked at Wynn.

"You think I wouldn't know?" Wynn asked quietly as Kiki took his seat across from her. "Step out of this game while you have the chance."

She folded her hands in her lap and twisted them.

"What's going on?" Kiki asked, glancing between them.

"Father-daughter chat. Right, Stephanie?" Wynn replied.

"Yeah," she managed. "Just getting to know one another."

Kiki gave her a long look.

"She's definitely my child," Wynn said in satisfaction.

Stephanie's appetite fled. She hadn't considered the consequences of breaking Andre out and wasn't at all certain Wynn wasn't going to send Kiki to Hell after all. Worse, he knew of her involvement in the rescue. She'd fallen right into his trap – again.

Feeling like the world was closing in around her, she pushed away from the table and walked to the door. By the time she hit the hall, she was in a run. Stephanie raced through the corridors until she reached the exit to the back lawn. She stopped and threw her head back, sucking in the evening air.

Where did she go from here? How did she juggle a world so foreign to her let alone survive it?

She sank onto the stairs and held her head.

"You're in over your head." Wynn's voice made her tense. He sat beside her and held out a glass of amber liquid. "Your instincts are good."

Stephanie studied him for a moment before lifting her head and taking the drink. She wiped her eyes with her other hand.

"What's your next move?" Wynn asked and sipped from his glass.

"I really don't know." Stephanie swirled the glass, wishing the liquid inside would either poison her or put her to sleep until this was over. "Are you going to send Kiki to Hell?"

"Darkyn gave me a day to decide which son to send," Wynn replied.

"How could you send any of your children? I mean, isn't the parent-child bond supposed to be the ultimate bond?"

"No one dies," Wynn said and shrugged. "When you have an

eternity, when you've lived an eternity, you begin to measure outcomes differently. There's always a way to change your circumstances. You've learned this. In time, whomever is in Hell will have something Darkyn wants. When that time comes, he'll negotiate for release. Everyone lives. Everyone gets what they want eventually."

"That doesn't make it right."

"What does right and wrong matter when no one else is playing by those rules?" Wynn countered. "If the game is rigged, do you refuse to play or find a way to win?"

Stephanie said nothing.

"Kiki will go to Hell tomorrow night, unless you figure out a way to keep him out of it," Wynn added.

She knocked back the whiskey with a grimace. "What would you do?"

"It depends on how far you're willing to go to save your brother. If you're going to play by human rules then there's nothing you can do. You'll tell me in the morning you're out of the game, and you'll do exactly what I say from here on out, and what happens to Kiki is no longer your concern," he replied. "If you're willing to become your father's daughter, you will do whatever it takes to save someone you care about."

She listened, surprised to hear him sound as if he were capable of caring for anyone.

"Darkyn claims another deity was set loose as well," Wynn continued. "Any idea how that happened?"

"None at all," she mumbled.

"Good." He took her glass from her hand and rose, returning to the interior of the fortress.

"Wait," she called. "What deity was it?"

"It's not your concern now, is it?" He left.

Stephanie dwelt on the brief conversation. Wynn was right. Her distress came partially from the conflict between what she as a human would do and what an Immortal wouldn't do.

She had her own limits, namely moral ones, and wanted no one hurt in whatever route she pursued. Leaving Kiki's fate, or her own, up to Wynn was terrifying. Was it worse than taking on Wynn? Than refusing his directive to do what he wanted?

She needed help. Stephanie wiped her eyes once more, exhausted after her long night, and sifted through everyone she'd met who might be able to help her.

"Deidre," she whispered finally.

Seconds later, the demoness appeared on the lawn before her with a smile.

Stephanie rose and approached her. "Hey. Thanks for coming."

"How can I help?" Deidre asked.

"I'm wondering if there's any way I can see Fate."

Deidre considered. "You want an invite into Hell this time?"

Stephanie's breath caught.

Deidre laughed.

"Maybe I shouldn't have contacted you," Stephanie said sheepishly.

"C'mon. I'll take you to see him."

"Really? You're not mad?"

"I thought it was funny. Oh, and if someone offers to take you to Hell, make sure you specify they have to bring you back immediately after your visit is over." Deidre winked. "Demons will take you to Hell in a heartbeat and leave you."

"Seriously. I'm not in trouble with you-know-who?" Stephanie pressed. "He scares the hell out of me."

"He doesn't get mad," Deidre replied. "He does get even, though. You made his short list of people he'll one day corner."

"That sounds absolutely terrifying."

"Yeah. It is." Deidre opened a portal and waved for her to follow. "You coming?"

Stephanie hesitated.

"You don't have to be afraid of me," Deidre said.

I don't think it matters at this point. Stephanie trailed her, at a loss as to what to do next without Fate to offer some sort of insight.

Deidre led her once more into Hell, this time emerging from the place-between-places somewhere Stephanie didn't recognize. The narrow hallway ahead of them was lined with open doorways every six feet. She could see nothing in each room aside from darkness.

"Third on your right," Deidre said and pointed. "Stay in the middle of the hallway until you reach his door. Don't talk to anyone else who tries to talk to you. I'll wait here."

Stephanie absorbed the odd instructions and followed them until she reached the third doorway.

"Hello?" she whispered, pausing before it.

She held her breath and heard nothing for a long moment. Finally, stirring originating from the cell was followed by, "You shouldn't be here."

Fate's voice was lower, rougher, pained.

Stephanie froze, her imagination running wild with all the horrible possibilities of what had been done to him. Realizing she was dumbstruck and standing stupidly in front of his cell, she spoke. "Are you okay?"

"Relatively speaking." His amusement was back. "He's been messing with me. These cells are on auto-torture. I think he's probably softening me up."

She squinted into the darkness without being able to see him. "I came to complain about my own issues but … that's probably not the right thing to do," she admitted.

"I'm happy to hear your voice. Have a seat. Tell me what's happening."

She hesitated then sat cross legged before the doorway and whispered her latest adventures to him. Fate listened until she was finished – and then laughed.

"You are amazing," he said.

"I don't feel amazing. You're here, and everything else is falling apart," she replied. "Andre and Kris are in the wind, and Wynn's onto me. I need a vacation."

"Me, too. Where should we go?"

"Someplace with nice weather and no Immortals." She squinted once more, hearing him shift but unable to see him. "Are you really okay? I mean ... I know it's a stupid question. You're in Hell."

"Don't worry about me. Worry about keeping your head focused on your goal."

"Which is ..."

"Staying one step ahead or away from Wynn."

She bit back her response, hating the way it sounded in her head. She wanted to tell him it'd be easier if he were with her, and she thought her goal was freeing him, even if she were taking a rather indirect route to get there.

"You disagree," he guessed.

"I'm screwing everything up."

"The best lesson you can learn as an Immortal is to survive. It's not an easy lesson."

"How can you be so calm about this? If not for me, you wouldn't be here."

"This was part of the chain of events I foresaw," he replied.

"Really? Being tortured by Wynn and sent to Hell?"

"I believe this is penance. I'm working off my karmic debt," he said with a grunt.

"None of this is fair! It's not right to be stuck with you, then not stuck with you and kinda wish I was, at least long enough for you to show me how to deal with all these assholes."

He chuckled. "Things change rapidly."

"I'm out of ideas and worried about what Wynn will do."

"In this situation, I like to throw in a wild card," Fate said. "Someone to distract Wynn."

She listened, fascinated by the idea.

"Find Rhyn."

"Karma is looking for him. I haven't heard from her in days, so I assume she's not having any luck," Stephanie said, disappointed.

"She won't be able to find him," Fate agreed. "But you can. Describe the man you freed during your adventure into Hell once more."

She did so.

"Perfect. You're going to summon him and cash in your favor, along with one of mine," he said. "He knows where Rhyn is, and he can offer you what I currently can't: protection that can hide you even when you have your soul."

"Really? Who is he?"

"His name is Raphael, and he's the head of the guardian angels."

"Angels are real," she murmured, surprised. "Are they uh, normal? Or like everything else, kind of twisted?"

"They are neither cherubs nor innately good, if that's what you're asking," he replied. "They protect. It's what they do, and how they do it has no restrictions."

"So Raphael killing six demons is normal around here."

"Angels and demons always massacre one another when they meet." Fate's voice was sounding fainter, and concern for him caused her chest to tighten. "Summon him and ask for the two favors. Be certain to specify you want a mature protector, not a baby."

"No baby angels," she repeated, once more feeling overwhelmed. "What about you? How do we get you out?"

"Concentrate on Immortal business. I'll handle the deity side."

"Maybe I can break you out, too."

"No," he said firmly. "Even if you made it this far, these cells can be opened only by Darkyn's will."

She started to respond then stopped herself, considered briefly, and spoke. "I really do want that date. Please tell me you have a plan."

"Stephanie, I always have a plan."

The tension in her belly had uncoiled. Whether it was a result of hearing his voice again or his advice, she wasn't certain. But for the first time in weeks, she felt like she, too, finally had a plan.

"Go on. I think my break is about up," Fate said with a grunt.

She hesitated, not wanting to leave him knowing he was going to be in pain. "Thank you," she said.

"Everything will work out," he said with forced lightness.

Except you can't see the Future to know that. Stephanie frowned and stood. Gaze lingering on the darkness of the cell, she stepped away and joined Deidre in the hallway beyond the row of cells.

Dread was heavy in her stomach, and she had the urge to fling herself into his cell and hug him until the world melted away.

"Good?" Deidre searched her features.

"Yeah. I think so."

The demoness led her away and opened a portal. "Go on through. I can't do this again, but I wanted you to be able to talk to him at least once," she said quietly.

Stephanie smiled. "Thank you. Really."

Deidre mirrored her smile and stepped aside.

Stephanie breathed a sigh of relief when she crossed into the place-between-places and paced to the glowing portal leading back to the castle. She dwelt on Fate's advice, grateful for his help, while feeling equally guilty about leaving him in Hell. He claimed to have a plan, but … well, he wasn't the kind to tell her if he didn't. She didn't feel reassured about his chances of making it out of Hell, of them ever going on a date. She hadn't thought she wanted anything to do with him and yet found herself praying he survived.

She blinked out of her thoughts when she entered her bedroom once again. It was evening, and the chandelier and torches of her room beamed happily. Stephanie looked around, doubting this place would ever feel like home, and grabbed a bottle of chilled water out of the small fridge near the living area. She sat and sipped, reviewing what she'd learned fro Fate.

She didn't feel at all ready to confront yet another new angle to the Immortal world. Being back under Wynn's influence, however, left her unnerved, scared he meant to act, to trade her to Hell or worse.

Stephanie rose, hands trembling with anxiousness, and drew a breath. "Raphael," she breathed the summons.

Moments later, the man from Hell with the white eyes appeared. "You figured it out," he said, smiling.

"My mate told me," she replied.

He cocked his head to the side, as if to discern her mate by looking at her.

"Shai," she said.

His eyebrows went up. "Intriguing. A deity and a half-breed?"

"Yeah. I, uh, want to cash in my favor and one of his."

"I'm listening." The lean man with penetrating eyes had the intensity of a demon. For a moment, she was caught in one of her old thought patterns, in wondering how any of this shit could be remotely real and when good and evil became indistinguishable from one another.

Stephanie shook her head. "I need to find Rhyn. That's one," she said. "Two –"

"Wait. Rhyn," he interrupted. "He's under our protection. I can't give him up."

"But you owe me."

"You're new at this. This much I can see," he stated. "What I can do is offer to set up a meeting with him, as long as you understand he has the choice of whether or not he wants anything to do with you. I can't force him to come. Immortals have free will, too."

"Okay. That makes sense."

"In order to arrange a meeting, I must have an oath from you, signed by your soul, that you won't harm someone under my guardianship."

"Easy. I need his help. I don't think I could ever hurt anyone."

"Good enough. Two?"

"I need your protection. But not a baby angel. An older ... I mean, really mature angel," she said.

He gazed at the ceiling. "Smart. As always. Shai doesn't make mistakes. I imagine a mate wasn't in his plan, or he wouldn't be cashing in a favor."

"Something like that. And no unwritten terms or conditions or small print or catches or whatever."

"Agreed on both counts." He held out his hand.

She touched him, and a familiar streak of cold went through her.

"I'll deliver your protector within twenty four hours. Do you have a message for Rhyn? Something that might make him more willing to meet you?" Raphael asked.

"Tell him ... tell him his sister needs his help."

"Very well. A pleasure, as always." He turned and strode into a portal.

Stephanie waited until the tear in the universe was gone before sinking onto the couch. She'd phrased everything the best she knew how and managed to get him to agree. If she tripped herself up or fell into someone's trap, she'd never know it until it was too late anyway.

Drained after her day, she got ready for bed, a small bubble of hope helping her fall asleep optimistic for once.

CHAPTER EIGHTEEN

HER NEW PROTECTOR ARRIVED THE FOLLOWING AFTERNOON.
"Raphael called me out of retirement. He said you requested me specifically."

What the hell? Stephanie sighed and looked over the hunched, slender, elderly man with a cane and thick glasses. White hair created a halo around his head. She went over her request to Raphael, stuck on the word *older.* She hadn't meant it; she'd meant not a baby. But Raphael took her literally.

"I need to rest," the elderly angel said and walked to the couch. His cane clicked on the marble floors as he moved.

Was there any chance guardian angels didn't need to be able to physically protect her to do their jobs? This was yet another drop in her bucket of frustration. Instead of being angry, she felt resigned. "What's your name?"

"Mithra."

"Do you have a message for me?"

The ancient angel sighed as he sat and drew a slow, deep breath before answering. "Yes. Rhyn will meet you at noon on the Caribbean Sanctuary."

She'd given up two favors for one useful outcome. Was this

trickery common among deities? Was it why none of them trusted one another? "Is that noon Caribbean time or my time?"

"It's whatever time we are in."

My time. She checked the clock and did some basic math given the time differences. "Oh, shit. That was, like, hours ago!" she exclaimed and spun to face him. "You just got here. How the hell was I supposed …"

The angel's head had nodded forward in a doze.

Furious about being duped twice by an angel, Stephanie called a portal and hurried through it.

The thick, humid, midday air on the other side of the second portal smelled of the ocean and sunshine. She paused, gazing up at the open wooden doors of a small fortress perched at the center of a tiny island surrounded by aqua hued water.

She stepped into the Sanctuary. Someone was waiting for her in the courtyard, a towering, muscular figure with liquid silver eyes, the penetrating stare of a demon and shimmering intensity of a deity. There was no mistaking the cheekbones and skin coloring they'd both inherited from their father.

Stephanie hesitated. Rhyn appeared less than eager to be there. She approached and stopped a short distance – if there were such a thing! – from her exiled half brother.

He said nothing and glowered at her.

"I'm a half breed, too," she blurted out.

His eyes narrowed.

"Let me start over." Stephanie drew a deep breath. She repeated her story as succinctly as possible, from being discovered by Fate and Kiki, to her introduction to the politics of the Immortals and meeting a half-brother who was supposed to be dead.

Rhyn's stance changed as she spoke. His arms unfolded, and he looped his thumbs through his belt loops. His silver eyes, however, remained pinned to her face with intensity she glimpsed from Fate in the little time they'd spent together.

When she finished, she waited.

"Okay," Rhyn said in a low, gravelly voice.

It was all he said before turning away and striding towards the interior of the Sanctuary.

"Wait!" she cried, startled. "That's it?"

"I have to tell my mate where I'm going," he replied over his shoulder.

"Does that mean you're –" She blinked when he slammed open the door to a hall too dark for her to see into.

Stephanie stood dumbly, staring after him. What had she missed this time? She hadn't even asked him for anything. Suspecting she'd fucked up both of her tasks from Fate, she rubbed her face and sought the shade to escape the hot sun.

Soon after, Rhyn emerged from the hall and approached her. "I'm ready."

"For what exactly?" she asked, watching him pass her and open a portal.

"You came here for my help, didn't you?"

"Well, yeah."

"I'm going to help." He strode into the place-between-places.

She trailed him. "You have a plan?"

"I tried planning once. Hated it." He paused at the second portal and glanced back at her. "Are you coming or not?"

Stephanie scrambled after him, not at all reassured she was doing the right thing.

He disappeared into the second portal and she hurried through before it could close.

She looked around when they emerged, not recognizing their surroundings. Rhyn strode down a dirt driveway leading to a humble bungalow situated in the middle of a large, green lawn. She guessed they were somewhere in the Midwest by the fields of corn across the street.

He didn't knock but opened the door and paused in the doorway. "What the fuck are you doing?"

Stephanie couldn't see around his large frame and held her breath, prepared for something horrible to happen.

"Minding my own damn business," answered a familiar voice.

Rhyn walked into a small yet modern living area.

Stephanie paused in the doorway to see the white-haired Kris standing from his position seated at an armchair.

"Why the fuck would you let *our* sister deal with that asshole alone?" Rhyn demanded.

"My brother. Demon in a henhouse," Kris replied.

The two regarded each other intently enough Stephanie started to step back onto the porch.

Suddenly, Rhyn threw his arms around Kris and slapped him on the back in a tight embrace.

"Good to see you, little brother," Kris said, distant affection in his tone.

She frowned, puzzled by the abrupt switch from animosity to warmth. "Look, I have like a few hours until Kiki gets sent to Hell by Wynn. Is someone going to help me or not?" she asked, at her wit's end.

"Send him," Rhyn said. "He won't die."

"Am I the only one who thinks it's a big deal?"

"Wynn's bluffing," Kris replied, extricating himself from his burly brother's embrace. "Please have a seat. Both of you."

"How do you know that?" she asked.

"Because Wynn's end of the deal has been fulfilled. He sent a son to Hell, using a favor to manipulate Andre into volunteering for the privilege. If Andre escapes, it's not on Wynn. He delivered," Kris said.

"So Wynn was fucking with me."

"Probably to see what other tricks you have up your sleeve."

She considered this, unable to help the trickle of relief at the thought of Kiki being safe. Somewhat placated, Stephanie sat down.

A quiet settled over them, one that seemed out of place for the two. They were gazing at one another intently, and she frowned. Their silence stretched on.

"Um, you can't talk in your heads, can you?" she asked finally.

"Yeah," Rhyn replied. "You don't want to know some of this."

"But I want to know the plan and how not to end up in the catacombs."

Kris glanced at her. For a moment, he didn't speak. "I was telling Rhyn we have a problem."

"Just one?" she replied sarcastically.

"A new one. I've been doing my own research on how to checkmate our father," he continued. "Andre is laying low for now, but we spoke once already. Whatever Wynn wants you for, no one knows. Why he sent Kiki to find you now, no one knows. What he's willing to do to keep you in place … well, that much we can figure out. Rhyn gets his lack of limitations from Wynn, so we were brainstorming what he might be doing right now to force you to do what he wants."

Stephanie swallowed hard. "I should be involved in this conversation."

"Where's your family?" Rhyn asked.

For a moment, she wasn't able to speak. "They're human," she said hoarsely. "They're of no use to him."

"Unless he wants to manipulate you," Kris pointed out.

"I'd grab 'em in a heartbeat," Rhyn added.

"As far as I know, they're at home in Newport."

"When was the last time you spoke to them?" Kris asked.

"Last week. Before Tamer showed up in my living room."

"Wynn has them," Rhyn said without hesitation. "He's waiting to play the card until you fuck up."

She wiped clammy palms on her pants. She'd considered telling her family about the Immortals but feared their reaction or dragging them into the mess. Distance was supposed to keep them safe, and playing along with Wynn was supposed to guarantee their exclusion from his game.

"I've been doing what he wants," she said. "We don't know that."

"There is one thing we always know," Kris said firmly. "Wynn is always several moves ahead. It's what makes him dangerous."

"Assuming this is true, what do I do?" She looked between the two of them, quelling the panic bubbling inside her. "Try to find them?"

"You need to play along with Wynn."

"I am!"

"We're not yet in position to take him on. Rhyn will make sure nothing happens to you. Wynn has people hunting for Andre. Only I can move around freely right now, at least, until he discovers I'm no longer dead-dead," Kris explained. "We have allies. Namely, Wynn's enemies, and he has quite a few. Enough for us to pull away part of Wynn's power base. With the Immortals divided, we have a shot at wresting power away from him."

Stephanie listened. "But doesn't that put everyone in danger from the demons? I thought they just want to wipe out everyone."

"Yeah. We'd have to hope the castle has enough magic to hold together the breaches if we end up losing track of Wynn. His power sealed the second breach last year."

Her brothers were grim.

"But you have a plan for that, right?" she prodded. "I mean, the cost of getting rid of Wynn shouldn't be unleashing Hell."

"You sound like Andre," Rhyn grunted. "She has good political sense."

"And you have none," Kris replied to him with a smile. "Which is why you're going back to your enforcer role. You can Rhyn smash problems away again."

"Gladly. As long as you aren't in charge of the Council."

"Because I did so terribly the first few thousand years?"

"Omigod, really?" Stephanie snapped. "Andre is the only one of you I'd ever put in charge of anything, even making brownies! You people lack empathy, impartiality and any sense of the world beyond this fucked up family."

Rhyn laughed. "Definitely my sister!"

"Something about half-breeds," Kris said once more with mild disapproval. His gaze grew considering once more.

Neither spoke, but Rhyn looked at her, head tilted, as if the two of them were discussing something telepathically.

"Stop it!" she ordered. "So the plan is for me to pretend to do what Wynn wants, so he doesn't hurt my family, and until you all figure out what to do next."

"Pretty much," Kris replied. "It won't be long. I've got feelers out to a few more allies. It'd be helpful if your mate was somewhere other than Hell."

"Can't help you there," she replied. *At least I know where he is.* Restless, concerned for her mom and sister, she rose and began to pace. "There has to be more I can do than just whatever Wynn says!"

"Yeah. Keep him from figuring out you're plotting against him," Rhyn advised. "I was in charge of the Council when he blindsided me with the news I'd been voted out. To make sure I didn't threaten his position, he sends the occasional herd of assassins after my family."

She gazed at him. "I'm so sorry, Rhyn."

"Not as sorry as the assassins when I get done with them." His silver eyes gleamed. "We are all risking something by being involved in any plot to get rid of Wynn. The best you can do is stay in line and provide us information when we need it."

"And protect Kiki. He's purposely oblivious," Kris said. "Wynn's in charge, but Kiki controls everything. He knows what's at risk if he's not there, but that leaves him vulnerable to Wynn."

"Don't give Wynn an excuse to use your family against you."

Her thoughts went to Wynn figuring out her role in releasing Andre from Hell. Was it enough to tip him into action? Or was he content realizing she had nowhere else to go?

"I still don't understand why he chose now. Why you. Why your mother. Why she's alive when no one else's mother is," Kris added pensively.

"He claimed not to be able to find us," she said.

"Lie," Rhyn said. "Unless she's not human. Humans couldn't hide from him."

"God, I hope she's not special," Stephanie said, distress for her family increasing. "I don't want them involved in this."

"We need to know, Rhyn," Kris said. "Wynn's eighth child conceived during his second incarnation."

"Ask Tamer. He's the research nut," Rhyn snorted. "I'm taking Katie and Hazel to a different Sanctuary. Toby is shielding them, but I want to be sure they're out of Wynn's reach. I'll come back when I'm done." He rose.

"Meet at the Caribbean Sanctuary Saturday morning," Kris directed. "I'll notify Andre. Rhyn, tell Tamer. Stephanie, drag Kiki away if you have to. It's time for us all to sit down and hash this out together."

"It almost sounds like a plan," Stephanie said somewhat hopefully.

"I'll know everything I need to by then," Kris said.

"Steph, summon me if you get in too deep before then," Rhyn told her.

"Keep in mind Rhyn's specialty is destruction," Kris said. "Call him for a situation where ultimate destruction is required."

"If not, call me anyway." Rhyn winked. "See you Saturday."

"Wait, Rhyn!" she called after him. "Has Karma found you by

chance?"

"Fuck no. No one has."

He strode out of the cabin.

Stephanie watched him go, not at all reassured things were going to break any better for her despite the addition of Fate's wild card to the mix. But at least the six of them were going to sit down and plan how to rid the Immortals of their father. She just had to play along for four more days.

CHAPTER NINETEEN

"M'LORD."

Wynn lifted his gaze from the daily report sent to him by Kiki.

The one-eyed Immortal guard, one of the few people he trusted, looked both ways before whispering the words, "We got her."

A jolt of satisfaction, mixed with excitement, shot through him. Wynn rose. "Which *her* exactly?" he asked.

"Karma."

Any disappointment he experienced knowing his first priority was still missing was smoothed over when he recalled Karma was the sister of one of his primary enemies. "Is she in the special cell?"

"Yeah. She's asking to see you. She fell for it, like you said."

"She doesn't know she can't portal out?"

"No."

"She'll figure it out fast. Keep her occupied," he advised. "I'll be right down. Send for my daughter. Bring Stephanie here."

The guard nodded and left.

Wynn stood in quiet for a moment. For a goddess whose power came from confronting people, Karma had been elusive. He had to assume she knew this was a trap. There was no real way to manipulate Karma or Fate, not when they retained their full power. Fate he'd smashed when he had the opportunity, and Darkyn had taken care of the rest. As long as he kept the deity out of his daughter's life, he had maneuver room.

But Karma was going to be a different challenge. A dangerous one. The goddess was classified as one of the soul-eating deities, which made her potentially lethal, if she fully understood her power.

He left his study and made his way to the catacombs, through the hallway lined with regular cells, past the chamber where his former body had been imprisoned for a thousand years, and to the area only he was permitted to enter.

Four guards stood nervously outside the cell disguised as an office, where they'd managed to lure the sister of Fate. Wynn touched the wall beside the door. The power of the fortress was stronger than it had been in years, thanks to his healing magic. His power was the only reason the second breach between the mortal world and Hell, caused by the Dark One a year before, had been fixed. The reminder of how long it had taken him, of how weak he was this time around compared to his first incarnation, rendered him far more cautious.

The fortress was strong, the seals on both breaches in place, but he had no way to know if the shield around the office would stand up to a goddess.

"Stay alert," he instructed them.

Wynn stepped into the office, aware there was a chance he wouldn't leave it alive, if she proved to be unstable like many deities were. The goddess was pacing at the far side of the room, her curly red hair and light eyes changing colors the moment his energy reached her. Beautiful and rumored to be quick to kill, she was of medium height and build, shapely, and dressed in jeans.

She faced him, and he picked up on everything he needed to know from her simple look.

She knew her power.

She was completely out of control.

"You're young for a deity," he said and motioned for her to sit. "How old?"

"I came into power just over a thousand years ago but have been alive longer than either of your lives," she answered.

She's a baby. Especially if it were true she'd been trapped in the Underworld for a thousand years. "Your age starts when you assume your duties. By this rationale, I'm older," he said with a smile. He sat across from her.

"If you seek to toy with me, I will –" She leaned forward, her eyes flashing black.

"Easy," he said and raised both his hands, staying as still and calm as possible. He picked up on her energy, the not-so-subtle shifts, the restlessness at odds with his quiet power. He was a man of control, and she was a loose cannon of the worst kind. "No one's toying with you. We're here to talk."

She searched his features and stood abruptly, returning to her pacing. "I want my brother back, Immortal," she snapped at him.

"That's not how negotiations work."

"I don't give a fuck. I'm a goddess, and you're … not." She waved a hand at him dismissively.

"You know I don't have your brother."

"I saw what you did to him." This time, her energy receded around her so fast, it nearly sucked the air from the room.

Wynn remained seated. The goddess was highly unstable, more so than any he'd ever run across in either of his lives. "He and I have a history," he said. "He killed me the first time around. At least I spared him."

She rolled her eyes, and her grip on her power loosened once more. "Your people said you had a plan to help me get him out of Hell."

"A deal," he corrected her.

She paused in her pacing and tilted her head curiously.

Sensing her relative receptiveness, he crossed to the alcohol staged on the edge of the desk and poured himself a drink. He offered her a glass, but she shook her head. "Are you willing to make a deal with me?" he asked.

She hesitated, scrutinizing his features hard.

Wynn had no doubt as to the stiff warning her brother had probably given her about deals.

"No," she said finally.

"Even to save your brother?"

Another pause. This time, she frowned, troubled. "He wouldn't approve."

"Is his life more important than his approval?"

"Of course it is. But I can't deal with one of you."

"Immortals?"

"Ancients."

"He warned you against me specifically?" Wynn was almost impressed he warranted a by-name mention.

She nodded. "But you can help me, or I'll balance you," she said, a predatory gleam in her gaze. "Something tells me you have a lot to atone for."

"Too much," he agreed with a small smile. "One day, I'm sure you'll serve me the justice I deserve. But not today. Today, we're having a civilized conversation about how to help your brother."

She planted her hands on her hips. "I won't make a deal with you."

"Have you been to Hell? Do you know how much worse it is than your cell in the Underworld?"

"Darkyn can't kill him."

"So it doesn't bother you he's there because of you. Interesting." He poured another shot of whiskey and sipped it, eyes on hers. His game of patience, of forethought, of control had gotten him this far.

She was dangerous, but he had come too far to cower before any goddess.

"What do you mean?"

"You balanced him, for one. It's the only reason I was able to exact my revenge and Darkyn is doing the same."

She glared at him. Before she could object, he spoke once more.

"Darkyn's called in every deity ever to have a bone to pick with your brother. He's letting everyone torture him. Do you know how many people that is?"

A flicker of worry was in her eyes. Wynn sensed he had her where he wanted her, assuming she remained focused on her brother's plight.

"It's pretty much every deity," he answered. "Your brother has a lot of enemies, and because of you, they're getting their chance to fuck him up."

She looked away and began to pace again. "But I'm helping him. Balancing helps people."

"As long as he survives."

She tensed.

"You want him to survive, don't you?"

"Of course I do!" Her emotion was in her eyes and tone, despite the distrust written across her face.

"One deal. It's all I need to help him," he lied smoothly.

"What kind of deal?"

"A favor."

She shook her head.

"What is his life worth to you? Or are you too afraid to deal with me?"

She went still. Wynn glanced up and realized he'd overstepped, confronted her directly instead of keeping the focus on Fate. The predatory look was back. She was young on the scale of deities – but wise enough to understand she had the upper hand.

"His life is worth more than yours," she growled.

Wynn stayed in place, not about to run when he knew he'd never reach the door before she reached him. He forced himself to remain calm outwardly.

Karma approached and circled him, close enough for her restless energy to graze his skin. "There is no balancing you," she assessed. "Not that I'd bother trying. I think I'll just kill you."

"Is that wise?" he asked softly.

"I don't give a fuck about *wise!* Your own daughter fears you, and my brother hates you. I would be pleasing both of them by ending you."

"And if I told you I'm the only reason the breaches to Hell are closed?"

She stopped in front of him and looked up at him. "I don't care," she replied in the same quiet tone. "I'd rather have your soul."

"Then you'd condemn your brother's mate to Hell. If I die, the breaches open, and Darkyn claims everyone."

They stared at one another, neither willing to back down, though he sensed Karma cared for Stephanie, if only because she loved her brother. For a split second, he had the sense he'd met his match when it came to there being no boundary he wouldn't smash to get what he wanted.

And then she stepped back. "You would do it, wouldn't you?" she murmured.

"I would," he replied. "Would you?"

She appeared to be arguing with herself. He didn't dare relax, not when he couldn't use his secondary power on a wary deity to play upon her fears.

"Yeah. I would."

Before he could react, she'd snatched his arm with inhuman speed. Her eyes turned black, and cold fire tore through him.

But he didn't flinch, didn't cry out, didn't panic, no matter what she was doing to his insides, no matter how dark his mind was growing. He stared her down, tense and stiff, unwilling to lose when he was so close to winning.

Her power swirled around them, sucking the air from his lungs.

And then, just when he felt like his body was about to implode, she released him.

Karma retreated, staring at him. Her power pulled away, though the searing coldness remained in his system. His body began to heal itself – but this level of damage was new to him.

Wynn released a breath, uncertain why the goddess hadn't finished him off. She had the ability and the resolve. She could destroy him too quickly for him to recover.

She wasn't moving, wasn't speaking.

"Until further notice, you'll remain here," he said with calmness he didn't feel. "If you reconsider my deal, summon a guard." He turned his back on her and left, sealing the door behind him. "Remember, no on goes in. Communicate through the speaker system," he told the guards.

They nodded.

Wynn left this wing of the basement. He waited until he was out of sight of any of them to lean against the wall and assess the damage she'd done. Pain rippled through him, and he gritted his teeth against what remained of her power. Five seconds more, and he'd be dead-dead.

Why wasn't he? Had he grown careless or reckless? He gripped the wrist where she'd grabbed him. Everything was healing, except this wound. It still burned with cold fire. Holding it, he left the catacombs.

He hated mysteries and the unknown or any variable with the potential for unpredictability. Returning to his study, he began scanning through his books for the secret diaries he had created about the deities his first time alive. He had never crossed paths with

Karma before, but there was a chance he picked up knowledge about her secondhand, somewhere, sometime.

If there wasn't a reason for her sparing him in his journals, he'd have to uncover the truth as to why he was still alive another way. Normally capable of discerning a person's motivation, he was drawing a complete blank with the wild goddess in the catacombs. There was no room for error in his plan; he needed to understand what made her stop.

On the slim chance it was his Immortal power, the ability to heal, he would find a way to use it against her before he subjected her to the wheel and the one-eyed Immortal who headed his interrogation program.

"You wanted to see me."

He'd forgotten Stephanie. Wynn lowered his hand from the bookcase and turned to face her. With some unease, he realized he wasn't back to normal from Karma's attack. His insides were shaky, and sudden movement caused the room to blur and his mind to start to close in on itself again. His power was working hard to fix him, but he wasn't ready to deal with anyone.

"Um, I can come back," she said, a terse note in her voice.

"I'll only take a moment of your time." With a deep breath, he faced her, his charred wrist behind his back.

Stephanie eyed him. "You look ... unwell."

"It's been a rough week," he said. "Have you reconsidered inviting your family here? Our spies say Darkyn is becoming more active. He's interested in you and might consider your family a target."

She flushed, and her eyes lit with fire. She spun and started to leave.

"I'm not finished," he said quietly.

Stephanie froze in the doorway.

Wynn took a moment to assess his options. Stephanie would

never reveal the whereabouts of her mother or invite her to the fortress. He was surprised her mother hadn't made an appearance yet. The amount of stress Stephanie was under from all directions was immense, not to mention the natural rivalry existing between Stephanie's mate and mother.

He'd increased the pressure on by grabbing and imprisoning Stephanie's half-sister in the hopes having both girls under his control would drive their Unseen deity mother out of hiding. Still, the goddess was silent. If Fate's claim, and Wynn's emergence into Stephanie's life, hadn't flushed her out, he was going to have to take more drastic measures.

Measures he didn't want to, especially not to the daughter he'd always thought he'd wanted.

But … he'd expected this to be the case. He was still disappointed by it, by the discovery Stephanie was everything he had hoped she'd be, just like his sons were. With her soul, she'd be the one child he'd place money on who was capable of carrying on in his place, of keeping the breaches sealed with the magic inherited from him and her mother, and preventing the Immortal society from crumbling.

She'd be able to undo the damage he was doing in order to return to the place he'd been right before he died-dead. He took no joy out of hurting his children, even if he was never able to openly mourn them either.

"Never mind," he said. "Enjoy your day."

She glanced at him, perplexed, and walked away.

He grimaced and gripped his wrist, unable to soothe the burn.

CHAPTER TWENTY

THE MANDATORY FAMILY DINNER WAS TENSE AND AWKWARD AS usual. Kiki appeared to ignore everyone, his iPad beside his plate and eyes glued to the screen.

Stephanie looked from him to Wynn, wanting so much to tell her father what she thought of him after his threat to send Kiki to Hell, of how much she hated the feeling of terror nestled at her center. She'd tried calling her sister and mom no less than two dozen times today without reaching either.

As the day progressed, she began to believe Rhyn and Kris.

The idea of her mother and sister in Wynn's clutches, however, sent her emotions spinning out of control whenever she dwelt on it. She'd managed to push aside her fear during petitions, but seated beside Wynn, she couldn't stop thinking about them. About where in the castle they might be, about how he was going to torture them like he had Fate.

Her sister would fight, and her mother …

Images of his torturers stripping Fate's skin from her body made her stomach revolt.

Stephanie dropped her utensils, vaguely aware of being close to hyperventilating. Kiki was staring at her, though Wynn's unconcerned glance pushed her closer to exploding. She pushed away from the table and bent, placing her head between her knees and breathing as steadily as she could.

Her brother knelt beside her. "You get used to feeling like this." Kiki's whisper was accompanied by the cool, wet cloth napkin he draped across the back of her neck. "You shouldn't let Wynn know what he's doing to you."

She squeezed her eyes closed, hearing the wisdom in his words, as usual, without being able to reel in her emotions. "I hate him," she said hoarsely. "I *hate* him!"

"Sssshhh."

"Does she need a healer?" Wynn asked coolly.

"No," Kiki replied. "I think she's still adjusting."

Stephanie focused on control, on being more like her brothers, who seemed generally immune to the cruelty of their world. Kiki remained beside her until her breathing grew steady, and the urge to vomit or pass out or scream was gone. She tugged the napkin from her neck with trembling hands and repeated the advice the others had given her mentally. She wasn't used to feeling trapped, to being so out of control of her life and circumstances.

And her family was in the clutches of a psychopath who was waiting for her to fuck up so he could torture them in front of her.

"Thanks," she said, glancing at Kiki. "I'm okay."

He nodded and rose, returning to his seat across from her. Stephanie took another deep breath and straightened in her chair, tugging it closer to the table once more.

"Everyone keeps telling me not to piss you off," she said to Wynn. "But not telling you how I feel is like swallowing poison. I can't do it."

Wynn looked at her fully for the first time since dinner began. Traces of whatever illness he'd had earlier remained in the tightness around his mouth and the lines beneath his eyes.

"You threatened to send my brother to Hell, to find my family, to kill my mate. There is no place for someone like you in any world, mortal or immortal, and I pray for the day when you really see and understand how many lives you've destroyed and how little you really are."

Kiki's mouth was agape, and even Wynn appeared not to be expecting her scorching words.

Stephanie felt better than she had all day, even knowing the consequences of her short speech were probably going to be very bad.

Only Mithra's quiet snores from his position dozing at the other end of the table broke the silence.

"I'm sorry to hear you feel that way." Wynn placed his napkin on the table and stood. Without another word, he left the dining hall.

Stephanie barely remained in her chair, her fear stirring again. Was he going to order her mother tortured? Kidnap her sister and send her to Hell?

"Kiki, I need you to tell me something," she said quietly. "Does Wynn have my mother and sister in the catacombs?"

"He wouldn't tell me if he did."

"But you know everything that goes on around here. Maybe more rations are going to the catacombs? Extra electricity? Something?"

"Was I the brother he wanted to send to Hell?"

"What does it matter?"

"I have to decide if I want to help you or stand back and let Wynn fuck you up after your speech."

"Yeah, you were."

Kiki studied her. "I suppose he would've fucked you up anyway. You might've expedited it." He picked up his iPad and a roll from the basket. "I'll let you know what I find out. Enjoy your last meal." He motioned to the spread with his roll.

Knowing the danger of her words, she nonetheless didn't regret them. No one spoke the truth to Wynn. Whatever his plan for her, she hoped he focused his rage towards her and not her family.

She could handle anything but him hurting her loved ones. Allegedly, the elderly angel was supposed to help protect her.

"Mithra!" she called to the sleeping guardian angel.

He stirred without waking fully.

"Mithra!"

He jarred awake. "Dinner is over?" He staggered to his feet and blinked, squinting at his surroundings. "I don't remember walking here."

"Holy shit." Stephanie squeezed her temples briefly and stood. Her hope of having any defense standing between Wynn's anger and her melted. "I'll show you back to our room."

"The demon has to stay here."

"There's no demon here."

He lifted his cane and pointed towards the balcony, one of whose doors was propped open to allow the cool, woodsy air to circulate.

She faced the balcony. "Mithra, there's ..." *something there.* Startled the sleepy angel got anything right, Stephanie snatched a knife from the table and hurried to the angel's side.

The familiar frame of Trayern moved into the room. "I've been assigned to you," he said, glancing around in thinly veiled disgust. "Darkyn's orders. Seems he doesn't want you sneaking into Hell again."

"This isn't Hell, and I don't give a shit," she replied. "Leave, before I call the guards."

"Call them. Wynn granted the Dark One's request." Trayern gave a fanged smile.

"This day can't get any worse."

"I can think of many ways it can."

"Mithra, is this true?" She glanced at the angel.

He drew a deep breath. "Perhaps. He could not be here without Wynn's permission."

"I'm unarmed." Trayern held out his hands and slowly

approached the table. "What is this? Food?" He picked up a handful of roast beef and scowled at it. "No wonder your kind is so weak." He tossed it into the fire.

Stephanie gazed at him, unable to determine if the demon was purposely fucking with her or serious. She wasn't entirely surprised the Dark One was taking measures to prevent her from returning to Hell, since he couldn't sense her enter his domain. Neither did she think Wynn would refuse the demon guard, since he, too, seemed to want to keep her in check.

Trayern's unwelcome presence made too much sense for him to be lying. He was going to make it impossible for her to slip away anymore. She could wait for Mithra to doze off when she wanted to disappear, but something told her Darkyn's favored demon wasn't going to be as easy to evade.

"You two can handle being around each other, right?" she asked.

"He is alive because I am ordered to observe not interfere." Trayern growled.

"Same," Mithra replied and slammed his cane onto the ground. "But that can change, demon."

"Bring it, old man."

Stephanie didn't know what to do about her unfriendly and unhelpful entourage. The idea of being in the company of a demon made her stomach less stable. The deeper she walked into the Immortal world, the more she wanted to flee.

She left the dining hall, shoulders hunched for a demon attack, and strode through the fortress, needing air.

Wynn was on the stairs where she'd gone to breathe the night before. She stopped the moment she recognized his form, anger and fear stirring once more. She wanted nothing to do with him, especially not this night.

"Your mother did you a disservice," he spoke before she could leave.

Stephanie tensed, fear fluttering through her at the mention of her family. "I think I turned out better without you in my life."

He glanced back at her. "Walk with me."

"No."

"Walk with me, and I'll tell you where your sister is."

Stephanie glared at him, unable to know when he was bluffing and when he was truthful. Gritting her teeth, she joined him on the steps. He descended at a trot and waited for her.

They began walking towards the forest, trailed by the silent demon while Mithra sat down heavily on the stairs of the fortress. Stephanie's gaze lingered on him before they slid to Trayern, who seemed to move through the shadows. Which was worse? A demon or Wynn?

"How long have you had my sister?" she asked.

"Several days."

ABplan was right. Wynn was always so far ahead. His speech about giving her a chance to back out of their game was hollow. He had already trapped her in it. How was someone like this dealt with? Uncertain what to do about someone who had already outsmarted her, her attention went to their path. Wynn was leading them towards the lake.

"Did you really agree to let a demon follow me around?" she asked.

"I did."

This is so fucked up. "Where is my sister?" she asked, managing to keep her voice level.

"Safe. She put up quite a fight. Almost killed two of my Immortal guard."

It definitely sounded like Sammy. Stephanie shoved her hands in her pocket, canning her panic before it could bring her to tears.

"I had hoped you'd back down. Realize your place. Stay out of the game," he said. "You're too much like your mother."

"I think I'm more like you," she replied.

"You are so much more like me than you know. But you share traits with your mother as well." His smile was knowing. "Tell me about her. Tell me how different from me she really is."

"In every way," Stephanie said vehemently. "She's hard working, kind, smiles a lot. Beautiful inside and out. Smart like you but not evil." She sighed, the image of her mother in her mind saddening her. "What did you do with her?"

"Your mother eluded me, as usual. Left your sister exposed and alone for me to pluck up."

"My mother has no idea what you are," Stephanie replied. "She'd defend us both to the death if someone tried to hurt us."

"Then you know nothing of your mother. If this is true, why hasn't she appeared to help you yet?" he challenged.

"Because she has no idea this weird sub-world exists! I haven't told her anything!" she cried in exasperation. "How many times do I have to tell you this?"

They reached the lake, and he paused, facing her.

"You think I'm stupid?" he asked.

She shook her head.

"You think I wouldn't know you're sneaking around with your brothers? Plotting to overthrow me?"

Stephanie's mouth went dry. But this time, she didn't take his bait. "I don't think the plotting around here ever stops, no matter who's in charge."

His smile was unusually warm. "You are my daughter. As much as I hate to say it, you're cut out for this," he said. "I'm certain your mother hated that about you."

"What are you getting at?" Stephanie asked, perplexed. "You guys had a horrible divorce or something? You're pissed at her twenty three years later?"

"Fate didn't tell you?"

"Stop trying to drive a wedge between me and him!"

"Then you're accepting your place with him."

She hesitated. "I don't know. I haven't had time to think about anything. I'm stuck in this insane spider web with a dozen different spiders getting ready to eat me. The only thing I know is I can't trust you. I can't trust him. I can't trust anyone, except maybe Kiki, because he's just trying to keep everything from falling apart."

"What do you know of Fate?"

Stephanie grappled with the answer. "Everything and nothing."

"It's not possible to understand a god fully," Wynn said. "Fate has the power to bring the world beneath his thumb and the discipline not to use it. What does that make him?"

"I don't know," she whispered, struggling with the same question.

"Neither do I. But after many years, I have a way to motivate him."

"Me."

"The deities require a much harsher approach than humans and Immortals. They have eternity, and some have lived for an eternity. Every once in a while, you can catch one off guard, and you have to act when the chance appears."

"I get it. You've been waiting for Fate to slip."

"Not just Fate." Wynn gazed around them, as if expecting company.

Stephanie's head was beginning to hurt trying to figure out his game. "What're you talking about?"

"I wish we'd started off on better terms or perhaps, a better understanding of one another," Wynn said. "If I'd found you sooner, I could've raised you correctly."

Her eyebrows shot up at the ridiculous claim.

He pointed to the sky. "What do you see?"

It's one insane moment after another. But Stephanie looked, because she didn't know what else to do or say. "The moon. A bunch of stars."

"I had hoped it wouldn't come to this, but your mother drove me to this point."

She dropped her gaze just as hot fire slid between her ribs. Stephanie's body exploded with sensation: agony, warmth blooming at her chest, horror. She looked down to see Wynn's hand around a knife buried to the hilt into the side of her ribcage.

She gasped and pushed at him. Wynn pulled the long knife free, and Stephanie dropped to her knees. Darkness was already starting to form around the edges of her mind, and blood gushed over her hands as she tried to stop the bleeding.

Too shocked to understand what was happening, she stared at the darkness spreading across her light t-shirt, at the black-red blood gleaming in the moonlight …

Wynn moved away from her and tossed the knife, arms crossed as he watched.

"What … what the fuck are you doing?" she gasped out. Tears sprang into her eyes.

Trayern stood nearby, surprise on his features. After a moment of indecision, he knelt beside her. "Darkyn will torture me eternally if I fail him again." Did he say or think his deepest fear aloud? The line between her mind and the world was blurring. He pressed both hands against her wound.

This isn't right. This isn't fair. Dizziness swept through her.

"Lie back." The demon pushed her onto her back and whipped off his shirt to reveal a muscular chest covered in tattoos. He tore the shirt into strips with his fangs.

"Summon her, daughter," Wynn said, drawing near. "You will die if you don't."

Stephanie gave a strangled cry of pain as Trayern shoved a wad of t-shirt against her wound.

"He has struck your artery, a favorite source of food for demons,"

Trayern said, leaning his weight against her. "Bad for you, though, human."

Her eyes drifted closed, and her thoughts began to race erratically, out of her control.

"Human, stay awake." Trayern shook her.

She opened her eyes and stared through a layer of tears at Wynn, who towered above them both.

"C'mon. You're my daughter but you're also hers. Summon her," Wynn said and knelt beside her. "Only you can."

The image of her mother was in her head, but whatever Wynn wanted her to do, she didn't know. "Andre." She whispered the name of the brother most likely to help her and started to slide into darkness.

"Awake!" Trayern barked, shaking her again.

"Summon. Her." Wynn ordered through clenched teeth.

This time when Stephanie's eyes closed, she couldn't open them again. She began to float and then fall and then … nothing.

CHAPTER TWENTY ONE

IN HELL, FATE FELT A JOLT OF SOMETHING BEYOND ANYTHING HE'D experienced yet. Hot, cold, tearing, searing ... the sensations woke him from a brief reprieve from his auto-torturous cell. His body convulsed, and sweat broke out on his brow.

He assessed himself quickly and went over the types of pain he'd so carefully categorized.

This wasn't one of them. This was new – and worse, for it felt like he was being shredded from the inside out, like every molecule in his body was trying to escape the others. He curled onto his side, waiting for the sudden seizure to stop, unable to understand what this newfound horror was. It emanated from his core and spread throughout him, a maddening anguish with no particular source – but at home all over his body.

His sluggish mind cleared with adrenaline and pain. Her nerves were screaming, and he sought some explanation from anything he'd learned over several hundred thousand years. What could possibly cause him to feel as if the soul within him was exploding?

Stephanie.

Fate's eyes flew open, and he stared into the darkness of his cell.

His bond with Stephanie would hold traces of the power of her lineage, even if she couldn't access her deity power without a soul. Their bond would contain what part of her magic Stephanie inherited, the dormant power she couldn't access.

In the darkness of his cell, with his mind pushed to its limits, one name came to his mind. There was only one power that could single handedly produce a body with no soul and tear apart a soul, the way his was being shredded now.

Stephanie's mother.

He clawed his way into sitting, doubled over, and gasped as his soul thrashed within him. Of all the deities he could call upon for an emergency favor, only one stuck in his mind, the one he wouldn't have to promise the universe to, the sole goddess capable of creating Stephanie when he took every precaution possible to ensure she didn't exist. His triumph at figuring out the mystery of Stephanie was fleeting, replaced by newfound agony.

Go to your daughter, he willed the elusive deity he suspected was Stephanie's mother.

He hissed as another wave of pain tried to tear him apart. He huddled on the floor, holding himself together with pure will.

Gradually, the screaming of his soul and body grew weaker until it finally stopped. Fate collapsed against the floor, gasping. Tremors worked their way through him.

Better late than wrong, he told himself.

"My turn."

He lifted his head. Yet another deity stood in the doorway. He had no chance to summon Deidre or anyone else who might tell him what happened to Stephanie to cause this level of pain. The sense of helplessness cored him, but he refused to let it shake his confidence and purpose. He wouldn't be able to help her if he didn't survive Hell.

Whatever was happening to her, it had stopped. For now. He had faith the goddess in question wasn't going to let Stephanie suffer again.

"Darkyn sent invites to the bottom of the barrel, I see," he said and pushed himself to his knees. "Have at it. But remember – when this is over, I tend to be vengeful."

"I'll take my chances Darkyn never lets you out," was the smug answer.

Fate smiled, as much because he wasn't going to show fear to anyone as from the knowledge he had a plan, even if it took a while for him to execute.

Hang in there, Steph.

CHAPTER TWENTY TWO

THUMP. THUMP. THUMP.

Stephanie snapped awake at the strange sound and into a sitting position, gasping in air. Her vision cleared. She was back in her room at the fortress. She touched her side without feeling any wound or bandage and yanked her sleeping shirt up to see the damage.

There was none. Not even a scar.

It felt so real. She looked again and began to calm.

Her guardian angel was on the couch, watching talk shows. On the opposite side of the chamber, in front of the door, the guardian demon leaned back precariously on a chair and flung knives into the closest wall. They landed with soft thumps and small bursts of dust as he chiseled away at the stone.

"So the demon part was real." Stiffness lingered in her side, as if her body were recalling the pain from her dream.

She stood. She was dressed normally in a soft t-shirt and her underwear, except she didn't recall getting ready for bed let along falling asleep here.

"Well, you're alive." The demon glanced at her. The front legs of his chair slammed to the ground. He stood, tucking his knives away as he approached her.

"What're you ... hey!" she swiped at his hands. A wave of dizziness made her stumble when she tried to move away.

"So fucking hungry." He gripped her arm and yanked her into place before him. "You know what I want to do to you?"

She lifted her hands to protect her neck.

"Then I suggest you don't fucking fight me. Your mate warned you."

She didn't have the energy to resist anything.

He tugged her shirt up to check the nonexistent wound.

"It was real?" she asked uneasily. "Wynn stabbed me?"

"He'd make a good demon." Trayern released her and moved away, back towards the door.

A chill swept through her. Kiki had said Wynn wouldn't hurt his children, just exile them. The memories of what happened were fuzzy, unclear. She recalled accompanying Wynn to the lake, talking to him, sharp pain when he stabbed her and then ... nothing.

The bored demon sat in his chair again and began throwing knives at the wall.

"Dude, that's not your wall and I doubt you'll pay to fix the damage you're doing," she snapped.

"Why do you give a shit? It's not your wall either." He glanced at her with a low growl and began flinging knives again.

"Whatever. Why am I not dead?" she asked.

"It's almost seven. Don't want Wynn to stab you again if you don't show up where you're supposed to be."

She gave him an icy glare. So it wasn't a dream, and her father had just randomly decided to stab her. A quick look at the fading light told her it was almost time for the evening dinner, which was going to be a nightmare.

"One day soon, I'm going to snap and take every single one of you with me!" she snarled and went into the bathroom. She slammed the door and screamed, not caring who heard her.

When she was breathless, she sucked in a deep breath and leaned against the marble counter, staring at herself in the mirror. She looked super healthy considering she'd been stabbed near death. Memories of the pain lingered, and her thoughts took on a grimmer track.

Was that what Fate was going through in Hell every second of his day? Pain so bad she couldn't think of it without flinching? How had he survived Wynn?

Her anger slid away, and a different kind of ache filled her at the thought of the enigmatic deity who had volunteered to go to Hell in her place. Mate or not, she was grateful to the stranger who sought to spare her what she went through at Wynn's hands.

After witnessing what he'd do to force her to listen to him, she was considering bowing out of whatever game she had entered. "Just do whatever will keep Wynn off your back," she told her reflection. She rested her palm on her abdomen, and she thought of her sister, imprisoned somewhere in the castle. The rage inside her was beyond repression. "No. Fuck that. Fuck *him*. He's already tried to kill you, Steph. We're not doing that again."

Not that she knew exactly what to do. Whatever it was, she wasn't backing down from him like everyone claimed she should. Backing down got her sister kidnapped and herself stabbed. She'd play nice until she knew where her family was, and then, all bets were off.

She got ready for another grueling family dinner, oddly energized despite her near death. If anything, Wynn had crossed a line, and some of her fear of him was gone. She no longer had to wonder what he'd do to her; she knew.

She whipped open the door to leave and found Kiki in the hallway with no iPad in sight.

"How are you?" he asked anxiously.

She smiled, touched by his concern. "Good. Thanks."

"You're not a real member of the family until you've been dead-dead or tortured." He stepped aside for her to exit.

She joined him, and together they began walking. "Good to know."

"What exactly happened?"

"I don't know." She dwelt on the fuzzy memories. "We were talking then bam. He stabs me, and I wake up in bed."

"He's never done this to any of us. I don't have a fucking clue what he was thinking. Andre brought you back here. He wouldn't tell me what happened either. "

She gazed up at him. "Did you find my family?" she asked.

He glanced over his shoulder at her demon escort and shifted closer. "Your sister is here. Not in the catacombs. He's got her secluded in a tower."

"Can we get her out?"

"She's under heavy guard and the tower is sealed against portals."

Stephanie was quiet, thinking. "Sounds like a job for someone specializing in destruction."

Kiki started to smile. "You might want to consider a subtler approach with Wynn."

"No. I'm done with subtle. He won't have the chance to lay a finger on my sister. Rhyn can get her out."

"I'll contact him."

"I thought no one knew where he was."

"News spread fast about Wynn stabbing you. Of course everyone reached out to me and totally fucked up my schedule," he said, irritated. "You've been out for three days, and tomorrow is the reunion."

"It's Friday," she murmured, uncertain why that made her heart race. Fate had promised to meet her for their date. She clung to the idea, too traumatized by Wynn to face the idea Fate couldn't come if he was trapped in Hell. She needed hope in any form.

"I haven't found any evidence your mother is here."

Stephanie hesitated. As sure as she was about today being special, the unwavering instinct telling her that her mother wasn't in danger was just as mysterious. "Get my sister somewhere safe," she said. "Please."

"I will. I promise," Kiki said.

They paused out of earshot of the guards outside the dining hall. The sight of the double doors filled her with dread. Already her heart was racing, and her hands were clenched into balls.

"I can tell him you're still recovering," he offered.

Stephanie shook her head. "No. I refuse to be afraid of him anymore. I can make it through dinner." *Even if I throw up afterwards.*

"Let's do it." He strode forward and opened the door for her. The scent of hot food made her stomach grumble, and she stepped towards the feast awaiting them.

"Stinky human food," mumbled the demon trailing them.

Stephanie was two steps inside the door before she wished she'd listened to Kiki and stayed upstairs. She froze in place. Seeing Wynn was bad enough, but the sight of the slender woman with dark hair and bright blue eyes standing at the mantle nearby smashed her newfound defiance.

"Mom?" she squeaked.

Panic wrestled with surprise. Neither emotion won, and she stood in place until the demon knocked into her as he passed.

Stephanie rushed to her mother with a scared look towards Wynn. "What are you doing here?" she demanded in a whisper. "Did anyone hurt you? Are you okay?"

"I'm fine, sweetie," her mother said with a warm smile. "Are you?"

"Never mind me," Stephanie took her mother's hands and led her farther from the others. "Mom, you have to get out of here. These people are dangerous!"

"I can take care of myself, Steph." Her mother replied. "I'm so happy to see you're okay." She rested her hands on Stephanie's cheeks and kissed her on the forehead.

Stephanie sighed, happy to see her mother but horrified of dragging her into the Immortal mess. "I'm so sorry, Mom," she murmured. "I tried to protect you all."

"I should've warned you."

Stephanie frowned.

Her mother glanced towards the table, where the others sat quietly. "Come on. Let's sit down." She moved away, leaving Stephanie by the fire.

Stephanie watched her, suddenly aware of how calm her mother was. On her first night in the Immortal world, she'd had a meltdown, but her mother sat down at Wynn's right, appearing unfazed by any of this.

"What's going on?" Stephanie asked. She sat on Wynn's left, beside Kiki. "Mom?"

"I think we know why Wynn picked your mom," Kiki whispered.

"I don't understand."

"Your mother's not human." Wynn's first words made her tense. She looked at him hard. "You're a half breed still. Half-deity, half-Immortal."

Stephanie waited for her mother to refute Wynn. Nothing came.

"Your mother is one of the Unseen deities, those whose singular purpose expired, or who retired or who otherwise no longer had a position as a god or godling," Wynn explained. "Your mother is Chaos, a creator goddess, from the time-before-time, one whose purpose was no longer essential once creation began. It took me two lives to find her. The Unseen remain unseen for a reason."

Stephanie stared at her mother.

"I had hoped you'd be able to live a normal life." Her mother said with a sad smile. "I kept you protected for as long as I could."

"You're saying this is real." Stephanie wanted to explode, and yet, it was just one more veil being lifted from her world. Her anger turned to pain, and she resigned herself to having another layer of her feelings sent through a cheese grater. "You knew what I was."

"I did. Wynn was clever. I didn't know when we met what he was." Rachel Jennings' gaze slid to the man beside her. "When I figured it out, I left him and hid both my daughters from a world I never intended you to know. We moved often to keep him from finding us."

"You're ... Chaos. What does that mean?"

"I came to be celebrated as a bringer of disorganization and mayhem. But originally, your grandmother was one of the first deities, a primordial soul with no body, an eternity of nothing and everything."

"I don't understand," Stephanie whispered.

"No one really can. Think of it this way. Before there was time, there was Chaos, the goddess capable of creating order and disorder," her mother said. "I'm third generation, born after the purpose of Chaos was obsolete, but retaining some influence over disorder and order."

"So Grandma was primordial stew and you are Chaos." No one was who or what they seemed in either world.

Kiki was texting madly. Stephanie assumed every one of her brothers would know about this by the time was dinner over. Of all the insanity in her mind, she couldn't think of anything to say. Wynn had been right all along – and she *hated* this most of all.

"I'm sorry for hurting you," her father said. He even managed to appear sincere, further driving her into her confusion. "I've never purposely hurt any of my children."

"It's my fault," Chaos said sadly. "I was in denial. I wanted so much more for you, Steph. You and your sister are the only good parts of my life. I wasn't ready to lose you and kept hoping Wynn would just let you go."

"He'll never let any of us go," Stephanie whispered hoarsely. "Ever." She gazed at her father.

"I won't," he agreed. "This is where you belong. As for your mother …"

As if sensing Stephanie's fear, Chaos smiled. "He can't kill me like the others. Don't worry."

Stephanie sat in silence, uncertain how anyone was so calm about any of this. Her mother seemed resigned rather than angry, and Wynn wasn't cheering at finally bringing her mother to the fortress.

The grandfather clock above the mantle chimed seven thirty, and abruptly, she didn't care whether or not Fate was able to make her date. She wasn't going to sit here and witness the rest of her world fall apart.

"I have to go," she said and stood.

Unable to speak to anyone, she fled the dining hall, trailed by her demon guardian, and raced through the hallways. She didn't slow until she was outside, and the cool night air helped calm her feverish thoughts. She walked into the forest, towards the lake, recalling when she'd last been there with Fate.

He'd promised to return. If ever she needed a miracle, it was tonight.

Wild desperation made her ignore the fact he was in Hell, while deep confusion prevented her from wanting anything to do with anyone in the fortress.

She reached the lake and paused, holding her breath to listen to her surroundings. The sounds of night – swaying trees, rustling animals, hooting owls – were accompanied by the restless pacing of a hungry demon behind her.

"I thought you'd forget." Fate's deep voice came from her right.

Stephanie faced his direction. The moment her body registered his presence, she began to lose control. Feverish desire flooded her. It was a hundred times stronger, rawer, than anticipating her first kiss at the age of fourteen. Each meeting entrenched the instinct she belonged with him, that he was the only real home she'd ever have.

He appeared well, though exhausted. "I didn't think you could come," she breathed, silently fighting back elation, the latest emotion she wasn't certain what to do with.

"The power of a vow between mates, conveniently made before I made my deal with Darkyn. He had no choice. But, like Cinderella, my time is up at midnight," he added.

She approached him. Heat bloomed within her in anticipation of his touch, his scent, his heat. She watched his eyes change colors, mesmerized by them, by the draw that only grew stronger between them, by the acknowledge of how his touch alone was able to quiet her confusion.

The tension between them had grown almost thick enough to be seen.

"I almost died this week," she said in the heavy silence.

"Me, too." Fate smiled. "And here you thought we had nothing in common."

She almost smiled. His sense of humor was growing on her, as twisted and inappropriate as it was. As always, when they were together, she was also no longer alone. She was the eternal companion of a man who controlled the Future. Whenever she looked at him in this light, she was able to pull up her barriers and combat the charismatic man who made her heart flip in her breast.

"Is it bad I trust a man no one else does and distrust everyone I should?" she asked, thoughts on her family. Pain flickered through her at the idea of her mother hiding such a secret. She wasn't ready to face this new reality. Not yet. Not when she had Fate muddling her senses and could think of nothing more than feeling his arms around her.

"Nah."

"I hate that," she said in frustration. "I ask a serious question. And you know what? You could give me any answer in the world, and I'd just want to accept it."

He stretched for her hand and drew her into his body, until they barely touched, and the sparks of their bond flashed between them. His gaze was on her face, waiting for her reaction to their nearness.

Stephanie was already melting, already tumbling into him. His effect grew harder to resist every time they met. She craved him physically with need that terrified her to feel so out of control. When they touched, she had a difficult time justifying why she shouldn't just throw herself into the bed of the man she barely knew.

"Are you okay?" he asked and touched her cheek.

"No," she whispered honestly. Caving to the primal instinct that took over whenever they were together, she flung her arms around him, shivering as the familiar flash of energy raced through her. "I can't do this."

His hard body, and familiar scent, threw her senses into disarray and managed to make more of a mess of her thoughts. The baffling attraction between them, the sense of being drawn to someone who scared her, crippled what was left of her resolve. In his arms, she was safe enough to want to cry.

"But you *are* doing it," he whispered, warm lips against her ear. He nuzzled her neck. "You're stronger than I am."

"Stop teasing me."

"Really, you are. The other day, I saw a rat in my cell and screamed for an hour."

She started to laugh. "I'm being serious!"

"And I'm not?"

She pulled her head back to look at him. He was smiling.

"You'll find the strength because you know these fucked up people, and their fucked up world, need you," he said and cupped a cheek in one hand.

"They don't need me."

"They're self destructing and have been for quite some time. The daughter of Chaos and Wynn is probably the only person in the universe who can return order to the Immortals."

"You knew about my mother?"

"I suspected she was one of the Unseen without knowing which one until you dying almost tore me apart."

Her breath caught. "I'm so sorry." She reached up to touch his face instinctively and trailed her fingertips across his firm jaw as she'd once fantasized doing. His warm skin was rough with stubble. The longer they were in contact, the more she wanted to mold herself against his lean frame. His intensity, the edge she glimpsed often of the man solidly in command of something as dizzying and unpredictable as the Future, scared her, and yet, she wanted to be closer to him now more than ever. "Are you okay?" she asked and studied him.

"I am now."

The reminder of the temporary nature of their time together disturbed her. They stood in silence, gazing at one another. She could pretend the rest of her world didn't exist when they were touching. It had always been so easy to dismiss anything outside of them, to trust the instinct rejoicing over the fact she'd finally found where she belonged.

"This scares me," she admitted.

"It's unsettling," he agreed. "But not bad."

I don't know if that's true yet.

Desire rocked through her, warmer and warmer, the longer they touched. Her eyes went to his lips and the memory of what it had been like to kiss him. He wasn't just her home. He could also become an escape, a refuge from herself and the world that grew more terrifying each day. He understood their world in a way she never would.

Stephanie rested her hands on his warm cheeks and drew his face to hers. She kissed him lightly, uncertainly, waiting to see what he wanted. His passionate response left her breathless, weak in the knees and without a kernel of doubt.

"I have a plan," he whispered. "Step one, we need to get rid of our clothes. Step two, we talk. Objections?"

She hesitated, understanding exactly what he meant. Her body screamed for her to agree. "Go easy on me. I don't have a billion years of experience," she said with an uncertain laugh.

"Easy? No. Gentle, yes," he said with a slow smile.

A thrill shot through her and added to the furnace blazing in her lower belly. "No objections."

"Open a portal. We aren't walking that far," he said with a husky laugh.

Stephanie shifted away. His arms remained around her, and it took two tries for her to open the portal. Moments later, after kicking out her angel and locking the demon out, she stopped fighting the flood of need, embattled emotions and confusion and melted into the arms of her mate.

CHAPTER TWENTY THREE

FATE SUSPECTED A NIGHT WITH HIS MATE WAS GOING TO BE UNLIKE sleeping with anyone else. However, the truth floored him. The fusion of their bodies, her flavor and husky voice, the look in her eyes when she climaxed ... every second was borderline orgasmic, and every climax greater than all of those he'd ever experienced as a deity combined. Even the simplest sensation of his skin against hers was mind numbing. Combined with desire amplified by his human state and several hundred thousands of years studying the female form, fucking his mate was all he'd ever know of peace or heaven.

When he'd worn her out, he wrapped her in his arms, unwilling to let go of the single greatest discovery he'd ever made. Any confusion as to why any almighty deity would take a mate sizzled away in soul-deep passion. For a species incapable of feeling, a mate became as necessary as air or water or any of the other essential elements.

Stephanie's ragged breathing grew steadier, her sweat-slicked skin cooling. He was aroused again already and doubted he'd ever be able to touch her without being ready to rip off their clothing. He breathed in her scent and admired everything from her smooth skin to her warmth to the faint smell of lavender in her shampoo. He did his best to absorb everything about her, mesmerized by the experience and understanding his parole from Hell was possibly the only reprieve he'd ever received.

"Why did we wait so long to do this?" he whispered and nipped her earlobe.

"I think you were in denial."

He smiled at the saucy response. "I apologize for torturing you for so long then."

She laughed quietly and lifted her head from the nape of his neck to see his face. Hers was flushed, her lips roughened from kisses and eyes sparkling. It was the most relaxed he'd seen her. Her pliant body was his to command, and he sensed this was a release for both of them.

Fate pushed away the nagging instinct that drove him to be concerned about the time for the first time in his life and instead, studied the woman he was destined to share a life – and power – with, assuming he outlived Hell.

"I don't want this to end," she whispered, and shadows darkened her gaze.

"But it will. At least, for tonight."

Her smile faded.

"Stop," he chided. "We both need this. We both need each other right now." He traced her high cheekbones and forehead with his forefinger.

"Please tell me you have a plan."

He considered telling the truth but found the words stuck in his throat. Stephanie's vulnerability, the emotions in her eyes, left him feeling raw as well, afraid to reveal just how bad their situation really was. "I always do," he lied. "But it's going to take some time."

"I think something bad is coming."

He said nothing, aware of the same.

She told him of all she'd done and seen, including Wynn stabbing her, since her visit to Hell. Fate listened, sorting through the events and placing them – when possible – in the chain of events leading to the possible Futures he'd been tracking before he lost his power.

When she finished, he hugged her more tightly. "The good news is the Future isn't set," he whispered. "There's time to change the worst from happening."

"The worst being ..."

"Civil war among the Immortals. Darkyn isn't the only one who would leap at the chance to take advantage of their disarray. As poorly effective as they are, they are at least a major speed bump standing between any ambitious deity and humanity."

"Makes me hate Wynn more. He must know what he's doing is going to hurt everyone."

"Wynn would make the quintessential deity. No one has ever understood the source of his madness, not before his first death, and not now," Fate mused. "He's brilliant and lethal and driven towards an end we've been speculating about since he emerged as a figure of power among the Immortals."

"How can gods not know what he's thinking?" she asked and propped her head up to peer at his face.

"It's generally suspected he's an illegitimate half-breed, the son of a deity and Immortal."

"Like me."

Fate smiled. "Yeah. Although, you were raised as a human. You lack the edge prevalent among my kind and theirs."

"You mean, I'm not an asshole," she said.

"Precisely."

"So no one knows his parentage or what he wants."

"He's killed anyone who did. Everyone took an interest in him when he united the Immortal factions and families under one roof. He wiped out entire races of Immortals who refused to capitulate and exiled others. But he did the impossible – he united them. In the process, he killed anyone who knew his true origin. He took on deities as eagerly as Immortals, which was unheard of before him. The lines between deities and everyone else were very clear, very rigid, before Wynn upset the balance of every realm he touched," Fate explained. "It was then that the rumors spread he must be part deity in order to cross those lines, to survive as he did."

Stephanie's gaze was pinned to him. She rested a hand on his neck, absently stroking the sensitive skin beneath his ear.

"When the Immortals were obedient, he stopped the wars and took seven mistresses over the course of several thousand years. After each gave birth, he killed her. He himself was murdered after a very complicated, long standing plot involving no less than six deities."

"You were one."

"I saw his madness first," Fate said. "I saw what it would do if he wasn't stopped." He dwelt on the Future he'd Seen many ages before. "But Wynn had an ally of the second most powerful deity in existence, Death. He foresaw his own murder and they worked together to achieve mutually beneficial outcomes."

"The twin Deidres," she said. "Why didn't you stop him?"

"It's complicated."

Her eyes narrowed. "You and your secrets. Will there ever be a day when you can share them?"

"No," he replied. "There are things that can never be spoken about, deals which will never be recorded, events and Futures only I can ever See and even Seeing them, still may not choose to prevent."

"Which is why you've always been alone."

"The Future is a burden. A beautiful one, but a burden nonetheless."

She nodded, pensive, chewing her lower lip. "And you don't like sharing your power."

"No."

"How does this work?" she asked carefully.

"Us?"

Another nod.

"I don't know yet," he replied. "I cannot share some things with you, ever."

She drew a breath. "Okay. I can live with that. I saw some of what you do when I asked the Oracle. I … I don't think I want to know everything you do. But it would be nice … I mean, if this all works out," she rolled her eyes, "and it's not just amazing sex, then it'd be cool to have, you know, a partner."

Fate understood what she was trying not to ask, namely, if the man who worked alone were capable of sharing himself with someone else. It was another question he didn't feel ready to answer.

"Sorry. I went all serious on you," she said, her blush deepening at his silence. "We can just do the sex thing."

"I kinda like it," he teased.

"How did I stack up to a trillion years of lovers?" she asked.

"You surpassed all of them combined."

Her gaze warmed.

"Do you trust me yet?"

"Not really," she replied.

He chuckled. "I love your honesty."

"Maybe I do. I guess I must if I'm in bed with you," she said, puzzled. "I don't know what to think. I just know I really like being with you here like this."

"I want you to listen to me," he said and rested his hands on her cheeks. He nudged her onto her back and settled between her legs. Her breath caught, and she gazed up at him. "You are my mate, and I claim you in every way possible, by the laws from the time-before-time and the laws of our world."

She listened with rapt attention, and he resisted the urge to fuck her until he'd said what he had to.

"But there are rules, and you must follow them. You can never reveal the Future to anyone, other than me. Whatever the Oracle showed you, you can never share it. Do you understand?"

Stephanie nodded.

"Second, I alone can interfere with the Future and do so at will. No matter what you See, you cannot act. Ever, and you cannot ask me to change something, no matter how much pain it may cause you."

"I don't plan on looking again," she murmured.

"Third, I will never allow anything to come between us, and you must promise me you will do the same."

"What do you mean?" she asked.

"I don't know if I can be the person you need, expect or deserve. I will act in ways you won't understand and perhaps may not be able to accept or forgive me for. I will keep secrets, and I will push you away to protect you from what I know I am."

Uneasiness flickered through her gaze.

"Everything I do is to protect you and the Future. It won't be easy for you to witness, and people are going to try to exploit you and your fears."

"You want me to promise not to be a liability," she said.

"Yes."

"Because you can't trust anyone else, even your mate."

"Because there may come time when you must choose between me and say, your family."

"That's not how this works," she said and ran her fingers through his hair. "But I will promise you can trust me, and I will do everything in my power never to betray that trust."

Ever cautious to the wording of deals, Fate dwelt on her declaration, uncomfortable with it. But he suspected his true concern was the vulnerability she created by simply being in his life.

"I wouldn't know how to trust," he said finally.

"Just say okay. This is how you start," she replied, smiling.

"Okay. We'll try it your way. Fourth rule, don't return to Hell. I need a promise for this one."

She hesitated once more. "I have hopes of breaking you out."

"No. It would interfere with the deal I have with Darkyn," he said. "Promise me."

She nodded unhappily.

"Fifth, whatever happens, try to prevent the Immortals from falling into a civil war. That will mean sacrifices, possibly even siding with Wynn against your brothers."

Stephanie studied him. "Is it that bad? Whatever you Saw?"

"It could be. I know what deities like me would do if it happened."

"When you say things like that, you terrify me."

"It's the truth."

"It's not. At least, not for you. Whatever you are, you're not cruel. You're not the monster Wynn is."

The simple observation, spoken with hushed confidence, intrigued him.

"You sacrificed your freedom for me twice. I don't know what to think about your duty to control the Future, or the things the Oracle showed me, but I know you're not doing them out of malice. You care on some level," she said.

He didn't respond. Her insight was too personal, too intimate, for him to know what to say.

"I know ... well, I suspect, you lie to me sometimes," she said. "I need an honest answer to something."

He waited.

"Is this the only night we'll be together like this?"

Something inside of him broke. He'd been carefully avoiding such a thought, unable to handle the idea of a single night with his mate. Hope, edged with pain, was in her eyes. Knowing she wanted more was torture when he was blind to the Future.

"I don't know, Stephanie," he whispered. "If it is, it won't be because I don't want another. I will always want another, and I will always protect you, wherever I may be."

"You're the only person who makes sense in this fucked up place."

He laughed despite the ache in his chest. "I've never had anyone tell me that."

"It's true. Crazy but true. I think I could handle this, if you could stay with me."

"I've never heard anything so beautiful."

She swallowed hard. He saw the fear in her eyes. "We're almost out of time." She pulled his head down to hers and kissed him hungrily.

Fate wasn't about to resist, not when he sensed the same desperation from her kiss he, too, was experiencing at the idea of never holding her again.

CHAPTER TWENTY FOUR

HE DIDN'T TRUST HER, MAY NEVER SEE HER AGAIN, AND SHE'D slept with him anyway.

The next morning, Stephanie remained in bed later than usual, breathing in the scent of Fate lingering in the sheets. She was sore in places she didn't realize had muscles, but it was her heart that hurt the most. She didn't know what to think about the man she couldn't keep her hands off of, his cryptic warning about civil war, or the idea their one night stand was all they may ever have.

Was all this how the Immortal world worked writ large? Two strangers were thrust together as mates then wrenched apart just when they started to fall for one another?

It seemed ... wrong. And terrible.

But if she had the choice between being in his bed for one night, without his love and trust, and not being in his bed at all, she already knew she'd choose him every time. And that frustrated her more than anything, the powerful bond trapping people in a world where they were already fucked.

The boom of thunder drew her gaze to the French doors leading onto a balcony. The chandeliers of her bedchamber trembled. It was clear and sunny out, without any sign of a storm lurking.

Sensing something was wrong, Stephanie flung off her covers and dressed hastily. Pulling on her shoes, she tied her hair back as she hurried to the door. When she opened it, her two unwelcome guardians were both across the hallway at the windows.

"What was that?" she asked, squeezing between them to see.

Black smoke billowed into the sky from a part of the fortress she wasn't able to see. She strained to see more, thoughts on the promise Kiki had made her the night before about getting her sister out of the tower where Wynn trapped her.

She couldn't see what was going on from this angle and darted down the hall to the nearest stairwell, not slowing until she was standing on the back lawn. The Immortal nobility living in the fortress, along with quite a few guards, were gathered, pointing and whispering. She joined them, trailed by the demon.

"Hey." She tapped the arm of one of the Immortal guards. "What's going on?"

He started to brush her off but looked back at her, recognition in his face. "Someone attacked the north tower. You should be inside, my lady, where it's safe."

Safe my ass. She hadn't been safe since landing in this nightmare. Unable to see what tower he referred to, she returned to the interior of the fortress and went to the second floor, open only to members of her family, where a flurry of guards were moving in and out of Wynn's study.

Unable to decipher what she felt for the man destroying her world, she hesitated to approach him and instead, went down the hallway around a corner, to a quiet area.

"Chaos." She summoned her mother, partially hoping it wouldn't work, and the part about her mom lying to her for the entirety of her life was wrong.

"Hi, sweetie," her mother's voice was warm and friendly, as always.

Stephanie's heart fell. "Hey, Mom." She faced the direction her mother came from and watched the portal close behind her. "Sammy okay?"

"Someone grabbed her before the tower collapsed."

Kris hadn't been joking about Rhyn destroying things.

Kiki crossed the hallway and paused, retreating his steps and waving to catch her eye. Stephanie glanced towards him. He gave her a thumbs up, which she assumed was a sign her sister was safe, and then tapped his watch.

Stephanie recalled it was Saturday with some dismay.

"I think we should talk," her mother said, pulling her thoughts from the meeting she was supposed to attend.

"Yeah, probably," Stephanie replied. "Would be nice to know why no one told me my mom was a goddess and my dad a psychopathic Immortal."

"To be fair, I did tell you he was a psychopath."

"Calling an ex-lover a psychopath and talking about a real live psychopath are two different things!"

"After I check on your sister, we'll all sit down and talk," Chaos promised and began walking away.

"Wait, mom. Is her father a psychopathic Immortal?"

"No. He was pure human. A good man."

Stephanie bit back the anger flaring at the sight of her mother walking away, as if today were normal and not the day she crushed the hearts of both her children with the truth.

She turned away and breathed deeply, calmed by the scent of Fate on her skin. How fucked up was her world that the man who could comfort her was him? She called a portal and started through, stuck in her thoughts, when someone snatched her neck.

"Escaping?" Trayern growled.

"I'm not escaping!" she strained to be away from him and then stopped when his long nails bit into her skin. "You're just slow."

"I'm not slow," he said, offended. "Where do we go?"

"To a Sanctuary."

He pushed her into the portal. "Lead on."

"Where's Mithra?" she asked, facing him.

"Dead-dead. Or not. I don't give a fuck."

Stephanie shook her head and strode forward to the yellow door beckoning to her. She slid through, followed closely by the demon, and emerged into the morning brightness and heavy air of the Caribbean Sanctuary.

Four of her five brothers were waiting outside the Sanctuary's walls. She slowed and glanced back at the demon guardian trailing her.

"I'm not going to escape, but they'll probably kill you if you follow me," she told him.

He was quiet, taking in the four. "Fine."

Surprised he agreed, she strode away anyway. Whether it was the beefy size of Rhyn and Tamer, or something else, she didn't know.

The sight of Andre caused her muscles to relax of their own accord. Stephanie smiled at him and approached, hugging him with a sigh.

"Good to see you," he said and squeezed her. "We're waiting on Kiki before we start."

She released him and stood back, observing her brothers. Rhyn was pacing, Tamer frowning, and Kris staring at the demon.

"Hey, you get in trouble?" she asked Tamer.

"Eh. Fired," he replied with a shrug. "Better than the alternative. Gabe usually kills those who fuck up."

"Fired doesn't sound so bad," she agreed.

"Your sister's safe," Rhyn told her. "Freaked out and crying but safe."

She started to smile. She would've liked to see Sammy – a kickboxing champion, perfect student and the only one in the family who remembered to send birthday cards – freaking out. It made her feel a little better knowing her tough sister was having a hard time coping, too.

"What is he doing here?" Kris asked, indicating the demon with a lift of his chin.

"Wynn agreed to let Darkyn's minion stalk me so I don't break into Hell again," she replied. "He saved my life the other day, after Wynn tried to kill me."

This brought the attention of all her brothers on her. Stephanie explained what happened.

"I knew your mother was special!" Kris exclaimed when she finished.

"Doesn't really help us to understand Wynn any better," Andre commented.

"Who cares? He has to be stopped," Tamer said.

"Hey, guys," Kiki emerged from a portal. "Had to make up an excuse to leave." He shook everyone's hands, and the six of them stood in silence for a long moment.

"How long's it been since most of us have been together?" Andre asked, a warm smile on his face.

"I'd like to say too long, but that'd be a lie," Rhyn replied, eyeing his brothers.

Stephanie watched them make small talk curiously. A tense edge, softened by the presence of Peace, was present, and their distrust of one another was clear. Their guards were up, with the exception of Andre. She dwelt on what she knew of Wynn, of what Fate and others had shared. He'd selected their mothers purposely over more years than she could fathom and today, they were plotting to overthrow him.

Just how smart was Wynn? Smart enough to know this day would come? Smart enough to already have the next move planned so whatever they did, it wouldn't matter?

"Down to business," Kris said. "I think we all know why we're here."

"To get rid of Wynn for good," Rhyn said.

"Out of curiosity, why can't one of you just walk up to him and ... I don't know. Shoot him in the head?" Stephanie asked.

"Wynn's healing gift makes him hard to kill. He has enough allies in place that such a move would start a war," Andre replied. "We can't afford a war."

"I think it's the only way to get rid of Wynn and those who support him for good," Kris said.

"We can't leave our people, or the humans, exposed to the demons."

"Then we make it a fast war," Tamer chimed in. "We walk in, take out everyone in a position to fuck us up, and it's done."

"And Wynn either opens the gates to Hell on his way down or doesn't try to stop the breaches from reopening. Anyone recall how Darkyn split the plane between the two worlds when his mate was taken to the Underworld last year?" Kiki countered. "And how Wynn's healing power has always been the source that kept the demons at bay?"

Silence.

"If Wynn leaves for too long, that breach opens back up. We have to go back to the old way."

"We get the point, Kiki," Tamer snapped.

"What's the old way?" Stephanie asked.

"When we kept his body in the basement so his magic formed a barrier the demons couldn't cross," Rhyn explained. "Our brother, Sasha, stole his body two years ago."

"His first body. Not the current one," Kiki added.

She frowned. They'd all imparted some part of their history to her since she entered the bizarre world. The details they spoke of, and how Wynn was alive twenty-three years ago to impregnate her mother, emerged slowly from the depths of her mind. His soul had been taken and incarnated into his second body by Past-Death as part of a deal they had made. Meanwhile, his first body had been kept at the fortress to repel the demons while Wynn 2.0 secretly roamed the human world.

"The castle sits on the site where Darkyn originally breached the mortal world, soon after the beginning of time," Andre told her. "The second breach was made mere months ago, but in the same area. Our castle is there to prevent them from coming through."

"Here I thought it was the beautiful surroundings," she murmured. "So we're sitting on two doorways to Hell."

"The fortress contains its own magic. Wynn's power amplifies it. We don't need Wynn, so long as the fortress can prevent the breaches from opening," Kris stated.

"We don't know how much of the seal on the second breach is linked to Wynn," Andre pointed out.

"Darkyn almost destroyed the fortress recently. We survived," Tamer added. "We don't need to overthink this. We just need to act."

"Well, let's vote," Kiki said. "All in favor of outright attacking Wynn and his allies, raise your hands."

Rhyn, Tamer and Kris raised theirs.

"Opposed?"

Stephanie reluctantly lifted hers. Andre and Kiki did as well.

"This is when it sucks to have an even number of siblings!" Tamer complained. "What the fuck are *you* thinking, Stephanie? Didn't he try to kill you and kidnap your mom and sister?"

"Yeah, and I hate him for it," she retorted. "Maybe it's different in your world, but no civil war is quick, and the scars it'll leave to wipe out Wynn's allies aren't going to heal quickly. I deal with those fucking petitioners every day. If you think there isn't a great deal of resentment toward any of us, you're stupid. The vast majority of the Immortals I've spoken to hate our family. Who's to say there won't be a second civil war once we get rid of Wynn?"

"Brava, little sister," Kris said. "I won't vote with you, but at least you're thinking like one of us. Our family is in power because we have a tendency to crush any opposition. It's what the enforcer role has been. I did it for years, and Rhyn took over."

"You know Kiki will never speak out against whoever's in charge," Tamer baited.

"Fuck you, Tamer. You've never had to deal with picking up the pieces!" Kiki shot back.

The two of them began arguing.

Kris said something Stephanie didn't hear, and Rhyn turned on him with a sharp response. Within seconds, all four were arguing.

"Is it always like this?" she asked, dismayed.

"Always," Andre said. "Wynn turned us against each other before we were even born."

"I don't understand. How have you all lived for so long like this?"

"We were born in a different time, a much harsher one. Combined with our father's selective breeding, we're incredible survivors. But very poor at working with anyone else."

His explanation managed to soothe the part of her that began to doubt they'd ever walk away from this without starting some sort of war.

"Your sister's inside." Andre pointed. "Go see her. I'll straighten our brothers out."

"You want help?"

He smiled. "I've played this role long before becoming Peace."

Good luck. Stephanie left and went into the fortress, towards the doorway he'd indicated. She knocked before entering and walked into a rustic cafeteria filled with well-worn, wooden tables, a stone hearth, and wrought iron chandeliers.

Two figures sat in front of a television propped above the hearth, and she recognized the shape of her blonde sister. A third person,

Hannah, the woman who had helped her break out of Wynn's at one point, was helping nuns in brown robes chop vegetables on a table nearby.

"Sammy!" Stephanie cried with more excitement than she wanted to show and raced to her sister.

Sammy rose and turned a split second before Stephanie tackled her in a hug.

"Please tell me this is a nightmare," Sammy whispered, bear hugging her in return.

"I wish."

"You get used to it," said the amused woman beside them.

Stephanie held her sister until certain she was real then released her. Sammy was ten shades of pale lighter than her with blonde hair and dark eyes. They were both tall like their mother, though Sammy was athletic where Stephanie was slender.

"You're really Rhyn's sister?"

Stephanie turned to face the woman seated by the fire with an infant in her arms. She was young, around twenty, with dark hair and large, blue eyes. The mating tattoo, *Rhyn*, scrolled around her neck.

"Yeah," Stephanie said.

"I'm Katie." She stood and held out her hand. "This is your niece, Hazel."

"Don't wake her up," Sammy advised.

"Awww, does she get cranky?" Stephanie shook Katie's hand then leaned closer too peer at the chubby face of the cherubic Hazel.

"Uh, not quite." Sammy pointed to a nearby table, where it looked as though a vase of flowers had exploded. "That's what happened when I tried to hold her."

"She has her father's temper and power," Katie supplied. "She tends to blow things up when she's throwing a fit, unless Rhyn or I am holding her."

Stephanie looked from the baby, who wasn't yet a year old, to the exploded vase. "Wasn't expecting a laser baby," she said after a pause. "I guess I shouldn't be surprised."

Katie laughed.

"She's so cute, though," Stephanie shook her head.

"The cuter, the more lethal," Katie said wisely. "You figure that out after you meet your mate for the first time. So sexy. So about to destroy your world." She sighed dreamily.

"Mate? What're you talking about?" Sammy asked, frowning.

It was Stephanie's turn to sigh. "Later, Sam. You guys are safe here, right?" she asked Katie.

"We are. And we have an angel, so he obscures whatever it is that trips off people looking for us."

"So that's what they do," Stephanie murmured. *Maybe I should make an effort to keep Mithra around after all.* She'd envisioned him fighting off demons with his cane and dying, then felt bad thinking she'd be responsible if that happened. But if him being with her meant no one could find her, he was more useful than she thought.

"They have access to libraries of information, too. Millions of years worth of memories from other angels," Katie said.

"Is that helpful?"

"Not usually."

Stephanie grinned. Of everyone she'd met, Katie was the first real person she could relate to stuck in the Immortal world.

The door opened, and Andre entered. He smiled at Katie as he joined them.

"How's my little niece?" he asked, eyes on the infant. He reached for Hazel, and Katie cringed as she handed her daughter over.

"Careful," Sammy warned and took a step back.

"She's sleeping. Maybe ... well, never mind." Katie said ruefully.

Hazel's eyes opened, and she peered up at Andre with the same liquid silver gaze as her father. Power sparked between her chubby fingers.

"You weren't joking." Stephanie moved away.

"You won't hurt your uncle, would you, sweetheart?" Andre asked with a smile and took one of the fists sparking with power.

Stephanie shrank back, uncertain how powerful the child was. But the baby smiled, and her power dissipated at Andre's touch.

The three of them breathed a collective sigh of relief.

"See?" Andre asked.

Stephanie wasn't surprised. She'd hugged him the first time they met, seconds after experiencing his gentle, calming power.

"You want to babysit?" Katie asked.

"My pleasure," he said with a chuckle.

"Steph, Andre! Your turn to vote!" Kiki called from the entrance to the cafeteria.

"Stay here, Sammy," she told her sister. "Mom's with me. She's okay, too. Just don't leave somewhere where you're safe."

Sammy appeared ready to rebuke her. The competitive older sister was even less interested in being told what to do than Stephanie.

Andre handed Hazel back to her mother.

"Laser baby and I will take care of her," Katie assured her before Sammy could speak. "Rhyn won't let anything near any of us."

Stephanie nodded, somewhat relieved to know the powerful half-demon was going to safeguard her sister. She and Andre went to the door, joining Kiki, who walked outside the walls, where the others were stewing in silence.

"Three for war, one no," Kiki reported.

"So no progress?" she asked.

"Rhyn and I traded sides."

She shook her head. "No to war."

"No to war," Andre seconded.

"Dammit!" Tamer snarled.

"As I said. Let's try this from another angle first," Andre said calmly. "Kris is working with allies inside the Immortal communities. I'm attempting to find deities who won't fuck us over too badly in the process of helping. We have some breathing room, at least for now."

"Wynn is too unpredictable, and he always, *always,* knows when something's going on," Kiki said. "Andre, we don't have much time. Why can't we go to plan B and assassinate him? Take the risk his allies won't act?"

"Because he probably has a fail safe for this situation. As usual."

Kiki sighed in exasperation and checked his watch. "Steph and I have to get back. He's constantly on alert around us. We can't make him more suspicious."

"Bet you're kicking yourselves now for voting me out," Rhyn said, arms crossed and glare on Tamer.

"Wynn would've killed you," Andre said. "It's the only reason you were voted out. To protect you."

"So I'm supposed to be happy with the status quo?" Kiki asked and raked a hand through his hair.

"No. But we need to be patient," Andre urged.

"Why don't we try voting *him* out?" Kris suggested. "It won't get him out of the castle, but it'll get him out of his position. If we're all there to keep him in line, he'll be more limited in what he can do."

"That won't stop him," Tamer replied.

"We could at least keep an eye on him," Kris said, though she heard his doubt.

"A knife through his skull. Even he can't heal that," Rhyn muttered.

"Vote him out, then kill him," Tamer agreed.

"Killing him could unleash the demons," Andre said with mild impatience. "You can't forget the bigger picture in your haste to exact some sort of revenge on him."

The four of them eyed one another in silence once more. Stephanie sensed they weren't going to agree on what should happen to Wynn, even if they did manage to vote him out. Despair drifted through her thoughts.

"We have to do something," she said. She looked up at Andre.

"Voting him out is a temporary solution," he said. "We can then decide on what to do with him. When is the next Council meeting?" Andre asked Kiki.

"We meet every morning at eight," Kiki replied. "Or ... we could all corner him at dinner, before he has a chance to sniff out what we're doing."

"If we present a unified front, we have a better chance, I suppose." Kris didn't sound convinced or supportive. "And we risk the chance he saw this coming and has a trap waiting for us."

The others were silent, glancing at one another.

"Let's vote. All in favor?" Andre asked and raised his hand.

Stephanie's hand shot up. The others did so reluctantly.

"I'm pleased to see we're unanimous. This is the first step we'll take," Andre said, satisfied.

"It's no use if we can't agree on what happens next," Tamer snapped.

"One thing at a time, Tamer. We'll decide his fate tomorrow."

The former death dealer snorted.

"C'mon, Steph. We can't be away too long or he'll get suspicious. Bring your fucking demon or the nuns will shit." Kiki stalked away, opening a portal as he went. "See you all tonight. Might be the last day of our lives."

Stephanie looked at Andre. "Go. I'll find you later," he said.

She trotted after Kiki, trailed by Trayern. They entered the place-between-places, and she caught up to her brother.

"Hey, what's up? You aren't usually the pissy type," she asked and took his arm.

"I get sick of Tamer giving me shit for trying to keep things together," he said and pulled away. "And for constantly being the guy who has to clean up after whomever is in charge flips out or leaves. Voting Wynn out with no follow-up plan has disaster written all over it."

She studied him, unable to help the flicker of warmth for her unappreciated brother. "You want a hug or something?"

He eyed her.

"You're doing amazing, Kiki," she said with a genuine smile. "I honestly don't know how you do it. Just don't stop, because you're the backbone of this family."

"What is this? Why are you saying these things?"

"It's called compassion, and it's what you do around family."

"I'm not sure I like it."

"Whatever." She swept past him through the portal and entered the gym at the bottom of the fortress. When Wynn didn't pop out of the woodwork to confront them, she released a breath.

"You have the morning off and petitions at noon," Kiki informed her. "Don't be late."

"Thanks." She left, afraid of being spotted with him and arousing Wynn's suspicion. She debated what to do with her free time, until she recalled the conversation she needed to have with her mother. *I don't think it's something you can ever feel ready for.*

Stephanie returned to her room and glanced at Mithra, who had resumed his spot on the couch. She paced briefly, ignoring the demon who took up position at the door and began throwing knives into the wall. When her heartbeat was no longer flying, she summoned her mother once more.

Rachel Jennings appeared with a sad smile, as if she, too, understood what they had to talk about.

Stephanie sat on her bed and grabbed a pillow. She wrapped her arms around it and breathed in Fate's comforting scent deeply, preparing herself for another round of shock. "Okay. Tell me everything."

The bed sank beneath Rachel as she sat cross-legged across from her. They'd sat this way a lot when Stephanie was a child, and her mother had told her fantastical stories to get her to take naps.

"There's a lot to say," Chaos said somewhat awkwardly. "Where should I start?"

"Maybe with how I'm alive when I have no soul."

"Because I wanted you," was the quiet, warm reply. "Because, at one point, I was convinced I loved your father. It was the only time I used my power, to ensure you came into existence."

"Your power is what exactly?"

"At the elemental level, to create form where there is none or to disperse form where it exists. I knew something was wrong the moment you were conceived, but I wasn't willing to let you go. So I did what my kind does."

"But why?"

Chaos laughed. "Because I love you. You're my daughter."

"But every deity I've met is psycho. Why are you not?"

Her mother shrugged. "Maybe it's the benefit of not being involved in the games the others play. My mother and I were left alone, viewed as obsolete. Retired."

"Did you plan on telling us?"

"Eventually. I hoped to give you both the space you needed to live your lives outside of all this." She waved to the room around them. "But ... I think I was in denial. I assumed, if you never crossed your mates, you'd never be mated or forced into learning about the Immortals and their world."

"I wish," Stephanie murmured. She was relieved to learn her mother hadn't created her as part of some sick game to manipulate others. "You swear I exist because you love me?"

"I promise." Chaos smiled once more.

"Did you know who my mate was before you saw the tattoo?"

"No." Her smile faded. "I'd have chosen otherwise for you. The

Fate family has a reputation carried over from the time-before-time."

"You don't have to tell me," Stephanie said quickly. "I can guess and if I'm wrong, I don't want to know." She cleared her throat. "Did I inherit any magic powers from you?"

"I can't tell, because you have no soul. Immortals can pass their unique talents, assuming they have any, onto their offspring. Deities pass down partial powers, about fifty percent of the time. Your true power lies in your family, both the one you were born into and the one you mate into."

"I'm an important pawn."

Chaos sighed. "I never wanted this for you."

They sank into silence interrupted by the thump of knives into the wall and the angel's snoring.

"He's, uh, not that bad," Stephanie ventured. "Fate."

"I hope he's treating you well. You're sacred, even to him."

Stephanie nodded, relieved once more to hear someone she trusted reassure her. "What happened to your mate?"

"It's a long story. Not one I care to retell."

At the hushed note in her voice, Stephanie looked up. Her mother's eyes were on her wringing hands. Sensing something dark in her mother's past, Stephanie was quiet, dwelling on just how much she didn't know about her parents. She quieted such thoughts. If she let herself grow paranoid about everyone, she'd become as caustic as her brothers. No, she needed to trust someone, or she'd go insane.

"Wynn used me to get to you," she said. "We have to get you out of here."

"I won't leave you, Steph."

"Mom, whatever he wants from you, it's probably horrible."

"No one invites Chaos in with good intentions," Rachel said. "He'll kill you again over and over to bring me back. If I leave, you must come with me."

"I, uh, well …" Stephanie squeezed her pillow harder. "I feel like

I need to stay. To help my brothers."

"Wynn has you trapped."

"No. I mean, maybe. But isn't it my responsibility to stop him? He's my father."

"It's not. This mess isn't our fight."

"I'm a part of this world, Mom, whether or not I want to be. My brothers are family, too."

Her mother pursed her lips.

"You can take Sammy and hide again," Stephanie said. "At least, until we take care of Wynn."

Agitated, Chaos stood. "I won't leave you here for him to torture."

"Then he'll torture us both to get what he wants!"

"Or we leave!"

Stephanie rubbed her face. When had she gone from needing to flee to needing to stay, to help her brothers? How did she have any loyalty to a family who didn't know what a hug was let alone how to care for one another?

You'll find the strength because you know these fucked up people, and their fucked up world, need you to save them, Fate had claimed.

"I can't leave," she said. "And I don't know what else to do."

Chaos sat beside her and took her hands. "Then we have to play Wynn's game."

"He doesn't lose."

"But he wants something, and that gives me leverage."

"Um, no offense, but if you've been retired, then are you ... um, rusty at this?" Stephanie asked.

"I don't think you ever forget how." Chaos smiled. "It's more a matter of how much damage I'll do in the process of remembering the details of how to handle the others."

This is a bad idea. "Just, uh, don't kill my brothers. Or my mate."

"Never thought I'd hear the day my daughter put in a good word for Fate," her mother mused. "Do you love him already? Despite what he is?"

"I barely know him. But there's something very …" Stephanie drifted off, recalling her few hours with him. "… he went to Hell for me. He's told me how to survive this disaster, and let Wynn torture him so I'd be left alone. He's … " She stopped. There was no way to describe the combination of profound awe and distrust or how her heart sang whenever she thought of him.

"So, yes," her mother said with a smile. "Love. Or something like it."

Stephanie shrugged, at a loss for words.

"Okay," Chaos said. "I'll get him out."

"What?"

"Your mom has a few tricks up her sleeves, retired or no." Rachel squeezed her hand and rose, headed towards the door.

Stephanie tossed the pillow and scrambled after her. "You're my mom. But deities and Immortals … yeah, I don't trust that side of you."

"As well you shouldn't," was the unsettling response. Her mother reached the door and faced her once more. "But I am your mother first and foremost. You and Sammy are my life. Your survival, and your happiness, are all that's ever mattered to me. If you need him, then I will bring him to you."

"Without destroying the world or anything like that."

"I make no such promises."

Stephanie gasped.

"I'm kidding." Her mother grinned. "Sorta. Just remember Wynn started this." She whipped open the door and left.

Stunned, Stephanie stood in place, uncertain she'd just heard what she did – her mother turning into a bloodthirsty deity.

"Good going. You unleashed Chaos," Trayern said from his position nearby.

"I think you're right." Stephanie's heart was pounding. "This could get very bad, very fast."

"But fun to watch."

She turned away, willing her mother not to do anything crazy.

CHAPTER TWENTY FIVE

STEPHANIE WAS GROWING TO HATE THE CONCEPT OF DINNER. IT didn't help she hadn't eaten a full evening meal in a week. It wasn't possible while seated at a table with Wynn.

She reached the dining hall right at seven, accompanied by her guardian demon. Mithra was sleeping when she left him. She fidgeted fiercely then shoved her hands into her pockets. Her mind raced with potential outcomes to the meeting, and she prayed her brothers were capable of a unified front and not torn from consensus by Wynn's maneuvering.

Barely daring to hope for success, she wasn't able to help the thrill that went through her whenever she thought about how this meeting might end with Wynn stepping down, and her soul returned to her. How different would life be with a soul?

The question was ridiculous, and she almost smiled, before recalling the mountain named Wynn standing between her and her soul.

She stepped into the dining hall, not expecting to be the last sibling to arrive. She paused, studying the six men. Wynn appeared little older than Andre, who looked to be in his late twenties at most. Being an Immortal was good on the skin, she noted absently. The two could pass as twins, with the exception of Wynn's shocking white hair, which matched Kris' rather than Andre's.

Closing the door behind her companion demon, she approached them where they were gathered around the burning hearth. Wynn alone didn't seem nervous, angry or uncomfortable, and this terrified her.

"You've managed to do what no one has to date," he spoke, glancing from the fire to her. "Unite your brothers."

"We have a common enemy," Rhyn growled.

"What brings you all here?" Wynn swirled his glass then set it down on the mantle, facing them. A white bandage was wrapped around his wrist and extended halfway up his forearm.

Stephanie glanced at Andre, who was looking at Kris.

"We want you to step down from the Council," Kris replied. "Permanently."

"You wish to expel me."

"Not exactly. No one knows for certain if the breaches will remained sealed without you."

"You wish me to stay, just hand over my power and position," Wynn said.

"Yes. Tonight," Tamer added firmly.

Stephanie held her breath, aware of Kiki, who stood beside her, doing the same. Her brothers were tense. The power rippling off Rhyn was visible as sparks in the air around him and being absorbed by Andre, who seemed to be focused on preventing anyone from exploding.

She didn't envy him the job.

Wynn met the gaze of each of his children. A small smile was on his face. Stephanie shifted weight between her feet anxiously, wondering what horrible fears and secrets he was gathering about all of them.

"I'm proud of you," he said. "All of you. I had great hopes for you, and you've exceeded them. We've never stood here like this, almost all of us together as a family."

"We're no family," Rhyn replied. "My mate taught me what family is, and it's not this, not *you*."

"You know what would make this better? If Sasha could join us, along with Erik," Wynn continued.

"Those are … my other brothers?" Stephanie asked.

"Yes. Sasha, who betrayed the Immortals to the Dark One, and Erik, who was planning the same."

Kris and Rhyn glanced at each other.

"Oh, you didn't know about Erik?" Wynn asked with mocking surprise. "I wonder what else you don't know about one another."

"This won't work, Wynn," Kris warned.

"Yeah, we know how fucked up everyone in here is," Rhyn agreed. "But we all want the same thing."

"You. Out." Tamer said firmly.

"Is the vote unanimous?"

Everyone nodded.

"Very well. I'll happily resign from my position, if you can tell me who my successor is," Wynn said. "There's important information to pass on."

Silence. Stephanie saw brief surprise on Kiki's features, as if he, too, hadn't considered the question of who would take over.

"So there isn't a successor. Interesting," Wynn said.

"We'll vote as soon as you're out of the way," Tamer replied.

"Let's look at this, shall we?" Wynn asked. "Tamer, you aren't cut out for leadership. Your temper interferes with any diplomacy you might learn, assuming you can learn it. Neither are you, Kiki. You're an incredibly effective manager, but you have no strategic sight and no risk tolerance, both of which are needed to become a successful leader. As Tamer says, you're good for cleaning up messes and that's about it. Andre isn't a contender, because he's a deity, and the

Immortals will revolt. Kris ... you were always my chosen successor. Until I found out all the deals you made on the side that undermined the society. Even I never commissioned so many assassinations, and the science experiments you did on human subjects?" Wynn shook his head. "Barbaric, even by my standards."

Stephanie listened, horrified. Every one glanced at Kris. Tamer's eyes were blazing, and Kiki was openly staring at Tamer.

"Kiki can verify," Wynn added. "We dug up Kris's mess when trying to clean up the disaster left in Rhyn's wake, which includes a second breach to Hell and the slaughtering of seventy percent of our Immortal warriors because Rhyn placed a deity's concerns over those of his people." His gaze rested on Stephanie.

She braced herself for whatever terrible things he had to say.

"Who would dare trust the daughter of Chaos and mate of Fate?" he asked.

She felt her optimism deflate. He was right. Always right.

The tension of those around her made her skin crawl. No one moved. No one spoke. No one even seemed to breathe.

"So tell me. Once I'm no longer in charge, what the fuck will you do?" Wynn finished with a flash of anger.

"War," Kris whispered.

"War," Tamer echoed.

"War," Rhyn agreed.

There was a pause, then, "War," Kiki said.

"No!" Stephanie cried. "This is what he wants! Andre, tell them – "

She had no chance to plea for her oldest brother to step in when Tamer withdrew a knife and lunged at Wynn.

"Tamer!" The closest to him, Andre shouted and leapt forward, smashing his brother into the wall before he could reach Wynn.

Tamer turned on his older brother, and Stephanie watched the worst case scenario unfold before her eyes. Kris tried to attack Wynn next, only for Rhyn to yank him away, and the two of them smashed to the ground, wrestling.

"No, no, no!" she whispered, stricken. Tears sprang up in her eyes.

Kiki was glaring at Wynn, who was watching calmly, once more sipping his whisky.

"Come here, stupid half-breed." Trayern gripped her arm.

"Leave me alone!" She tried to pull free.

He yanked her against him and all but dragged her away from the melee, to the corner near the door.

She wasn't able to look away from her fighting brothers. Wynn left the hearth, ignored by everyone, even Kiki, whose focus had turned to Tamer. She almost saw something within him snap, and the animosity she'd witnessed between the two, which Kiki had been suppressing, emerged.

He launched at Tamer, knife in hand.

Tears of frustration streamed down Stephanie's cheeks. She recalled Fate's warning with no small amount of urgency. Wynn hadn't just pulled apart their tentative coalition; he'd demolished it without lifting a finger.

Helpless to stop them or figure out what to do, she could only watch.

"Trayern, I suggest you confine her to her room," Wynn said, pausing beside them. "My sons have an appointment with a one-eyed man."

She froze, recalling the man from the vision of Fate being tortured. "No!" she cried, starting towards him. "You can't!"

The demon yanked her back, and she watched Wynn open the door and summon the guards. They rushed in, and Trayern pulled her out of the room. She began to fight him. He was tougher than those she'd met in the alley, strong enough to overpower her, without any concern about hurting her in the process. He slung her over his shoulder and trotted through the fortress to her room, slamming the door open.

With little ceremony, he threw her onto her back on the couch. "Do not fucking move, half-breed!" he snarled. "My duty is not to protect you, and if I must break your legs to do it, I will!"

She stared at him. "Protect me?"

"My master ordered it as part of the deals he made with your mate. But I am so fucking close to fucking you up. Do *not* test me!"

"Back off, demon." Mithra was on his feet, cane pointed at the infuriated demon.

Stephanie blocked out their short argument and began to cry out of impotent fury.

Part of her hoped Wynn never let his sons out of the catacombs, or the civil war Fate warned about would begin. The other part of her couldn't live with knowing they were going to suffer horribly at his hands, and by extension, so would Katie and Hazel and anyone else who made the mistake of loving one of her brothers.

Wynn was always one step ahead, and the only person who could outsmart him, the only person she could ask for help, was stuck in Hell, along with her soul.

What the fuck do I do?

CHAPTER TWENTY SIX

"GUESS WHO'S NEXT?"

Fate bit back a groan. Panting from his previous tormentor, he was in no shape to face a new one so soon. Darkyn had done away with his breaks upon his return from a night with his mate.

But he forced himself to his feet, no matter how rattled and wobbly he was from the last round of pain. He rubbed his eyes to clear them from blood and sweat, then peered out at the woman standing in front of his cell without recognizing her.

"You'll have to forgive me, but I don't recall what I did to you," he said with mild amusement.

"You stole my daughter," she replied and folded her arms across her chest.

"You'll have to be more specific. I've stolen many daughters." And then it clicked. Fate registered the shimmer around the unfamiliar face too late.

The goddess glared at him, her look similar to those Stephanie gave him on occasion. "Yet another reason why our families have never gotten along," she said icily.

"It's a pleasure to meet my mother-in-law," he said, wanting to laugh but knowing how wrong the timing was.

"You have no idea what it was like seeing your name on her back."

Fate stretched back. The worst part of his cell wasn't the round of auto-torture between his vindictive visitors. It was how it healed him after every horrific event, so only the mental scars remained. Darkyn liked his subjects to be fully healthy when he tore them apart again. The mind-fuck was working. He was starting to dread the thought of eternity stuck here.

"You're here to punish me?" he guessed. "I think there's already a queue. You may have to wait a few months."

"It'd give me a great deal of pleasure to watch you suffer." Her eyes flashed from human blue to black.

"Ah. There you are," he said with some satisfaction. "There's the goddess my father helped strip of her power to create unparalleled disorder."

"He promised me an eternity of being only half-whole. You don't know what that means."

"My father was a brutal man, but he had a reason for his actions. If he hurt you, it was to prevent you from hurting others," Fate said, studying her. "And you're wrong. I do know what it means. It means you live in pain, because half of what you are is gone. I'm sorry for that."

"My love for my daughters is the only thing capable of filling that void. To know the son of the man who sentenced me to living hell now claims my daughter ..." She shook her head. "If I had warned her, she'd never be able to love you."

"We aren't to that point yet, if that helps."

Chaos began to glow darkly. Her magic was absorbed whisked away by Hell's magic, but her eyes were solid black.

"She loves me?" Fate asked, more surprised by this than the appearance of Chaos at his cell. The night with her had been beyond incredible, but he considered their circumstances far too fucked up to risk there being more. Or perhaps, he was hoping there wasn't more, because he was stuck in Hell for the foreseeable future. He alone should suffer, because knowing Stephanie was hurting, and being helpless to do anything about it ...

It was worse than anything Hell could throw at him.

Chaos appeared ready to explode. Her features were flushed, and she was starting to hover inches off the ground rather than stand. At war with the powerful buffering magics of Hell, she'd be unable to unleash any of her remaining magic at him, but she was fighting it hard.

With an angry goddess before him and Hell's magic creeping in, Fate's mind was completely elsewhere, on the mate he hadn't wanted to exist. Some foreign emotion fluttered inside him. It was pleasant, warm, and ran him through like an internal hug, even if he didn't quite know what to call it.

He was also smiling absently, and just a little bit unnerved. It struck him he'd been holding back from letting himself fall completely for Stephanie. They were both fucked as it was, without the added emotion.

"I came here to free you." Chaos' words pulled him back from the warmer thoughts in his mind.

His eyebrows lifted. "Free me?"

She had calmed. Her eyes were human blue again, her magic suppressed by Hell. "My daughter needs you. I know what Wynn is, and I don't have the power or will to stop him if he hurts her again."

"I'm at a disadvantage," he said. "I have no power."

"Your family is known for its political brilliance," she said with reluctant admiration. "Stephanie is smart, but she doesn't know what you do, and she's too good to have the stomach for manipulation I know you do."

It wasn't a compliment, he sensed, though she was right. "The

Dark One is enjoying this too much to free me."

"I've taken care of Darkyn."

His eyes narrowed. "Care to clarify?"

"Hostage exchange. I take your place."

Fate shifted closer to the doorway. "I can't allow that."

"Stephanie needs you more than me right now."

"You misunderstand. I know what Darkyn would do with the opportunity to have Chaos in his debt. I don't need to see the Future to know he would use you to further any number of his plans," he said. "You put more at risk this way than by letting me stay here."

Chaos hesitated then shook her head. "I would do anything for my daughters. This makes sense. I can't protect them, but you can."

"Rachel, please consider. You ..." He stopped, instinct wriggling. A mother with her power wouldn't hesitate to confront Wynn, unless ..."Wynn threatened them, didn't he?"

She averted her gaze. "Not just them."

"Meaning ..."

"He has your sister, too."

Rare fury trickled through Fate despite his exhaustion. He didn't have to be told to know how Karma ended up confronting Wynn. His sister didn't think before she acted; with him in Hell, it was probably only a matter of time. Wynn had trapped Karma and manipulated Chaos into Hell. What kind of favor would the Dark One grant the Immortal for a chance to control Chaos?

The second chain of events he'd feared was happening. Karma had crossed paths with Wynn, and soon, the Immortals would topple into civil war.

"You still shouldn't do this," he managed to say. "You've been out of the game too long to understand the kind of pressure someone like Darkyn can put on you. Not to mention, Stephanie isn't going to take this well."

"Then I suggest you figure something out fast," Chaos said.

"There's so much more at risk here, Rachel."

"You don't understand," she said. This time, sorrow crossed her features. "I'd do anything for my daughters, even fuck up the world. But you … you killed your own father to alter the Future. You will do what I can't, no matter what the sacrifice is. And you will protect her with the same tenacity."

Fate was quiet. Dread sank into him, along with fear.

"I already made the deal," she continued. "Stephanie's life is in your hands and mine is in Darkyn's."

A chill ran through him. "You may have set your expectations too high."

"I know the blood running through your veins. Perhaps the mating bond has added what your kind has always lacked – the ability to see beyond your duty and yourselves."

The observation was too accurate for him to counter. He recalled wondering what kind of tool Stephanie would make in his manipulations, soon after they met.

At some point, he'd begun to consider her in a different light, one immune to what he normally was. Thinking back, he wasn't able to pinpoint the exact moment when his mate had gone from a useful tool to someone he cared about. But the shift had happened, and he innately understood what it meant for Chaos to place her daughter completely under his protection.

"How about that," he murmured, impressed as much by the subtle change in him as the woman at his cell. "Fate and Chaos have a common goal."

"You're free to leave," she said and stepped back from his cell. "Just so we're clear, if anything happens to my daughter, I will tear you apart, atom by atom."

"Nothing will happen to her," he replied. He stepped out of the cell, expecting Darkyn to be there to send him right back into it.

She peered into the cell with apprehension then sucked in a deep breath and entered the darkness.

Fate lingered. Chaos was a natural rival to the orderly progression of the Future, but he pitied her, as much for what Darkyn would do to her as knowing she'd be severed from any information about her daughters. If humanity had one curse he wouldn't miss, it was uncertainty.

He hated knowing Stephanie, and now his sister, were in danger, and he wasn't able to help them. Free, he'd be able to do more, to see more, to manipulate those he had to. He needed to be in the mortal world to stop the civil war that was coming.

There was nothing left to say to Chaos, so he walked through the corridor to the demon waiting for him at the end of the hall. He was led to the portal room and permitted onto the dais. The entrance to the place-between-places yawned open.

Someone was waiting for him. Fate crossed the cavern to Death, whose grim expression was the first indication of yet more trouble.

"No less than three deities have paid for hits on you. Oh, and Wynn," Gabriel said with wry humor.

"It's not entirely a surprise," Fate said. "But I can't talk now. I need to –"

"You're not listening. You can't go back to the mortal world, not until I can recall the death dealers hired to kill you." He held up his arm. "You're on my list."

Fate registered the information in some disbelief. To have made the list meant he was officially as good as dead. "Take me off your list," he replied.

"I'm working on it. But you can't go back until I get this fixed. I've already almost destroyed the universe once. I won't let your death be what finishes the job."

Fate bit back his initial response. Gabriel was helping him, or trying to. He couldn't know what was at stake, why Fate needed to return immediately.

"Come on. I'll keep you safe for a few days." Gabriel stalked toward a gray door that appeared only for Death and his death dealers.

Fate's gaze lingered on the lemon colored portals. His instincts pulled him towards Stephanie, while his rationale acknowledged how useless he was to anyone if he was dead-dead. Even knowing what he needed to do, it was hard to turn away from the woman he yearned to protect from all the dangers of the worlds. The resolve he experienced for ensuring there was a Future, settled within him when he thought of his mate.

I'm coming, Stephanie. Nothing will ever become between us again. I swear it on my soul, he promised in silence before turning to follow Gabriel into the Underworld.

RHYN ETERNAL

Gabriel's Hope

Deidre's Death

Darkyn's Mate

The Underworld

Twisted Fate

(untitled) 2016

Continue reading for a sneak peek of

OMEGA

In a modern day world torn apart by warring Greek gods, the fate of humanity rests in the hands of the teenage Oracle of Delphi and her unlikely allies.

CHAPTER ONE: ALESSANDRA

No man or woman born, coward or brave, can shun his destiny.
– Homer

FOR ONCE, TYCHE, COULD YOU GRANT ME A LITTLE LUCK? I slowed before reaching my favorite meadow in the forest, my heart racing and chest heaving. A grin stretched my cheeks, and I stopped to listen for the boy I'd challenged to a race. I heard … voices. Male and at least two females.

"I guess not," I muttered aloud.

The damn nymphs had him. My giddy excitement faded. I was the one who managed to lure a teen boy from the nearby campground into our forest and, as usual, the nymphs stole him. I couldn't compete with the beautiful women. There were thirty of them my age, all unusually perfect, feminine and graceful. Even my guardian said they weren't normal, and we'd coined the term *nymphs* to describe the other girls at the isolated orphanage where I lived under the thumb of strict priests. The other girls were all my age, too, each of them destined for positions befitting their beauty, according to the priests.

It was disgusting. I couldn't stand them.

I was an athlete, uncomfortable in anything but tennis shoes and yoga pants, terrible in school and bearing a scar from childhood across one cheek. No matter how much makeup I plastered over it or how far forward I brushed my dark locks, I wasn't able to hide it. I was always late to class, always the last to understand whatever torture the priests were teaching us, always trying to catch the first light of Aurora in the reflecting pool or scaling a hill to watch the last rays of Hersperides.

The nymphs laughed at me. I hated them for it and me for not being able to fit in no matter what I did. I couldn't change the fact I was shorter, smaller and otherwise imperfect compared to them.

"Lose another one, Lyssa?"

"Yeah." I heard my guardian's approach and looked up into his scarred, ugly face. A mountain of a man with bright red hair, Herakles had never once understood why I was so disappointed to lose every guy I looked at to the nymphs.

"If a man can't outrun you – "

"– I can't bring him home with me. House rules. I know." It was a stupid rule. Surely there had to be one man somewhere who shared my deer-like agility.

My guardian chuckled.

"He was so handsome!" I whined with a sigh, recalling the gorgeous brown eyes and smile of the teenage boy I'd met today. When he had looked at me, my insides turned fluttery and warm. "He almost outran me, too."

"Only because you slowed down."

I rolled my eyes and spun away, headed towards the compound in the middle of a forest where we all lived. "So what? Everyone here has kissed a boy and I can't even look at one without the stupid nymphs taking him away. They just bat their eyes and the boys fall all over them." I made a show of shaking my hips and blinking rapidly in mockery.

"I've never kissed a boy."

"You know what I mean!" Herakles was a jerk sometimes. His rules were designed to prevent me from ever having a boyfriend. My interests generally lay in martial arts and sports. If not for the nymphs conspiring to steal any boys I lured away from the campground and always taunting me about everything, I wouldn't look twice at a boy. But I shared one sole trait with the nymphs: competitiveness. I wanted so badly to best them at something and earn enough respect not to be bullied every day for the rest of my life.

"You could try studying harder," Herakles suggested.

"Right. Like that's going to get me a boyfriend."

"There is more to life than boys and whatever else it is your head is full of," Herakles reminded me. "You don't need a man anyway. You can take care of yourself. I've trained you to survive anything."

"I know I don't *need* one. I want one so the nymphs stop laughing at me. Just for a day, then I'd let him go like you free the rabbits I catch."

"You noticed."

I arched my eyebrow at him. "I figured it out after I caught the same one every day for a week when I was, like, sixteen. You know the nymphs don't have to hunt rabbits, don't you? They don't have to run every day or build their own campfires and shelters on the weekends. They get to go to town, Herakles, and see movies!" I sighed, tortured by my miserable existence. "Can I be normal? Just for one weekend?"

"Normal people aren't prepared for their world to change or to face the trials awaiting them."

"The zombies apocalypse isn't coming. The priests say the world has never known a time of greater peace and prosperity and the gods are happier than ever."

"An apocalypse is not required to announce itself," he stated.

I bit my tongue. I knew better than to argue with Herakles. He was of a singular mind and convinced the world was going to end any day. Nothing I'd ever said over the past twelve years had dented his obsession with self-reliance and survival. I learned to hunt game bigger than me, forage for berries, survive in extreme weather conditions and other skills the nymphs – and even my teachers – often ridiculed. Sometimes he blindfolded me or hobbled one leg or arm so I had to survive for a weekend alone in the forest with simulated physical impediments. He first dropped me off in part of the forest alone with no compass when I was nine. I bawled for a day until he came to get me. Instead of taking me back, we stayed in the forest, and he taught me to navigate by the stars.

No one understood why he made me do these things, least of all me. I obeyed him because, above all else, I loved my Herakles, as weird as he was. While we were accepted here, we didn't fit in at the school filled with nymphs and priests. We had to stick together, two dented peas in a misshapen pod.

"The man you want will be able to outrun, outhunt and outsmart you. When you meet him, you can marry him. Until then, no man will do," Herakles said.

"I don't want to marry anyone," I said. "I just want to kiss him."

"Then you can kiss the man who catches you."

His conditions for me seeing someone were impossibilities. Herakles alone was the only man who could keep up with me. It was his way of saying I'd never have a boyfriend as long as I lived under his roof.

I glanced up at the green canopy overhead. The blue sky resembled puzzle pieces from this angle, and not a cloud was in sight on this warm spring day. What torture did he have in store for me on such a beautiful Friday? I had to climb a rope or navigate whatever obstacle course he built before I was allowed to go to bed at night. Weekends were worse. I was exiled to the forest for more survival training until Sunday night.

He was conditioning and preparing me for something. I had no idea what, and I suspected he was just a little off. A former Olympian, Herakles was the toughest, most honorable person I had ever known. He swept the annual Olympics for three years in a row before he stumbled upon me, rescued me from the house fire that killed my parents and brought us here. He didn't respect anything but physical prowess. He could barely read, and he had an almost allergic reaction to discussing anything regarding emotions.

But he was my hero in every sense of the word.

To this day, I was unable to recall what exactly happened the night I turned six except it involved Herakles catching me when I fell from the sky. Why or how I was flying, I didn't know. I still occasionally dreamt of falling – but no fire. My life changed that night. Herakles was unwilling to talk about it even after I turned eighteen and was considered an adult by everyone but him.

Herakles tugged the sleeve I'd tucked under my bra strap back down over the strange birthmark on my bicep that looked eerily like a double omega. The omega was the final letter in the Greek alphabet, or, according to Herakles, a sign of Armageddon. "Keep this hidden," he reminded me.

"I know." I pulled both sleeves down so I didn't look stupid with only one up.

Picking my way through the forest back towards the compound where we lived, I considered the topic I'd been meaning to broach to him but hadn't quite figured out the best way yet.

"We haven't talked about graduation," I started. "It's in three weeks."

"The world might end tomorrow. You should not think too far beyond today."

"Omigods, Herakles! I'm eighteen, and I'm graduating in three weeks! I want to go home!" Too late I realized I'd told him what I had hoped to discuss in a calmer manner. I didn't look back at him but focused on the path at my feet.

"You know there is nothing for you there."

"So you've told me every time I asked. But I have to go somewhere," I pointed out. "College. Waitress at a fast food joint. Holy Zeus, I'd become an initiate at a temple."

"No temple would have you."

It wasn't the first time I'd heard that, either. The priests didn't consider me disciplined or selfless or motivated enough to refer me for a position in the elite initiate corps. Half of the nymphs were headed to temples of the Greek gods. The others were being sent to the households of influential politicians and nobles around the world. I could speak English, Greek and French like they did – a requirement to become an initiate – but my grades were sorry and my temperament deemed too unsuitable to be placed in a position where diplomacy and manipulation was required.

"You have more freedom here than the average person living beneath the thumb of the Supreme Magistrate will ever know," he said. "Why do you wish to leave?"

"Because that's what kids who graduate high school do. They get a life. Join the real world."

"Where did you learn this? Television?" He was genuinely confused. He rarely spoke of his childhood, but I'd assessed over the years that his own upbringing had been very different. "I must talk to the priests about censoring the programs they let you girls watch."

"They already monitor everything we watch. I guess I just want to know ... where do we go next? Because we are leaving, right?" I asked, sensing I was doomed to work at a fast food joint the rest of my life, if he let me leave at all.

"We are. But I'm not yet certain where."

"You've only had twelve years to figure it out," I shot back with some exasperation. "I want to see the world, Herakles, or at least somewhere beyond this forest."

"Until I know for sure –"

"– stay inside the boundaries." I wasn't allowed to travel beyond the red cord lining the perimeter of the priests' quiet property. Since arriving when I was six, I had never left. The nymphs went to town every weekend to shop or watch movies or eat food and whatever else they did that Herakles didn't approve of. It had to be more fun than navigating the forest in the rain with nothing more than a poncho and a knife. Meanwhile Herakles timed how long it took me to get home to make sure I wasn't slacking before the inevitable end of the world.

We reached the edge of the greens where the compound proper started. Daydreaming about what was to come when I finally graduated, I missed Herakles stiffening.

"This isn't good," he said.

Blinking out of my thoughts, I stopped to see him staring at the long driveway leading from the road to the massive manor house that acted as our home and school. The priests had erected two small temples, one for a Titan god named Lelantos and another for the Olympic goddess Artemis, behind the school, beside the stables.

An extra car was parked in front of the school, a black sedan with darkened windows. "We've had a lot of visitors lately," I said, unconcerned. "I imagine the employers of the nymphs are coming to interview them."

"It's not an employer."

The car wasn't there to take me away to the real world, and I doubted it was the first zombie from the apocalypse we were preparing for. Therefore, the vehicle's appearance meant nothing to me. "Okay. I'm going to my room."

Herakles paid me no heed and jogged towards the car.

I circled the house to the back entrance where the stairwell leading directly to our rooms were located. I took the stairs two at a time and strode down the landing of the girls' wing towards my room.

"Lyssa!" someone called as I passed.

"What?" I paused and stepped back, peering into the room of one of the nymphs, a willowy blonde named Leandra. She was finishing her makeup and wore a sparkly party dress.

"Wanna go to town with us tonight?" Leandra asked innocently.

"I hate my life," I muttered.

She laughed.

But I didn't leave. Playing on her television were news clips of the footage I'd missed two weeks ago when I spent my eighteenth birthday in the middle of the forest, shivering and buried beneath leaves in the final cold snap of spring, during one of Herakles weekend tests. The priests censored everything that reached us from the outside world, including the news. They removed what they didn't want us to see before letting us watch what was left.

"Hey, is that …" I asked and walked into her room.

"Yeah." A wistful note was in Leandra's voice.

It took a lot to make the perfect, beautiful nymphs envy someone else. For once, I understood where she was coming from.

"The Silent Queen," I said in awe, gazing at the television. The Queen of Greece, known as the Silent Queen because she hadn't been seen or heard from until this month, was plastered everywhere on the news. A girl my age, she was stunning with white-blonde hair, pale blue eyes and a jawline sharp enough to cut ice. "Wow."

"She's just a symbol of the unity of gods and mankind. No real power." But even Leandra sounded enthralled by the woman on the television. "She can't speak. She gave her first address in sign language."

"Wow," I murmured again. In a sparkling diamond tiara and radiant silk dress, the teen looked more godlike than human. She was flanked by the Supreme Magistrate – the powerful political representative of humanity – and the hooded and masked Supreme Priest – the gods' advocate on Earth. The three most powerful figures in the world were known as the Sacred Triumvirate, and each had his or her own private security force, according to the priests, which was how they balanced their power.

I couldn't look away from the Silent Queen. The priests had drilled the history and importance of the hereditary Bloodline into us since we arrived. The Silent Queen's ancestors were touched by the gods, and it was said only she could appeal directly to them in a way that defied even the priesthood. Throughout history, once Greece fell as a global power, the most powerful nation on the planet was given the sacred duty of protecting the Bloodline and housing the royal leader, which was how she ended up here in the United States. "She's amazing."

"I'm sure she's been Photo-shopped for television," Leandra said somewhat defensively.

I rolled my eyes. The nymphs knew they were special. There was something strange about thirty orphaned women of extreme beauty and charm, all born within three months of me, all under the strict protection of an orphanage run by priests who didn't hold weekly worship ceremonies but taught us instead the Old Ways, as they called them. They were positioning the nymphs in places of eventual power, where they could then share the Old Ways with others.

If our world was strange, we had no idea. As far as we knew, this place and its customs were normal.

"I've been assigned to her court," Leandra said.

"Seriously?"

"Yep."

It made sense. Leandra was a hair prettier than the others and quite a bit smarter, according to the priests. I was suddenly crushed that I might end up taking food orders from hung over college students the rest of my life while the others went off to positions I could only dream of.

"Where are you going?" she asked, green eyes finding me. "To live with the Mountain Man on some isolated peak?"

"He's not a Mountain Man," I said, bristling. "He's the greatest Olympic athlete in history."

"A disgraced one who ditched his wealthy benefactor to live in a forest with us. He's absolutely mad, and he's turned you wild and ruined any chance you had at a decent future."

My anger bubbled. I knew better than to cause a fight. I had stopped that nonsense when I was fifteen, but sometimes I wanted to sock the pretty, perfect women around me.

My biggest issue with Leandra wasn't that she was mean. It was that she was often right, and her words about Herakles stung. Something was wrong with him, and I sometimes thought maybe that meant there was something wrong with me, too. It was why I didn't turn out like Leandra and the others and why I was definitely not going to the Silent Queen's court.

I squinted to see the ticker at the bottom of the news. *Civil unrest grows. Supreme Magistrate places five more states under martial rule over SISA's objections.* That made about forty states under martial rule by my count. The priests refused to tell us about the civil unrest when we asked, but sometimes, like today, tiny pieces of information slipped through their censoring and made it to us. I was dying to know what the world outside our boring forest was like.

"When I get to court, I'll find you a job chopping wood or something," Leandra said with a wide grin.

I stormed off to my room, followed by the sound of her laughter. I loved Herakles like the father I couldn't remember, but sometimes I was really embarrassed to be me. I hated that feeling. I had trouble making friends, more so because Herakles often had some bizarre requirement for me to hang out with someone. Boys had to be able to outrun me, and girls had to solve a riddle. No one ever succeeded at his challenges, except for the perfect little nymphs who hung out with me only to laugh at me.

Basically, I was always alone, and he seemed determined to keep it that way. I felt even more isolated knowing the nymphs all had plans of where they were going after graduation and I didn't.

I went to my room and closed the door, sitting on my bed. I had barely pushed off my shoes before a tap sounded at the door. "Come in," I said and tossed myself onto my back.

"Lyssa, I have to leave for the weekend."

Startled, I immediately sat back up. "Where? Why?" I demanded of Herakles, who had never left me for half a day let alone a weekend. "Is something wrong?"

"No." His features were scarred beyond recognition, his smile lopsided and frightening. Everyone else winced when he looked their direction, but I loved every knotted scar and burnt piece of flesh on his face. He was my protector, my friend, the only father figure I knew. He had always been beautiful to me. "You are to travel to the eastern boundary and back this weekend. Here's your surprise pack. Open it when you get there." He tossed the satchel onto the bed beside me.

"Ugh." I eyed it warily. He no doubt had planned another weekend of torture. I'd probably have a hat and spoon and nothing more to survive two days in the forest alone. Technically I should have had only three more weeks of this madness remaining, except I had a feeling his plans were always going to trump mine. "You're sure there's nothing wrong? You've never left me before."

"I'm going to scout someplace where we might settle after you graduate," he told me.

I looked up, thrilled. "I won't be trapped here for the rest of my life!"

"No, but you might one day wish you had been." He frowned. Every once in a while, my guardian had a mood I didn't understand. Naturally open, upbeat and focused, his features were now grave and unreadable.

I studied him, wishing I could read his thoughts or make him smile again. "Something is wrong," I assessed.

"Not wrong. It's always complicated to move from one place to another." He shook his head. "Anyway, you have a treasure hunt to complete this weekend. Your tasks are in the bag. You will not wish to wait until morning. I put up several traps and obstacles."

I muttered curses I'd learned from him under my breath. As long as we had been together, I never really knew what to expect on these adventures. "I'll see you Sunday night," I said reluctantly.

"Heed the boundaries and rules."

"I know." I pulled on my shoes obediently and a camouflage windbreaker. When I stood, he smiled at me again.

"Good girl. Don't get lost out there."

It wasn't possible and we both knew it. I'd been over every inch of that forest multiple times. "Have fun in town."

He turned and left.

I grabbed the bag and left my room for the forest once more.

No boys. No future. No town.

There were days when I wanted out of my life so badly I wanted to scream.

Want to read more? The "*OMEGA BEGINNINGS MINISERIES*" short story series is FREE on ebook wherever you purchase ebooks!

"*OMEGA*" will be released October 2015.

Join the Omega Fandom for exclusive giveaways, updates, and excerpts!

OMEGAFANDOM.COM

ABOUT THE AUTHOR

Lizzy Ford is the author of over forty books written for young adult and adult paranormal romance readers, to include the internationally bestselling "Rhyn Trilogy," "Witchling Series" and the "War of Gods" series. Considered a freak of nature by her peers for the ability to write and release a commercial quality novel in under a month, Lizzy has focused on keeping her readers happy by producing brilliant, gritty romances that remind people why true love is a trial worth enduring.

Lizzy's books can be found on every major ereader library, to include: Amazon, Barnes and Noble, iBooks, Kobo, Sony and Smashwords. She lives in southern Arizona with her husband, three dogs and a cat.

CONNECT WITH LIZZY

Website: LizzyFord.com

Facebook: www.Facebook.com/LizzyFordBooks

Twitter @LizzyFord2010

Instagram: @LizzyFordAuthor

Also By Lizzy Ford

History Interrupted – time travel romance
West
East
North (2016)
South (2017)

Omega Beginnings Series
Alessandra
Mismatch
Phoibe
Lantos
Theodocia
Niko
Cleon
Herakles

Omega Series
Omega (2015)
Theta (2016)
Alpha (2017

Non-Series – 2014 & 2015
Black Moon Draw (about a reader sucked into her book)
Highlander Enchanted (2015)
The Door (2016)

Sons of War – contemporary military romance
Semper Mine
Soldier Mine
SEAL Mine (2016)

Starwalkers Serials (with Julia Crane) – new adult science fiction serial
Severed
Trapped
Exiled
Revealed
Escaped

Heart of Fire – sexy dragon shifter
Charred Heart
Charred Tears
Charred Hope

Incubatti – Buffy meets 50 Shades
Zoey Rogue
Zoey Avenger

Rhyn Trilogy – new adult paranormal with demons
Katie's Hellion
Katie's Hope
Rhyn's Redemption

Rhyn Eternal – Death finds love
Gabriel's Hope
Deidre's Death
Darkyn's Mate
The Underworld
Twisted Fate (2015)

War of Gods – paranormal with gods, guardians and exceptional humans
Damian's Oracle
Damian's Assassin
Damian's Immortal
The Grey God

Damian Eternal
Xander's Chance
The Black God

Hidden Evil – paranormal with angels and four horsemen
Hear No
See No (2015)
Speak No (2016)

Unnamed Series
Unnatural (2015)
Unmade (2016)

Omega
Omega (2015)
Theta (2016)
Alpha (2017)

Anshan Saga – new adult science fiction romance
Kiera's Moon
Kiera's Home (novelette)
Kiera's Sun

Santa's Ninja Elves (short stories)
Natasha & Hunter

Non-series titles – 2011 - 2013
Star Kissed
A Demon's Desire
The Warlord's Secret
Maddy's Oasis
Rebel Heart

Witchling – young adult paranormal
Dark Summer
Autumn Storm
Winter Fire
Spring Rain

Broken Beauty Novellas – new adult dramatic fiction
Broken Beauty
Broken World

Voodoo Nights - young adult paranormal
Cursed
Chosen (2015)

As SE Reign, erotic romance writer
101 Nights
Claimed
Tainted
Crushed
Volume One Box Set (Serials 1-3)
Tempted
Captured
Twisted
Volume Two Box Set (Serials 4-6)
Cornered

Trial Series
Trial by Moon
Trial by Thrall
Trial by Blood
Trial by Heart

Made in the USA
Charleston, SC
31 August 2015